Dear Reader,

What would you do if you were a long way from home, in a place that felt unfamiliar and dangerous?

Would you be able to trust your instincts and survive? Well, this is the position Jack finds himself in.

But Jack's not just trying to stay alive. He has a bigger mission to save not only himself, his friends and his parents but also the WORLD.

Our planet is already under threat, without more bad guys trying to destroy it. But it only takes one hero to make a difference.

So get ready for the most explosive adventure of your life . . .

Yours sincerely,

Wilbur Smith and Chris Wakling

THE JACK COURTNEY ADVENTURES

Cloudburst
Thunderbolt

Look out for more . . .

WILBUR SMITH

with **CHRIS WAKLING**

CLOUDBURST

A JACK COURTNEY ADVENTURE

Piccadilly
PRESS

First published in Great Britain in 2020 by
PICCADILLY PRESS
80–81 Wimpole St, London W1G 9RE
www.piccadillypress.co.uk

A CIP catalogue record for this book is available from the British Library.

ISBN: 978-1-84812-853-8
Also available as an ebook and in audio

2

This book is typeset using Atomik ePublisher
Printed and bound in Great Britain by Clays Ltd, Elcograf S.p.A.

Piccadilly Press is an imprint of Bonnier Books UK
www.bonnierbooks.co.uk

'*How far that little candle throws the beams! So shines a good deed in a weary world.*'
William Shakespeare

I dedicate this book to all my young readers
whose hearts are in flame for the right to win.
Wilbur Smith

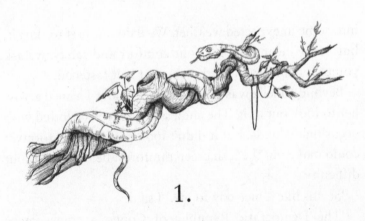

1.

I was asleep when the airliner hit turbulence. It must have dropped a hundred metres in half a second. The swooping up-rush launched my stomach into my chest and my head grazed the ceiling before my bum slammed back into the seat. I opened my eyes as an electronic warning bell started pinging above us. The 'fasten seat belts' light came on.

'Bit late for that,' I said to Amelia beside me.

'I never unbuckle mine,' she explained, showing me the snug clasp before returning to whatever she was doing on her phone. Reprogramming it, probably.

'Of course you don't,' I said, just as the plane bounced hard again.

Mum craned round from the seat in front. 'You OK, Jack? Amelia?'

'Just fine . . . Why wouldn't we be?' we said over the top of one another.

The co-pilot's voice oozed out of the speaker, full of reassurance: 'Ladies and gentleman, we seem to have run

1

into some unexpected weather. We'll do our best to skirt it, but in the meantime, for your comfort and safety, we ask you to remain seated with your seat belt fastened.'

Beyond Amelia was the porthole window. I leaned across her to look out of it. The endless blue sky was dotted with occasional clouds, but it didn't look particularly stormy. I could make out the lush green rainforest below us without difficulty.

'Seems like a nice day to me,' I said.

'The Democratic Republic of Congo averages more thunderstorms per year than anywhere else on earth,' Amelia replied.

'Good to know. Still, not today, eh?'

As if to prove me wrong, at that moment the plane hit another airborne speed bump, hurling me sideways in my seat. I burst out laughing. Up until this point the trip from London to Kinshasa via Brussels had been long and boring. This was fun.

Mum, however, is a nervous passenger at the best of times. Through the seat gap ahead, I glimpsed her neck, rigid with fear. More loudly than she meant to, she said, 'Will the plane cope, Nicholas?' to Dad, who was in the seat next to hers.

'Of course,' he said, stroking her hand on the armrest.

Unfortunately, Amelia heard what Mum said too. Amelia always means well, more or less, but has a knack of saying the wrong thing. Now she leaned forward and said, 'Mrs Courtney, the wings on an Airbus A330 are tested to more than 5.2 metres of displacement. It would take an extraordinarily abrupt pressure differential to rip them off.'

Mum withdrew her hand from under Dad's, her knuckles white.

'Where do you get this stuff?' I asked Amelia.

'What stuff?' she replied, genuinely confused.

Amelia's mother met mine on the maternity ward fourteen years ago; we've known each other since we were babies. How her mind works, though, I'll never understand. It's not short of processing power, I admit, but she uses that power for the strangest things.

'Amelia means we're perfectly safe, Mum,' I said, as another wedge of turbulence lifted me, grinning, from my seat. 'The wind's just giving us a helping hand. We'll be in Kinshasa in no time.'

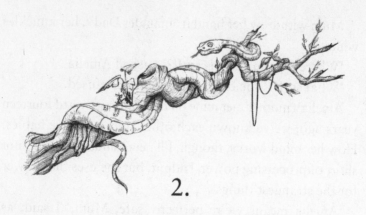

2.

I was wrong about that. The jagged air got worse. Someone a few rows back threw up (and I mean up) and somebody near the front lost it completely and began wailing. A few minutes later, although I still couldn't see anything other than blue sky out of the window, the co-pilot's super-calm voice informed us that the weather had closed in on Kinshasa. For safety's sake, we were being diverted from N'Djili Airport to somewhere else beginning with *R*, or it might have been *D*. Either way, Amelia immediately informed us that it was five hundred kilometres away. This news turned Mum's fear to frustration: she forgot her concern that our wings might fall off and set to worrying that we would miss the first of the meetings she'd scheduled in the lead-up to the environmental summit she and Dad had flown all this way to attend.

I tried to placate her. 'It's only a few hours' drive, Mum.'

'On a tarmac motorway, yes,' Amelia pointed out. 'But that distance can take days on dirt roads, particularly in the wet season, which it is now,' she added helpfully.

Dad also tried to reassure Mum all would be well. We'd be there in time to make a proper impact on the big vote, he said, but his voice had the same tone he used when he told me boarding school would be a walk in the park – which it hasn't been – and I could tell she didn't believe him either.

This vote that Mum and Dad – Janine and Nicholas Courtney, joint founders of the Courtney Conservation Foundation, to give them the names by which they wield such influence among environmental campaigners – were hoping to help get passed, was the latest in a long line of interventions staged by the Foundation. Ever since they took early retirement from their finance jobs in the City, eco-activism through the Foundation has been their thing. It's a pretty generous way to spend their time and money, I suppose, but if I'm honest, although I completely back the whole save-the-planet thing, I can't get quite as excited about it as they do. Which was why Mum had insisted I come along on this trip. While my parents would be lobbying business leaders, government officials and ministers in the capital, Kinshasa, Amelia and I were set to go on safari in one of the country's national parks, to check out the natural wonders Mum and Dad were here to protect. Though she hadn't spelled it out, I knew Mum was hoping that once I saw first-hand what was threatened, I'd be more keen to do my bit to help. And maybe I would. I was certainly up for seeing some gorillas. Either way, the gorillas' habitat, and the big vote about whether to protect it or sell it off to mining companies, was the reason we were now coming in to land at the wrong airport somewhere in the Democratic Republic of Congo.

For ages there'd been nothing but trees visible below the plane. As Amelia pointed out, I was looking at the second largest rainforest in the world, after the Amazon, in a country roughly the size of western Europe, slap bang in central Africa. I couldn't help thinking that if the gorillas weren't able to sort themselves out down there, the Courtney Foundation would have its work cut out to help them, but I didn't say that to Mum, obviously. I'm not a total idiot. Instead I listened as Amelia, who – true to form – had done her research, gave a mini lecture on the 'endemic corruption' the citizens of the Democratic Republic of Congo have to put up with.

'It's rife,' she said. 'As in quite possibly the most corrupt country on earth. There's more mineral wealth in the ground here than just about anywhere else, and yet the people are among the world's poorest. Even those who do the digging for the gold, cobalt and tantalum – which is used in mobile phones – barely see any of what it's worth. Foreign companies from China and the West bribe corrupt officials, buy up what's dug out for a pittance, sell it overseas and pocket the profit. Unless the government steps up properly – which is what the vote your folks are here to influence is all about – the country will have lost ninety-five per cent of its rainforest within the next eight years. Add in the militia, who've turned much of the country into a war zone, and the deforestation for charcoal, and the threat to wildlife from poachers . . .'

She tailed off. Looking at the calm green landscape beneath us, it was hard to believe the scale of the issues. But Amelia doesn't lie – it's one of the things I like best about her – and Mum and Dad wouldn't be focusing their efforts here if it wasn't necessary.

The pilot hit the brakes hard when we did finally touch down. That was the scariest moment for me. As with any jump, landing is the hardest part. We juddered to a crawl at the end of the runway, the seat belt tight across my lap, and then doubled back to the little terminal.

Passport control was two guys. Ours was wearing a hat about four sizes too small for his head. When I made the mistake of nodding for Amelia to check him out she said aloud, 'That's for a child; it must be uncomfortable,' and for an awful moment I thought the man had heard, since he gave us one of those very hard stares. What Dad had told me about the country being sketchy – skirmishing militia, tourist kidnappings and an epidemic of street robberies – came to mind. Apparently Dad had arranged for us to be chaperoned on our safari by ex-military guides, to head off any threat. 'We Courtneys will not be intimidated, but I've taken every precaution to make sure you kids are kept safe. We can't be too careful here,' he'd said.

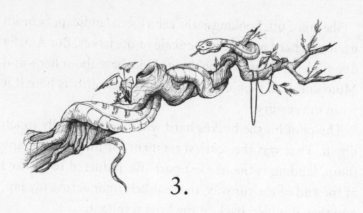

3.

It soon turned out that Dad needed to take his own advice. We collected our luggage (from the squeakiest baggage-reclaim carousel ever) and stumbled onto the hot concrete apron beyond the airport building, where a colourfully dressed crowd seemed, from the sound of things, to want something quite badly: money, of course, in exchange for taxi rides, hotel rooms, bananas, fake DVD box sets, and even, according to the little old lady wearing odd trainers, tins of glue. Fellow passengers from our diverted flight stood blinking in the harsh sunlight, trying to work out their next move. We fought our way through the throng to the kerb. The guy standing next to us looked as if he had brought everything he owned on the trip, including a set of golf clubs that toppled off his airport trolley when Amelia bumped into it. Clubs slid out, balls bounced away.

I helped her retrieve them while Dad, hands on his hips, legs apart, argued that we should check in to a hotel before deciding what to do. Mum wouldn't hear of that though.

'We have to charter a plane to get us to the capital right away,' she said.

'But the weather . . .' Dad was drowned out by the harsh rattle of an approaching motorbike.

'It will probably have cleared by the time we're back there!' Mum hollered over the noise. She'd changed her tune, fear of flying being no match for her commitment to getting on.

As I often do, I sensed something was wrong before it happened. The motorbike veered towards us. Neither of the guys on it were wearing helmets. I learned later that's the norm in Africa, but in that moment I was surprised to see beaded sweat on the driver's brow. His pillion passenger leaned out towards Dad as they got close. Dad goes to the gym three times a week and his reactions are still quick enough for him to beat me at ping-pong half the time, but he cottoned on to what was happening here as if underwater, and did nothing sensible to protect himself; he just stood there. The motorbike cut in and Dad staggered forward as the thief, having yanked his briefcase from his hand, shoved him to the ground.

The motorbike was ancient, its exhaust shot, its powers of speeding away pretty laughable. But it was able to pull beyond us before I could grab the briefcase back, and, as it flickered around the assembled crowd, I knew I couldn't catch it up.

Other than meeting my friend Xander there's not much my first year at boarding school has been good for, apart from learning how to play this game they call 'roofs'. It's banned and therefore popular, and involves throwing a tennis ball from the yard up onto the roof of our four-storey boarding house, the idea being that the next boy in line has to catch the ball when it comes down. That sounds simple, but the house is an ancient Victorian relic, and its roof is made up of all sorts of pitched hips, gables and buttresses. Throw the ball high and accurately enough and those weird slopes become a pinball machine, making it pretty hard to catch. Throw it even higher and you might break a slate, which is why the game is banned, and accounts for four of the six detentions I had in my first term.

As the motorbike wove its way through the crowd of bewildered passengers and clamorous hawkers, I realised I was still holding one of the golf balls I'd picked up from the spilled trolley. There was no way I could hit the bike, driver or passenger through the throng. But the road swept close to the side of the brick-built terminal building just beyond the crowd, and before I knew what I was doing I'd unleashed that golf ball with a year's worth of tile-busting roofs practice straight at the wall. Golf balls bounce hard. The one I threw was still flying level when it hit the bricks. I got the angle right: no doubt it was a lucky shot – Amelia wasted no time telling me that afterwards – though it must be said that I have a good arm. Either way the golf ball struck the guy driving the bike in the face, hard enough to make him lose control. He swerved into the kerb and both men fell off. By the time I'd made it through the crowd the driver was back astride the bike, revving hard. His passenger had to run and jump to make it back onto the saddle.

He'd dropped the briefcase in the crash. I picked it up and returned it to Dad. Subsiding adrenaline left me shaky as I did this, but, having done something so obviously helpful, it wasn't just the aftermath of having sprung into action that made me unable to meet Dad's eye. Weirdly, my achievement made looking straight at him even harder than usual. The awkwardness itself wasn't new; I'd not been able to face Dad properly in a long while.

'Thanks!' he said. 'My passport, laptop, all our money. How brilliant of you, Jack. What an amazing . . .' He tailed off. I felt his gaze upon me. He certainly sounded pleased, but when he saw me now, what did he actually see?

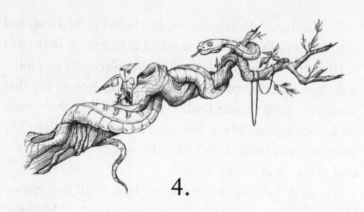

4.

To guess at that, I have to go back four years, to when I was just ten, and Mark, my brother, was twelve and a half. Mark was good at everything: sport, maths, art, the electric guitar, cooking pancakes, coding, walking on his hands, French, chess, pulling wheelies . . . the list goes on. But he was modest. When he did something well, the most he'd do was smile, run a hand through his shock of dark blond hair, give a little shrug. He wasn't even competitive. As often as not, whatever it was we were doing, he'd let me win. I loved him for that, but couldn't stand him for it at the same time.

We were walking home from school on a Friday afternoon. It was summer and we'd just had sports day. I still had sand in my socks from the long jump, which I'd won, for my year group at least. I'd also won the hundred metres. Mum and Mark both knew: they'd seen me triumph, but I still couldn't resist mentioning it again as we passed the hardware shop. I was only ten, but even then I understood that telling them

I'd won when they already knew was pathetic. Still, neither of them pointed that out. I could forgive Mum's kindness, but Mark's 'That's great' just made me feel more ashamed.

'Really great,' he repeated.

'I've got faster,' I said. 'Fastest in my year.'

He didn't reply.

'Yeah, I'm probably as fast as you.'

He smiled and pushed his fingers through his fringe.

'You don't believe me, do you?'

'I know you won your race.'

'I can prove it if you like.'

He turned to Mum and changed the subject. 'What are we having for supper?'

'I can. And I will,' I went on.

A recycling truck had paused at the entrance to our street, with men in fluorescent clothes sorting plastic and cardboard and glass into its sides. What traffic there was had snarled up behind the truck. We passed a convertible Mini with its roof down. Its driver had close-cropped hair and a glossy, trimmed beard. Classical music soared from his car, a swirl of violins accompanied by the crashing of bottles from the recycling bins. The driver was craning his neck to see what was up beyond the truck as the tang of engine fumes swam hot in the air.

'Fish and chips. How does that sound?' asked Mum.

'Lovely,' he said.

'I'll race you home, Mark. You'll see,' I said.

'But after this afternoon you must be all raced out.'

'I'm not. To the lamp post outside the house.'

'Well, I'm not sure I have the energy,' said Mark. 'In this heat.'

'It's not *that* hot,' I said. 'I think you're scared.'

'So I'm scared,' he said.

'If you won't race, you must be frightened I'll win. So in a way I've already won.'

'You've won then. Congratulations.'

Mark's refusal to rise to the challenge just made things worse. Since he wouldn't be goaded, I was embarrassed to hear myself begging instead. 'Please?'

Now turning me down would have been an unkindness, so he relented. He smiled and shook his head. 'Oh all right. But go easy on me.'

'No. You have to really race. Like it counts. Because it does!'

'Sure.' He handed Mum his school bag. She was already carrying mine, her phone in the crook of her neck.

From ahead came another crash of bottles; from behind violins surged, full of engine revs.

'To the lamp post,' said Mark.

'Yeah, the one outside the house.'

This wasn't our first race; we both knew where the finish line was.

'Want a head start?' Mark asked.

'No.'

He shrugged. 'You say go then.'

I looked up at him. He had our father's sharp features, softened by Mum's long eyelashes and wide mouth. The sun had brought out his freckles. His eyes were green, smiling yet somehow serious, giving me my due in the moment.

I took a deep breath, a step back, shouted, 'Go!' and hurtled off.

I really had improved. A growth spurt, or something new in my technique, had helped me win the sports-day race with ease, just as I would beat Mark now. I heard my feet pounding the pavement, felt my arms pumping me forward, was amazed by the sense of my own acceleration. My reflection flickered in the windows of parked cars. I was in the lead. I could hear Mark behind me, but as we rounded the postbox on the corner I was still holding him off. The pavement widened here. I took the middle line, ran for all I was worth, convinced I could beat him yet at the same time expecting him to surge past me.

The lamp post was in sight, right outside our house. To get to it we had to cross the street. Approaching the pavement-dip, our footsteps hit the same rhythm, but his stride was longer. I could sense him coming up alongside me, hear him breathing hard, gaining with each step. We were flying. In that moment I both loved and hated him with all my heart.

Somewhere behind us the man in the Mini had finally managed to swing around the recycling van. With his violins and his groomed beard and his convertible with the roof down in the sunshine, he must have felt freed, entitled to accelerate too. But I didn't know that. I didn't hear the engine pitch rise, or feel anything other than the straining of my own body at its newfound top speed. I knew nothing until I jinked off the pavement ahead of the crossing and heard an almighty screech, felt something huge and solid

15

swerving behind me, saw the reflected light from metallic green paintwork bouncing off windscreens as the Mini careened sideways into the rear wheel-arch of a parked Ford Fiesta, ramming it into Mark.

He wasn't killed instantly. When I realised what had happened and turned back to see the driver of the Mini climbing out of the passenger door, and Mum running as fast as she could up the pavement, shedding school bags as she came, Mark was still conscious, though pinned between the crushed Ford and a garden wall. I reached him first. He looked confused. His free arm struggled weakly as he fought for breath. It was as if I wasn't there. His eyes blinked straight through me and then his head slumped sideways against his shoulder, and Mum was screaming, and the Mini driver, to his credit, was tugging in vain at the Ford's back bumper. He was wearing pointy shoes with no grip. The last thing I remember is seeing him slip and sit down in the blood pooling beside the car.

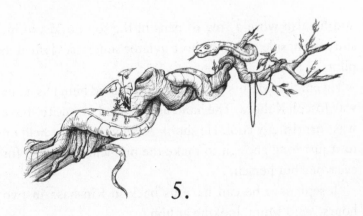

5.

'It was nothing,' I said eventually, head still down beneath Dad's gaze and the beating sun.

'That doesn't make sense,' said Amelia. 'Just because it was lucky doesn't mean it wasn't helpful.'

It was a relief to turn and roll my eyes at her.

'Thank God,' said Mum. 'Without passports and cash, we'd really be stuck.'

'True,' Dad agreed. He sounded more thoughtful than relieved.

'So let's not hang around.' Mum was in brisk mode now. 'Forget taxis and hotels. You guys wait back in the cool of the terminal. I'm going to find a pilot with a plane.'

Mum is nothing if not resourceful. Within half an hour she returned to where we were sitting on our luggage; that was one way of protecting it, I thought. She was accompanied by a smart young guy who had one of those freshly clipped lines by way of a parting in his hair. His jeans had knife-edge creases in them. Who irons their jeans? This guy, it seemed, and he also wore a row of pens in the top pocket of his shirt, alongside a pair of those aviator sunglasses issued to pilots at birth.

He put the aviators on as Mum introduced him. His name was Joseph Kahora. The hand he extended for me to shake was surprisingly cool. He shook Amelia's too; she held on to it just long enough to make the moment awkward for everyone but herself.

'Joseph says he can have us back in Kinshasa in two hours,' said Mum, looking at him.

'Of course.' He shrugged. 'Two hours tops.' His accent sounded French; it came out 'tups'.

'But the weather,' said Dad. 'We don't want you to take a risk.'

'What weather?'

'The storm.'

'No storm today.'

'There was a storm.'

'If there was one, it's gone.'

Dad looked sceptical.

Amelia turned to him. 'This pilot looks like he cares about himself, with his ironing and neat hair and everything. If he was endangering us, he'd be endangering himself too. That wouldn't make sense.' She said this at normal volume, though Joseph was right beside her, listening.

He just nodded and smiled.

Dad generally gets his way. You don't get to 'retire' at forty from investment banking by being a pushover. But as I've said, Mum also worked in the City back in the day, and Amelia makes her own special kind of concrete sense. Together they weren't pushing back; they were a brick wall.

So Joseph flew us to Kinshasa. His plane had six seats, two propellers and incredibly flimsy doors. The cracks around them let in daylight and wind, but this didn't seem to bother Mum; she was just pleased to have solved the problem of making it to the summit in good time. The run in to N'Djili was clear – not a cloud in the sky – and Joseph was an excellent pilot: the plane didn't even bounce when it hit the tarmac, just settled gently as if landing on a lake.

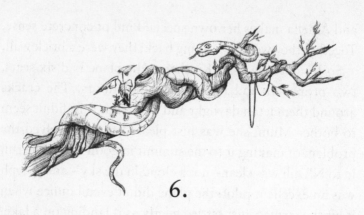

6.

The hotel was flashier than I expected. For starters, it had a pool. Also an armed guard on the door, with his gun slung super-casually over his shoulder. The big surprise though was that Xander had already arrived from Nigeria. To sweeten the offer of bringing me on the trip – mostly she just didn't want to leave me at home to ride my bike, watch YouTube and stare at the ceiling, though after a long first year at boarding school that's all I wanted to do – Mum had suggested back at Easter that I could bring a friend. She thought I'd pick Amelia, and of course I wanted her to come, but when I mentioned the trip to Xander at school he took it as an invitation too. Xander's dad is Nigerian and they live there. I'd told him about the safari and he was really up for that. So keen in fact that he had got his dad to put him on a plane from Lagos a day early. He was on a lounger by the pool, baggy shirt undone, hat on backwards, drinking Coke with an umbrella in it, when we turned up.

I introduced Xander to Amelia. It's always weird when

20

two people you know in entirely different ways meet, with you in the middle, and Xander, who's normally completely unruffable at school (he slept through a fire alarm in our first week) seemed instantly twitchy in front of Amelia. She'd changed into a swimsuit as soon as she clocked the pool, chucking her towel onto the lounger next to Xander's now, eager to get in the water.

'Nice to meet you, Amelia,' Xander said, so stiffly I laughed out loud. 'I've heard so much about you.' He immediately started doing up his shirt buttons with jittery fingers.

'How many of those have you drunk?' asked Amelia, twisting her long brown hair into a bun to fit beneath her swimming cap.

'It's Coke.'

'Yes, fully caffeinated and rammed with sugar,' she replied. 'You look wired.'

'Three,' he admitted, his face set to *Who-are-you-anyway?*

'That'll be why. Who's coming for a swim?'

Without waiting for a reply, she dived straight in, did four lengths of butterfly very quickly indeed – she's on the county swim squad – and stood up in the shallows to announce, 'It's approaching blood temperature in here, at least thirty-five degrees.'

'You'll get used to her,' I told Xander. 'Did you see the guy with the rifle out front?'

'I didn't notice him,' he said. 'But . . . you'll get used to it. I told you: Africa's different.'

'Yeah. We've already been robbed, sort of.'

'Don't stereotype.'

'It's true.'

'Well, that's either astonishingly bad luck or you were asking for it.'

I fought the urge to tell him how I'd hit the motorcyclist with the golf ball. I'm not ten any more and I've learned that a person's achievements sound more impressive if retold by someone else. It'd come out in time.

'Just bad luck, I suppose,' I said instead.

Mum and Dad came through the lobby. He was wearing a light blue suit, open-necked shirt and brown brogues. She also looked smart; I noticed she'd put on lipstick.

They knew Xander already because he'd come to stay with us for the February and May half-terms. Mum and Dad like him, mostly because he has this way of making everyone – adults included – think he's interested in them. It has something to do with asking questions and actually listening to the answers. Anyway, back home in England he'd done a job of showing an interest in the whole conservation thing and now he asked them how they thought the land lay, 'Looking ahead to the vote?'

Mum beamed at him when he said that. 'Well, we're off out lobbying this afternoon. The vote's still weeks away, but we need to get a groundswell of opinion among people in the right camp, and that means meeting with as many influencers as possible, right away.' That explained the lipstick.

'Yes,' said Dad. 'It'll be tricky: there are lots of people with a vested interest in exploiting the DRC's natural resources. Between now and the summit, we have to get as many of the good guys as possible onside.'

I nodded, but couldn't help yawning.

'And this evening your uncle's arriving to have dinner with us,' Mum said to me.

Dad pursed his lips. He and his brother don't exactly get on.

'Make yourselves comfortable here until then. Use the pool, feel free to order snacks on the room number, possibly catch up on some sleep,' she went on hopefully.

'Just keep out of trouble,' said Dad. Perhaps surprised by the harshness in his own voice, he added, 'Wish I could spend the day swimming instead of beating my head against a closed door.' It sounded like he meant it.

They set off. I realised I was hungry and ordered a club sandwich and chips. For a joke, I got Xander another Coke. Amelia ate salad with something local called *makemba*. 'It's a kind of plantain dish,' she explained. I must have looked what I felt: none the wiser. 'Cross between a potato and banana, idiot.'

'Sounds great.'

'It is,' she insisted. But she's a terrible liar, and couldn't stop herself adding, 'in small quantities.'

At this point a movement caught my eye and I looked up at the hotel roofline to see another armed security guard taking a stroll. I went to check the rear entrance of the hotel, and sure enough that was guarded too. These guys were obviously supposed to make the guests feel safe, but the idea that we needed protecting in the hotel at all was a bit unnerving.

On my way back to the pool I found a stray tennis ball.

It seemed there was a court here as well. Xander and I played catch in the pool while Amelia did laps. Xander's also pretty good at roofs. It got a bit competitive, with each of us chucking the ball harder and harder at the other, until finally I let rip properly, glancing it off the surface just in front of him at maximum speed. He missed the catch and the ball took out a tray of drinks on a poolside table – very loudly indeed.

Immediately the security guard on the roof had his gun trained on the pool area, and another one I hadn't seen before sprang through a nearby gate, his drawn pistol aimed right at me. For a nanosecond I feared he might pull the trigger. As luck would have it, Dad, who'd only been gone fifteen minutes, strolled back through reception just in time to hear the crash. He had his hands on his hips and a thunderous look on his face. *Here we go*, I thought, and sank beneath the surface of the water again.

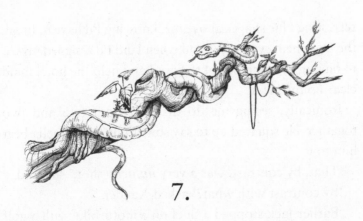

7.

In the aftermath of Mark's death Dad didn't blame me. He didn't need to. As soon as I realised my brother was dead, I knew it was my fault. Mum spent whole nights trying to convince me otherwise. When I didn't believe her, she even got a counsellor involved. Like the driver of the Mini, the counsellor had a beard, but his was more straggly. He kept a bowl of tangerines on his coffee table and offered me one when he saw me staring at them. That was kind of him; he was all kindness in fact, but none of it helped.

Dad did his best too. The week after the funeral, he bought me a BMX, took me to the bike park and sat in the car while I practised. Everything about him said, 'I am trying to forgive you.' That was the problem. There's no need to forgive someone who's done nothing wrong.

It turned out he hadn't seen what caused the drinks explosion; he was just irritated because he'd left his wallet in his other clothes and had to come back to retrieve it. But I didn't know that from underwater. I looked up at the scissoring blue shapes above me, knowing I'd have to break through them eventually, and when I did I'd resigned myself to having to climb out of the pool and help the hotel maid clear up the mess.

Ironically, seeing me do that, Dad put two and two together. He squared up to say something, but Amelia beat him to it.

'That, by contrast, was a very *unlucky* shot,' she said.

'By contrast with what?' asked Xander.

'Earlier Jack stopped a thief on a motorbike with a golf ball. It was a lucky ricochet.'

Reminded of this, Dad dropped his hands to his sides and explained that he'd left his wallet upstairs.

'You're not being very vigilant today, Mr Courtney,' said Amelia. 'It's unlike you. Maybe you're getting old. Early-onset dementia is a thing.'

Xander tilted his face into the water to laugh. Even Dad couldn't help smiling.

'I'll catch you later,' he said, pausing before delivering the truly bad news with a glint in his eye. 'Your uncle Langdon called. As well as meeting him tonight you can expect to see your cousin again. Caleb's out here for the summer on work experience at his father's mining company apparently. Try to be nice, eh.'

Caleb. Ugh. Just as Dad finds his brother hard to take, my cousin and I have never really got on. He's only fifteen, but that puts him two school years ahead of me, and when he condescends to speak to me at all he treats me like I'm a complete idiot. I tried to tell myself that he might have

26

changed in the six or so months since I'd last seen him, but no. When he turned up that evening with Uncle Langdon, he barely said hello to me, just nodded and then started asking Mum and Dad how their lobbying that afternoon had gone. The way he asked ('How *has* blah blah blah been going?') was ridiculous; I could hear his father's opinion – that Mum and Dad's conservationism was a waste of time – lurking behind his apparently interested question. It made me feel protective towards them. He'd filled out and his hair was different: short on top and shaved at the sides. Was he trying to look like a US Marine?

Uncle Langdon wears Hawaiian shirts and loves the sound of his own voice. I think he thinks the combination makes him unexpected and witty. Sure enough, his big thing today was not-so-subtly undermining the efforts of the Courtney Conservation Foundation (he's never forgiven Dad for putting the family name to such a venture) over drinks at the bar. He didn't exactly say that what they were doing was a bad thing, just that it was unnecessary.

'How can you think that?' asked Mum. 'The rainforest is disappearing at a rate of –'

'*Was* disappearing,' Uncle Langdon interrupted. 'But responsible outfits, like our own, are already leading the way as far as conservation is concerned. By showing the locals how to mine sustainably, safely *and* profitably, we're encouraging them to do the same.'

Mum said, 'I'm sure you're doing your bit,' in a voice that told me she wasn't sure of that at all.

She was probably right, I thought, and before I could

stop myself I stirred the pot by saying, 'You guys should go and see for yourself.'

'Not a great idea,' said Uncle Langdon. 'The bush is a dangerous place.'

Mum said, 'We've a lot on our plates as it is. And the thing is, although I'm sure you're mining sustainably, without proper legislation, passed and enforced by the government, there's no guarantee others will follow suit.'

Uncle Langdon, who had drained his champagne flute, refilled it without offering anyone else a top-up. 'Even if you get this vote passed, relying on the powers that be to enforce it is laughable,' he went on. 'This mob couldn't police a shopping centre, much less the jungle. A load of red tape is just an opportunity for already corrupt officials to make things much, much worse.'

Mum sat back. Dad sighed, but obviously felt he had to chip in. 'We take your point, Langdon, but a two-pronged attack by government and industry is generally considered to be the best way.'

Langdon did some earnest nodding, while conveying 'Yeah, right, I don't think so' from every pore.

Mum bristled, but Dad's *this-is-exactly-what-I'd-expect-from-you-Langdon* expression lacked bite. Disagreements between the two often escalate into proper arguments – they actually squared up to each other over a business deal that went wrong a couple of Christmases ago – but today Dad seemed content to let Langdon's condescension go.

Since Uncle Langdon's mouth was full of champagne, Caleb took the opportunity to chip in. 'Dad's point about corruption is key. Nothing gets done here unless the right people are paid.'

He shook his shaved head very man-of-the-world-wearily. It made me want to ask him how many bribes he – personally – had paid, but I bit my tongue. Instead I sat and listened to his phoney I'm-such-an-adult questions, sipping my drink, waiting for Mum to do what she always does, which is try to push us together. Sure enough, when Uncle Langdon started ribbing Dad for having given up his real job in favour of helping questionable do-good causes, she said, 'You and Caleb should go to join the others in the games room. You can take him on at ping-pong or something.'

'Others?' said Caleb.

'Jack's brought a couple of friends along for the safari,' explained Mum.

'That's nice for you,' he told me in a tone that made me want to punch him.

'Why don't you introduce him to Amelia and Xander?' Mum, oblivious, went on.

It wasn't actually a suggestion, of course. I did what I was told. I led Caleb through the marble lobby to the hotel's games room, where we found Xander and Amelia playing pool. Amelia is all right at pool. She was leaning over the table with just one red ball and the black to dispatch, while Xander, whose yellows were still all over the place, watched.

Amelia didn't look up until she'd potted both balls.

'Four nil,' she said. 'Another one?'

'Nah, I'm good,' said Xander.

'Good? But you lost four times . . .' Amelia trailed off as

she noticed Caleb. He didn't wait for me to say who he was, just launched right in, introduced himself and offered to play the next game. I didn't say anything, but I knew that Caleb has his own pool table at home. He's annoyingly good at it. I watched him out of the corner of my eye as Xander and I played table tennis. He let Amelia get ahead, then reeled her in, then snookered her again and again, drawing the game out. All the while he was chatting to her in a way that made my skin crawl, though I don't know why. It's not as if Amelia can't look after herself – she's as resilient as she is honest. I just didn't like that my cousin was making me feel that she might have to watch her back.

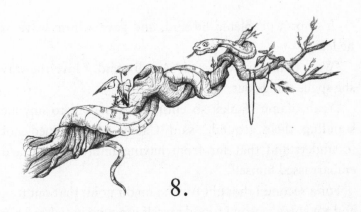

8.

'Well played,' she said, when he eventually beat her. I was pleased when she added, 'You made a bit of a meal of it, but won all the same.'

At this point two guys aged about eighteen walked in. One of them had dreadlocks; the other was wearing a vest top revealing tanned, bulging arms. He obviously worked out and was keen to let everyone know. 'Mind if we use the table?' the gym-built guy asked. He sounded American.

'Actually, yes. We've not finished,' said Caleb, puffing himself up.

Xander shot me a look.

'But we have,' Amelia pointed out.

'That game, but not the next one,' said Caleb, staring from one newcomer to the other.

A pause followed.

'Whatever,' said the guy with the arms, eventually. 'We'll come back later.'

'But –' Amelia began.

'It's not a problem,' he said, and gave a little wave as he left.

'Well, that was awkward,' Amelia said. I love the way she spells things out.

'Yeah, damn Yanks, so entitled. Not used to anyone standing their ground,' said Caleb, who seemed not to understand that far from having impressed us he'd embarrassed himself.

For a second I thought Amelia might point that out too, and for some reason I found myself jumping in to head her off. 'It has to be dinner time,' I said.

'Sure, let's go and eat,' said Caleb, and led the way back to the bar as if it had been his suggestion. When we passed the two Americans in the main lobby, Caleb's big-man walk turned into an actual swagger.

But if that episode was annoying, things got worse when we sat down in the hotel restaurant. Mum explained that she'd learned Caleb wasn't due to start his work experience for another ten days. What that had to do with us, I couldn't guess at first. Uncle Langdon, who had ordered king prawns, paused as he was ripping the head off one to make things clear.

'So, Caleb, to save you kicking your heels here in Kinshasa, I thought you might like to go with these guys, on their safari.'

'What, as a chaperone?' said Caleb.

Langdon shrugged. 'If you like.'

Thankfully Mum corrected him. 'There's no need for that. We've sourced one of the most experienced safari guides in the country. He's ex-military and heads a team that has a perfect record in keeping clients safe. They know the hotspots to avoid and how to defuse trouble, in the unlikely event they run into it. There's an element of risk in everything we do, heightened here in the DRC, I concede, but life is all about minimising risk to optimise outcomes. The outcome we want here is for you youngsters to come away inspired to defend the planet. You're its inheritors after all.'

Mum can be a bit preachy at times, but you have to admire the fire in her eyes when she goes off on one. This safari she and Dad had organised for us, with all their precautionary research and risk assessment, well, it obviously mattered deeply to her, and Caleb's 'Whatever you say. I don't mind going along for the ride' set my teeth on edge.

Langdon made things worse by saying, 'Obviously Caleb's been on safari before. He can show you the ropes.'

Caleb, who was smiling at Amelia now, had definitely decided the plan wasn't a bad one. If I hadn't known how much it would disappoint Mum, I'd probably have chosen not to go at all rather than have him tagging along thinking he was remotely in charge. But the arrangement already had a sort of bike-crash inevitability. It felt like that split second when you lose control and time slows down to give you a chance to wonder, before you hit the ground, how much it's going to hurt.

Langdon went on. 'Yes, despite my reservations about your little eco-crusade –' he looked from Mum to Dad and back to Caleb again – 'it won't do you any harm to see the flora and fauna everyone, including those of us who mine

33

responsibly – in fact *especially* us, for the sake of business as well as the chimps and whatnot – wants to protect. You need to learn about the industry from all sides after all.'

The fire in Mum's eyes had turned to ice. She looked away from Langdon. 'This will be a chance for you boys to get to know each other better,' she said. She could tell I wasn't overjoyed, I know, because now that she was focusing on me, her face wore the anxious expression that always makes me feel a bit sorry for her.

'Sure,' I said, and patted her hand.

'That's settled then,' said Langdon. 'I'll dock the cost of the safari from your first pay cheque, Caleb,' he added, and chomped down on another prawn.

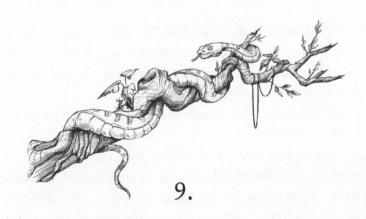

9.

A couple of days later we flew from Kinshasa to a town called Goma, having spent most of the intervening time in the hotel games room or at the pool. Fun enough, with Caleb out of the picture, but I kept asking to see something of the place, so eventually Mum organised for an armed hotel guard to ferry us out on one brief trip to the national museum. The place was tiny, and I mean that as a compliment. In standard-size museums I generally feel like lying down for a sleep before I've even started. Here I more or less made it to the end, though I was a bit vague about what we were looking at, since the signs were all in French. Xander did some translating. There were some tribal masks in the gallery, and a couple of statues outside. One was of an explorer called Stanley who discovered Congo. I'm pretty sure it was here before he found it, but still. Then Amelia gave us a fascinating – it actually was – lecture about another man made out of bronze: King Leopold II of Belgium. This guy was on a massive horse and had a huge, wedge-shaped beard. Needless to say, Amelia knew a load of dates about him, but all I can remember is that he helped put 'Belgian' before 'Congo' after Stanley 'found' it, declared the entire country was his, and ran the place for a while until they kicked him out.

'Although by "ran" I really mean "looted",' said Amelia.

'If you say so.'

'Just as the West, and China, with the help of local warlords, continue to rob the country of its natural resources today. If you think about it, this country, the heart of Africa, has been pillaged pretty constantly for a hundred and fifty years. From King Leopold to your uncle Langdon, outsiders have always wanted to slice up the pie.'

She can get earnest pretty quickly, Amelia. A bit like Mum; they share an admirable passionate streak. But lumping Leopold – who declared the whole country his – in with Langdon – who on his word at any rate just wanted to do sustainable business here – seemed a bit harsh. But whatever. I wasn't about to defend him.

I looked over Amelia's shoulder at the most impressive thing we saw that day: a view of the city spilling down to the river, which lay massive and brown in the distance. If the Natural History Museum in London makes the Kinshasa National Museum look like a shed, the Congo River makes the Thames look like a streak of dog wee. I unholstered my camera and took a few wide-angle shots before one of the museum staff told me I had to pay extra for the privilege.

Caleb joined us again for the trip to the airport, where Uncle Langdon, wearing a lime-green Hawaiian shirt, made a big show of the fact that we'd be travelling east in one of his charter jets. Caleb got in on the act, telling Amelia, 'This country has one of the worst air-safety records in the world: all its airlines are blacklisted in the developed world,' loudly enough for other passengers in the terminal to hear.

She wasn't impressed. 'Statistically, flying here is still safer than riding a bicycle at home, by a factor of about ten.'

This should have put him in his place, but he just shrugged and said something else to her, too quietly for me to hear. Annoyingly, whatever it was made her smile. She sat next to him on the plane. Just because a person knows a lot, doesn't make them a good judge of character.

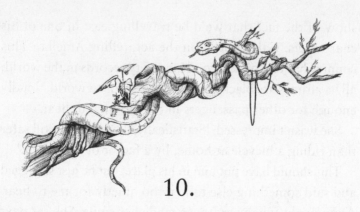

10.

It was only after we'd landed in Goma that I really started to think about what we were about to do there, namely trek into the jungle in search of chimpanzees and gorillas. I have to admit I was looking forward to it: I'd have the opportunity to take some good photos. Our safari guide picked us up from the airport with a placard that spelled 'Courtny' wrong, and introduced himself as Innocent.

Amelia said out loud what I was thinking: 'Unusual name. French, I suppose.'

Thankfully he took no offence, just said, 'That's right,' with a big smile, and led us to a battered Toyota Hilux among the sea of motorbikes and pickups parked haphazardly in front of the terminal. He was quite young, thirty at most, with thin stubble on his chin but not his cheeks. It was as if his face was saying this was all it could manage for now, beard-wise, but he moved quickly and authoritatively, which persuaded me he knew exactly what he was doing. This guy was a former soldier after all.

A small girl was leaning against the pickup's tailgate. Instead of telling her to clear off, Innocent introduced her.

'This is Patience, my daughter and right-hand man. She'll be coming with us. She's learning how to track and is already ten times better than I was at her age,' he said proudly.

This Patience only looked about ten, but she stepped forward with a confidence that made her seem much older. She had the biggest, steadiest eyes I'd ever seen, and she gazed at each of us in turn without blinking – the absolute opposite of being nervous to meet us. Caleb had put his pack on the floor. Without asking him, Patience – who couldn't have weighed much more than the pack – swung it up into the back of the pickup in one clean movement and motioned for the rest of us to follow suit. We climbed in ourselves after our luggage, at Innocent's instruction. Caleb tried to assert his authority by telling us – pointlessly – that all this was normal. He'd done something similar before, many times. What 'all this' was, I don't know.

'Rest assured,' he went on, 'my dad's people will have done thorough due diligence on this safari outfit.'

Apart from cringing a bit – he'd said this right in front of Innocent and Patience – I didn't react to this statement. The truth was, I didn't know exactly what 'due diligence' meant. Amelia must have noticed, because she said, 'He means Langdon's done background checks on our guides, but we know your mum and dad did that before they booked us onto the trip, so I'm not exactly sure why he said it.'

'Belt and braces,' Caleb said, looking away.

Before we set off, Innocent introduced our driver,

explaining that although he was brilliant at negotiating dirt roads he spoke no English. In the Toyota's big wing mirror I saw the man had bloodshot eyes. He did speak French as well as the local language, but it seemed he did that grudgingly; after he'd fought the pickup through the weaving motorbikes to our hotel Xander offered him a '*merci beaucoup*' and said something about the traffic and got just a grunt in reply.

I say 'hotel', but this place was nothing like where we had stayed in Kinshasa. That one was posh; this one was not. Like just about every other building I saw on our way into the incredibly busy town centre, it was low-rise with a corrugated roof, and bits of it hadn't yet been built. Someone had put plastic flowers on the reception desk though, and the floor looked clean enough.

After we'd checked in, Amelia, Xander and I went to explore the hotel garden, which was also half finished. In the middle of an incomplete patio stood an empty fountain with rocks in the bottom. There being no chairs, we sat on the concrete lip, dangling our feet into what would have been water if the fountain had been full. It was late afternoon. In Kinshasa the heat had been constant and oppressive; Goma, today, was cool by comparison. The sky above us was the colour of a fresh bruise and there was a sulphurous rotten egg smell coming from somewhere. When she heard me mention it to Xander, Amelia said, 'It's because of the geography, not a lack of sanitation.'

'Meaning?' asked Xander.

'We're on the shore of Lake Kivu. Its depths are full of

pressurised gas. Mostly carbon monoxide, which doesn't smell, but there's some methane down there too and that does. Both are lethal if released in large quantities.'

'That's all right then,' said Xander.

'But it could just be the volcano.'

From the looks on our faces she could tell we didn't know which volcano she was talking about.

'Nyiragongo. It's only twenty kilometres away. Hasn't erupted since 2002, when it took out half the city. It's still active.'

'Great,' said Xander, but I could see he was impressed with how much she knew.

Amelia looked for a moment as if she might be about to correct him, but she stopped herself and instead went off in a different direction: 'But that's still quite a long way for a smell to blow, I think. Actually I don't know: how far do smells carry? A strong wind can blow for thousands of miles, but surely if it was a real gale it would disperse the smell? You don't ever hear of tornadoes carrying smells. Breezes do though. Wolves and bears can smell things wafted at them from miles away, but we're not them, we're humans. I've never thought about it much before, but what's the furthest distance a human being can smell, do you reckon?'

Amelia's monologues make me smile. But neither of us had an answer to her question. I was staring at the green plastic fence running round the edge of the garden, thinking, or at least pretending to, when a movement caught my eye. From behind what looked like a water butt in the corner of the garden a rat ambled into view. I hate rats. This one was large and grey and in no hurry. Xander saw it at the same time as me. Without saying anything, we both leaned forward and each picked up a rock from the pile at our feet. I expected the movement might make the rat scuttle away, but it just stopped and eyeballed us. The horrible thing was less than ten metres away. I drew my hand back slowly, preparing to unleash, and Xander did the same. But I hesitated. The shot hardly seemed fair. It wasn't until Xander threw his stone and missed, startling the rat – it jumped high in the air – that my revulsion kicked in. I aimed at the gap between the water butt and the fence and hit the rat squarely as it fled. I'd thrown a fair-sized stone. I'm not sure if you'd call it instant, but by the time the three of us had crossed the patio to have a look, the twitching was over, the rat dead.

Innocent, Patience and Caleb came into the garden at that moment.

When Caleb worked out that it was me who'd killed the rat he made a good show of being unimpressed. 'Not really an act of conservation as such, was it?' he said.

He had a point, but I didn't bother answering him.

There's no way I'd have touched the thing with my bare hands, but Patience, completely unfazed, picked it up by the tail.

'It was old,' said Innocent. 'Grey hair, look.'

Whether that made my having killed it better or worse I didn't know.

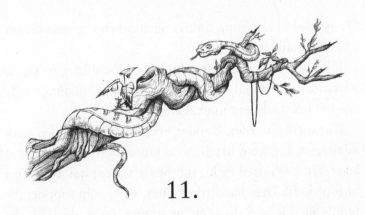

11.

The following morning we set off in search of chimpanzees. Innocent said the national park we'd be visiting was 'local', but the journey still took all day. The easy bit was crossing the lake by boat. After what Amelia had said about the gas in it, I expected the lake to be bubbling, but it was just a huge green-brown mirror reflecting a sky full of enormous clouds, pinpricked with birds. Innocent pointed out a pair of eagles riding a thermal and handed round his battered binoculars for us to take a better look. The birds were huge wedges of black with wide, ragged wings and short white tails. While I was watching them, the bigger of the two dived down to the other and seized hold of its talons and the pair spun towards the lake like a huge sycamore leaf, only breaking apart just in time to stop themselves from hitting the water.

'They're friends,' Innocent explained. 'Male and female.'

Caleb, who'd brought his own binoculars with him, had also watched the birds fall. I overheard him tell Amelia,

'They could have hung on to one another a second longer and still made it.'

If I'd said anything that stupid, she would have given me a lecture on terminal velocity or something, but annoyingly she left his statement unchallenged.

During the journey, Xander, ever the smooth talker with adults, got Innocent to tell us his life story – or some of it at least. He was raised by his mother in the capital, the eldest of four kids. They had little money, so to help support the family he'd joined the army as soon as he could. This, he ruefully suggested, was, 'Very silly, a big mistake.'

'Why's that?' asked Caleb.

Smiling, Innocent simply shook his head.

'How old were you when you joined up?'

Still with the faraway smile, Innocent replied, 'Very young, very young indeed'.

'Where did you serve? And in what capacity?' Caleb asked, in a voice that seemed to imply he'd be able to relate to Innocent's experience, whatever it had been.

'Here and there. Mostly they sent us to fight in the east.'

Amelia nodded. 'Makes sense. That is the part of the country that has been most at odds with itself. And it still is, with all the militia groups fighting each other for control.'

'That's why Innocent here is the best man to keep us out of harm's way,' said Xander. 'Isn't that right? We're lucky to have you.'

Innocent's face said, *Oh yes, for sure*.

And with that the conversation would have ended, if Caleb

44

hadn't ploughed on. 'I bet you experienced some stuff, eh,' he said. 'What was the sketchiest action you saw?'

Now Innocent's smile faded. Rather than answer, he turned to Patience and said, 'Our guests must be thirsty. Pass round the water.'

Caleb jerked his head back, annoyed to be ignored. For an awkward nanosecond I thought he might insist on an answer. But as Patience pulled bottles of mineral water from the cardboard box at her feet, Xander cut in with, 'How did you make the switch to safari guiding?'

Innocent's face lit up. 'It's my passion,' he said. 'Ever since I was small I loved animals. Stray dogs, cats, chickens, even little mice.'

I felt bad about killing the rat, but didn't say anything.

He went on, 'My mother tore her hair out over the number of creatures I brought home.'

'Very David Attenborough,' said Amelia. 'He's a TV naturalist on –' She cut out when I dug my elbow into her side.

'Yes,' said Innocent. To Caleb he continued, 'Only one good thing came from the army for me. It was that I saw this beautiful country, the national parks, Virunga and so forth, the paradise of them. And also I saw the threat to it all, from bad and greedy men – desperate men. In time I will tell you how we resist them if you like.' Turning back to Xander, he continued, 'So the first thing I did when I escaped the army was to train as a ranger, using my skills to help protect the park and its animals. I did that for five years. Then, because I had learned to speak

45

English, I could start with the tour guiding too. And now I do both, guiding and the ranger work. I help defend the parks and show them off. Because the more people who see what's actually in the rainforest, the more people will fight to save it.'

Mum had done well in her choice of guide. The gentle heat in his voice as he made this speech was heartfelt. I'd already warmed to him. The fact that he'd put himself on the line as a soldier in defence both of his country and its wildlife made me like him even more.

If the lake crossing was a smooth, comfortable ride, the road more than made up for it. A streak of orange dirt weaving through the emerald greenery, it had for years, according to Innocent, been cut to shreds by tyres and rain, then been baked hard by the sun and shredded by rain and tyres again. The result was a rutted, soupy, jolty, bumpy mess. We were in the back of another pickup truck, bouncing all over the place. When I could, I watched the driver in the wing mirror. His eyes, still bloodshot, were slits of concentration as he wrestled with the steering wheel, which was covered in fur that might once have been white but was now the colour of the rat I had killed. For some reason, the man unnerved me.

We spent the night in a permanent camp on the edge of the reserve. Innocent was in one tent, Xander, Caleb and I shared another, while Amelia bunked with little Patience. I think she wanted to take the young girl under her wing, but given where we were, I suspect Amelia had more relevant stuff to learn from Patience than the other way around. Hard rain fell in the small hours and the noise on the canvas woke me up. It sounded as if we were inside a drum. In the morning, after a breakfast of salted hard-boiled eggs and strangely sweet bread, Innocent introduced us to the porters he said would be hiking into the bush with us.

'Porters?' said Caleb.

'To help carry, track, et cetera.'

'But hold on. We're not fat old Americans, incapable of carrying our own gear.'

Under his breath Xander said, 'He should possibly can the racist stuff.'

Innocent had a wide, disarming smile, and deployed it now. 'I know. Strong young guys,' he said. 'And girl! But it's dense vegetation here and difficult underfoot. Also for the tracking, best to have more eyes.'

'But you've been employed to do the guiding,' Caleb insisted. 'We don't need extras. The four of us can carry whatever we need.'

'Does it really matter?' Xander muttered.

As if explaining the alphabet to a two-year-old, Caleb said, 'Age-old scam – rack up the cost with unnecessary extra help.'

'But Jack's parents paid in advance,' Amelia pointed out.

'Yes, but they'll all want tipping,' Caleb replied.

'OK, no problem!' Innocent waved Caleb's concerns – and three of the porters – away. Pointing to the last one he said, 'Just Marcel. He stays. Marcel is strong as two men anyway, also ex-army, and best tracker in DRC. After me, of course.' He pulled his handheld GPS navigation device from his pocket and waved it at us, attempting to divert our attention with the joke.

Marcel, who happened to have a semi-automatic rifle slung casually over his shoulder, helped him out by saying, '*Oui, mais moi je n'ai pas besoin de piles.*'

Amelia laughed at that and said, 'He says he doesn't need batteries.'

For a moment I thought Caleb might argue that all help was unnecessary, but Innocent, in his sing-song voice, cut him off by adding, 'Can be dangerous animals. Security!' And that seemed to get through to him.

Innocent then told us what to include in our daypacks. The usual: spare dry clothes, a hat and water for the day. I added a few bits I'd brought along: a penknife, matches, mosquito repellent, flashlight and a new roll of super-strong duct tape I'd packed because Dad once told me the stuff was capable of mending just about anything. We parcelled out what seemed to me to be more than enough food and water between us. I had to admit Caleb was right: we wouldn't need any help with what we had to carry. But that just left me with a nagging worry. I liked Innocent. He had a trustworthy face, and I knew Mum and Dad would have paid him properly. I didn't think he'd been trying to pull a fast one as Caleb had suggested, which meant he must have thought we needed extra local help for some other reason. What did 'security' refer to? Which 'dangerous animals' did he mean?

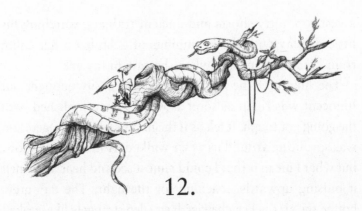

12.

Before we set off, Innocent gave us each a long stick to walk with, explaining that it might come in handy for bashing a path through the jungle. He and Marcel had straight-edged machetes. When Caleb saw them, he leaned his pole up against the gnarled tree we were standing beneath and ducked back into the tent to fetch his own machete from his kitbag.

'Almost forgot it,' he told Innocent. 'Thanks for reminding me.'

I could see doubt behind the guide's eyes, but he didn't object, just watched as Caleb strapped his knife, which came in a commando-style black rubberised sheath, to his thigh. When he drew it out, the blade flashed blue silver. He waved it around a bit, trying to look as if he used it often, but the machete was obviously brand new and, combined with the lime-green hiking boots he was wearing, also clearly just out of the box. He looked ridiculous. I wasn't the only person who thought so. I noticed Patience, dressed only in a vest top, tatty shorts and ancient trainers, watching his little display with the beginnings of a smile on her calm, round face. It vanished when she caught my eye.

The hike into the jungle started out easily enough, but Innocent was right, as soon as we left the established path the going got tough. It felt as if the impossibly lush vegetation was sprouting around us as we walked. And it was, I know, but what I mean is that I could almost see and hear and smell it pulsing upwards, reaching for the light. The day grew hotter, the air thicker, chewier. It smelled strangely like cooked broccoli. At one point I stepped over a moving line of bright green ants, each as big as a paper clip, some carrying leaves or bits of twig. Where were they going? Where were we, for that matter? There were no clearings as such, just patches of less dense tree-tangle. We had to push aside fronds and stalks and whole bushes to make progress, and despite the thick tread of my walking boots I slipped and slid when the earth beneath us became a reddish clay sludge. I wasn't about to complain though. Patience, carrying a load that looked suspiciously heavier than mine, was just ahead of me much of the time, floating along with ease, even pausing to hold the occasional branch clear of our makeshift path, and she didn't appear to have even broken a sweat.

With so much going on at ground level, as we pushed through the foliage I didn't really have time to look beyond my feet. But we hadn't been on the move long before Innocent paused, motioned for us to be quiet and pointed up at the canopy above us, indicating a group of brown and grey monkeys gathered among the branches.

'Red colobus,' he said. 'Resting now, after early-morning feeding.'

I craned my neck to get a better look. The name made sense; on closer inspection their brownish backs were more a coppery red. They looked thoughtful up there, meditative almost, and their fur was improbably stylish, like a show-dog's. Through the zoom lens of my camera I could clearly make out three young-looking monkeys dangling their legs over a thick branch – and closer to us still, a bigger, older specimen sitting in the crook of a branch, leaning right back, with his hands clasped behind his head. If the first lot looked as if they were on a park bench, he was definitely kicking back on a sunlounger. I snapped a few good photos while we watched them; by zooming in I could fill the frame with individual faces.

'That's a good sign,' said Amelia in my ear.

'Why?'

'Chimpanzees eat colobus monkeys.'

I know Amelia well. She was pointing out a fact, not hoping to see the beautiful creatures above us torn apart.

Xander, however, looked worried. 'And that's a good thing?' he said.

Caleb answered for Amelia. 'Means they might be close. If we're lucky we could even get to see them hunting, I suppose.'

Happily – on all counts – Innocent corrected him. 'That's unlikely,' he pointed out gently. 'If there were chimps nearby, the colobus wouldn't be so relaxed.'

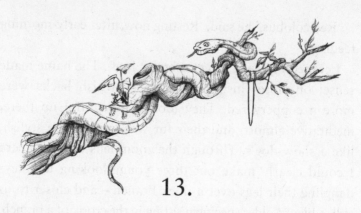

13.

We pushed on further into the jungle, with Innocent telling us the names of the plants and trees. They mostly went in one ear and out the other, if I'm honest, but the most common plant we had to hack through at ground level was a straggly thing about my height, with longish blue-green leaves. Innocent told us the pigment in those leaves was hypersensitive to light, little of which managed to filter through the canopy above.

Though I don't know what those straggly plants were called I do know the name of the bird responsible for the 'ka-ka-ka' noise that erupted close by while Innocent was telling us about the pigment. The kaka bird. Obviously. Later he pointed out an aardvark hole, twice the size of the entrance to the badgers' set on the north slope of Pitch Hill back home in the south of England, and later still he stopped beside an enormous mound, the surface of which was alive with termites, shimmering in the gloom like petrol on tarmac.

The heat pressed in from all sides.

My shirt stuck to my back, my trousers stuck to my legs, my boots stuck to my feet.

We walked for hours.

We didn't see any chimpanzees.

But just as I was about to give up hope and suggest we head back to camp and try again the following day (somebody had to crack; I wasn't too proud to do it), Marcel, who was leading the way, stopped dead mid-machete-swing. We all paused. I heard Amelia beside me take in a breath to ask what was going on, and held up my own hand to shush her, just in time. We all stood still.

'Bingo,' said Innocent.

All at once there was a mighty eruption of shriek-chattering and the canopy ahead of us shook as the troop of chimpanzees we'd walked all this way to see dropped and climbed and swung, hand over hand over hand, from branch to vine to branch, some lowering themselves all the way down to the patchy undergrowth, others ricocheting up into the treetops. Innocent motioned for us to squat down next to him and gave us each a blue paper hospital mask. As I fiddled to put mine on he explained that this troop, led by an alpha male called Bingo, were habituated to humans. The cacophonous display was a greeting of sorts. But although they were used to people, and therefore would tolerate us getting close, that made them vulnerable to catching any harmful bugs we might be carrying.

'By bugs, you mean pathogens,' said Amelia. 'That's the collective term for viruses and bacteria.'

'Smart-arse.' I smiled.

She gave me a questioning look.

'Just put the thing on!' I said, snapping the elastic round the back of my head.

Masked, we looked like a gang of surgeons about to perform an operation. If I'd been a chimpanzee I'd have run a mile. But Bingo's troop didn't seem to mind. If anything, by the time we'd put on the masks and stepped forward into the trees they'd been cavorting through, they'd calmed right down. Some were still milling about on the ground, but most were back up among the branches, ignoring us.

I'd seen chimpanzees before, at Whipsnade Zoo, and even though I was only about seven I'd found the fact that they were stuck in an enclosure a bit depressing. This was different. They might have been used to humans, but it felt as if we were visiting them on their terms. They seemed content enough to hang – literally – in the trees around us for the time being, but if they had decided to move off, we had no way to stop them and wouldn't have been able to keep up with them. That, and the fact that we'd searched for so long to find them, made me really focus on what I was seeing.

The youngster nearest me was picking at the shoulder of the one next to him, parting the long dark fur carefully in search of something or other. He rolled sideways to look more closely at what he was doing, and his short back legs stuck out towards me. I zoomed in on him. How thickly padded his feet were, how pronounced and distinctive the paleness of his face. And those ears. They really did stick out like saucers, comical brackets either side of a serious brow. His fingers mesmerised me most. They were so unhurried and precise. The ape he was grooming had his eyes half closed. The pair of them, sitting right there, not ten metres from us, looked blissfully content.

Having cottoned on to the idea that Amelia knew a fact or two about the natural world, Caleb now started telling her what he knew about chimpanzees. It wasn't much. 'You know they're five to eight times as strong as a man, pound for pound,' was the best he could come up with. As it happens, Amelia, Xander and I had already speculated about whether that clichéd statistic was true, back at the hotel, and three minutes on Google had dispelled it as a myth. They're strong, but not that strong. And anyway, looking at these chimpanzees, bumbling about among the vines and sitting placidly together, emphasised their gentleness, not their strength, for me.

I waited for Amelia to correct Caleb, but amazingly she just said, 'Hmm.'

I fought the urge to say something myself, and won by concentrating instead on what was in front of me again. A female chimpanzee on the ground off to my left had picked up a piece of wood. After inspecting it, she brought it down smartly on what I at first thought was a stone balanced on the tree root in front of her. In fact it was a nut. Once, twice, a third time she hit the nut, her face set in concentration, until the shell broke apart, at which point I swear her expression changed to one of satisfaction. I took a photograph of it. Delicately she swept the crushed shell off her anvil-root, retrieved the nut itself and ate it. And then she picked up another nut and repeated the process.

I gaped at Innocent, who smiled proudly. 'She's the best at it,' he said. 'Also fishing fire ants from a nest with a fine twig . . . she's champion of that too.'

'They hunt meat as well though, right?' said Caleb.

'Nuts, fruit, leaves, colobus. They're as omnivorous as you,' Innocent replied.

'We share ninety-seven per cent of our genes with higher primates,' Amelia said, then corrected herself: 'Actually it's between ninety-six and ninety-eight per cent, depending on how you calculate it.'

'Thanks for clarifying,' said Xander.

Amelia, missing the gentle sarcasm, took Xander's words as an invitation to expand and started telling him about humans and chimpanzees sharing a common ancestor dating back just six-to-eight million years. That seemed a long time ago to me. I tuned them both out. Undoubtedly there was something human about the apes. But it was more complicated than that. Being in the jungle with them filled me with two contradictory emotions. On the one hand, I felt as if I was connected, part of something larger than myself. On the other, looking through my zoom lens into the nearest chimp's black-brown eyes, I felt very, very alone.

I became aware that Innocent had got to his feet. Patience stood up too, beside him. A general restlessness spread among the chimpanzees. Their chatter was more urgent. In seconds they had all moved away. Whether Innocent and his daughter had triggered the change or were responding to it, I didn't know.

'Quickly, we must leave,' he said.

I turned just in time to see Marcel raise his gun to his shoulder. Something – or someone – was moving through the jungle towards us. One figure became two, five, six . . . nine men at least, half of them armed.

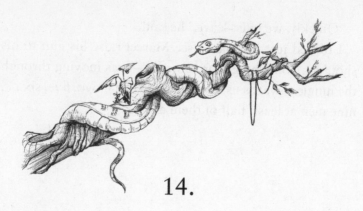

14.

Innocent said something in French and Marcel put his gun down.

'What's going on?' said Caleb. 'Who are these guys? What do they want?'

I took in the man nearest me. He was wearing stout rubber boots, a trucker's cap, and an out-of-date Manchester United football shirt. I noticed all that before fixing upon the rifle slung across his chest, the muzzle of which was casually but definitely pointed at me. The situation didn't seem real. It was laughable! Except that it was absolutely real and, I'll admit, frightening. Unable to stop myself, I took a step nearer to Amelia, at which point another of the men, this one wearing a khaki shirt and sunglasses – despite the gloom – shouted something and moved very quickly towards us, waving his gun at each of us in turn.

'Let's stay nice and still,' sang Innocent. 'Still is nice.'

The chimpanzee noise behind us evaporated as they moved off through the trees.

'What do these people want?' Caleb repeated. He was trying to sound authoritative but his voice was brittle.

By contrast, Innocent's murmuring was calm. 'Nice guys,' he said. 'Just hunters. Everything's fine.'

Amelia couldn't stop herself saying, 'Not if they're hunting us, it's not!' Her tone was flippant but I could tell she was terrified. I was too. Dad had warned us about the kidnap threat here; were we about to experience it at first-hand?

Innocent managed a chuckle. 'No, no, no! Everyone be still and quiet. I will have a nice chat, very nice. Everything's good.' He sounded fine but I noticed his hands, raised in front of him, were fluttering slightly as he took a step forward to talk with the last of the men to emerge. This guy was older, pot-bellied, unarmed, and his face was so black in the half-light that it seemed almost blue. Whoever these people were, he was clearly in charge of them.

Innocent and the man talked in French. I caught words but not enough to piece together the sense. However, I knew Xander would be able to translate, and when I leaned his way he whispered, 'Innocent's pretending he doesn't know they're poachers and they're pretending they don't know this is a wildlife reserve.'

'OK,' I said.

'Trouble is, they don't believe each other.'

Almost imperceptibly, Patience breathed, 'Shhh,' beside us.

The guy with the pot belly looked over Innocent's shoulder. And saw what? Four white kids flanked by a little black girl and a burly chaperone who had already lowered his gun. Innocent was doing his best to keep light-hearted and in control. But Amelia let out a sob and Innocent glanced around at her and seeing her terror he missed a beat, faltering in whatever he was saying. The fat guy he was negotiating with noticed. Even without understanding what they were saying, I could tell that the discussion had changed shape. Innocent had been reasoning and persuading, but now he was pleading. Everything bristled. The poachers, the rainforest, the bird-noise within it – a wave of anything-could-happen happened, and I was powerless to help.

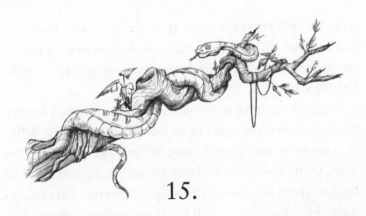

15.

Or was I?

I once saw a television programme about what you should do if you're confronted by a mugger. The best option is to run away. But though I'm quick, and I have a pretty good sense of direction, the jungle was ridiculously dense and I didn't know which way to run. And even if I had managed to get past the cordon of armed men, I'd be leaving Xander, Amelia and – yes – Caleb in the lurch, and I wasn't about to desert my friends.

Another option is to fight back, but, as the TV presenter said, that's a last resort, only to be used if you think you can win, and – let's face it – these men had guns. All I had was a long stick. It didn't even have a sharp end. Attacking them would be suicide.

However, the TV presenter – an ex-army type with thick sideburns and a moustache – had explained that there is a third way beyond fight-or-flight. In certain situations, unnerving a mugger by doing something unexpected – pretending to have an epileptic fit, say, or reciting the Lord's Prayer at top volume – can convince them not to bother with you on the grounds that there are better, more predictable people to mug elsewhere.

Without pausing to think the thing through, I started singing the first song that came into my head, 'Jingle Bells', in a stupid voice, squeaky one minute and fake deep the next. Quite loudly. Everybody looked at me and I looked back at them all in turn, still singing. No two expressions were the same. Amelia had her that-doesn't-compute face on. Caleb shrank from me in angry alarm. And Xander was grinning. Meanwhile, Innocent was shaking his head at me, mouthing, 'Stop!' and Patience's round eyes had narrowed to a glare as the guy in the Manchester United shirt took a step forward and aimed his gun right at my head.

'Over the fields we go, laughing all the way!' I yelled. Forcing each word out was like coughing up a stone. Out of the corner of my eye I could see one of the other men's shoulders shaking. I turned to him and grinned manically as I sang. He was carrying a long bamboo pole with a noose dangling from it. By the time I got to 'Oh what fun it is to ride . . .' he was laughing openly, jiggling the rope.

Out of nowhere, Xander joined in, but with a different song and in a completely flat tone, more droning than singing: 'Oh come all ye faithful, joyful and triumphant . . .'

Manchester United shouted 'Silence!' – in French it came out as *seelonce* – but the main man also advanced, waving at him to put his gun away. There were big sweat patches under the main man's arms and the buttons on his shirt were taut around his belly.

'Bells on bobtails ring, making spirits bright!'

'Sing choirs of angels, sing in exaltation!'

The leader's face was hard to read. His brow was furrowed, but more in disbelief than anger. Would he explode or walk away? Neither yet. He glanced back at Innocent for an explanation, and Innocent thought quickly enough to raise one hand and spin his forefinger next to his head, the international sign for 'beats me, they're mental'.

Amelia, having solved the quadratic equation of the situation, now chimed in with a screechy, 'Silent night, holy night, all is calm, all is bright!' and on the three of us went, murdering those carols in broad daylight.

I felt curiously weightless, as if I'd taken a leap and gravity hadn't bitten yet; I had no idea where I was about to land. The pot-bellied leader put his hands on his hips and looked to his friend with the snare, who was still trying not to laugh. I think this tipped the balance in our favour, as a smile flickered on the face of the main man himself. Not wanting to give in to it either, he puffed up his chest, shrugged, and said something I didn't catch, but that didn't matter because his body language spelled it out: everything about him said, *This really isn't worth it*.

Innocent, catching his attention, mimed a further apologetic *what can you do?*

The fat man brushed Innocent aside and strode straight past us, close enough for me to catch his acrid smell, and the rest of the group moved forward with him, although most of them gave us a wider berth. We kept on singing, our words a jumbled, discordant mess of 'infant so tender and mild in a one-horse open sleigh oh come and behold him' and the like. Not until the last man had disappeared did my relief make the words fizzle out of me, and then the others also fell silent, leaving us in the clicking, chattering hush of the jungle.

Innocent motioned for us to follow him. 'Quickly, in case he changes his mind,' he said.

We did as we were told, with Innocent leading the way and Marcel bringing up the rear. Nobody spoke, not until we'd been walking a good half-hour. Then Innocent called a water break. As I was pulling the flask from my backpack, Caleb, in his most offhand voice, said, 'Well, that little stunt could have gone either way.'

'It worked, didn't it?' snapped Xander.

'Could have really wound the guy up though.'

'I suppose,' I admitted.

'Yeah, well, I thought it was genius,' said Xander. 'Better than your non-contribution anyway,' he added, glaring at Caleb.

'Ah, but I *was* contributing,' said Caleb. 'Or trying to. I just had a less risky plan.'

'Which was what exactly?' scoffed Xander. 'Sit very still and try not to wet your pants?'

'The first bit, certainly. It's in all the manuals. Presented with a conflict situation, it's always best to play the grey man. Don't give an aggressor a reason to pull the trigger. Isn't that right, Innocent? Stay calm, stay reasonable.'

Innocent smiled and said, 'We're here. Whatever happened,

happened. The singing was very funny. But also your calm, Caleb. That was great.'

Xander bristled beside me. I could sense him wanting to call Caleb a liar and a coward, but I also knew that Caleb was already beating himself up for not having saved the day himself. His grey-man stuff might have worked in another situation, but today my response had succeeded. There was no need to rub his nose in it.

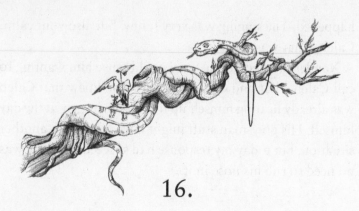

16.

'So what are we going to do about the poachers?' I asked Innocent.

'I'll report them. My ranger colleagues patrol the national parks. I'll give them descriptions, coordinates, direction of travel. Maybe they will be caught, but probably not.'

At this Patience dropped her head.

'Why do you say that?' I asked her father.

Amelia reasoned for him: 'The rangers have to patrol a slice of jungle roughly the size of Luxembourg. On foot. With pretty much nothing on the ground visible from the sky. If the poachers didn't think they could get away, they wouldn't have let us go.'

Under her breath Patience said, 'They know we will not follow them ourselves.'

'But those snares they were carrying,' I said, 'they're probably setting them as we speak.'

Innocent, blowing out his cheeks in exasperation, said, 'Bushmeat is valuable, people are hungry. They hope to catch antelope, but really such snares are, how do you say . . .'

'Indiscriminate,' said Amelia.

'Take her word for it,' said Xander.

'Literally.'

Innocent smiled.

Caleb was still smarting. His eyes, catching mine, blazed. 'Hold on,' he said. 'These poachers are about to disappear, setting snares all over the place, snares that might well kill the animals we're all so keen to see, and we're just going to let them?'

I could tell where he was going with this, and he did.

'I mean, Patience here has put her finger on it. They're banking on us fleeing, not following them ourselves. You said Marcel was the best tracker in the Congo, after you, am I right?'

Innocent kept his composure. 'Yes!' he sang. 'Very good tracker, but –'

'But what?' said Caleb. 'We've given them enough of a head start. We should track them down, find out where they camp, give the rangers something better than "we met some poachers, sang songs, and ran away" to work on.' He looked around the group, alighting on Amelia. 'You agree, yes?'

If I'd asked her the same question, the answer would have been something like, 'No, idiot,' though if she'd been in an expansive mood she might have added, 'Never mind Marcel's tracking skills – to suggest that two tour guides, a little girl and four kids from the English home counties should chase an armed Congolese militia through a jungle they live, hunt and kill in makes zero sense.' But I hadn't asked her. Caleb, with his stupid crew cut, lime-green boots and puffed-up chest had. And her response wasn't *no*; it was *yes*.

Innocent smiled harder. 'Number-one job is to protect clients. I will radio in coordinates. There is a chance –'

'No, there isn't,' said Caleb. 'Unless we go after them straight away, they're gone. Never mind antelope – right now they could be butchering the very chimps we were watching.'

The funny thing was, I could tell Caleb didn't really care about the chimpanzees, the antelope or anything much at all, beyond himself, by which I mean a combination of putting me in my place and impressing Amelia. I knew that, and yet I couldn't call him on it. In fact it seemed I had to do the opposite. 'He's right,' I heard myself say. 'We should retrace our steps, follow them, do something to stop them.'

Patience was staring at me hopefully. My heart beat louder in my ears because of it.

'Something like what?' asked Xander, incredulous.

'I don't know,' I admitted. 'As Caleb says, we could at least give their exact location to the rangers.'

'Let Marcel do it. He's the tracker. We don't all need to go.'

Xander had a point, but I guessed Caleb's reaction before it came.

'That's fine, good idea. You guys go back with Innocent. Marcel and I can track the poachers.'

Innocent laughed gently and said, 'No, no, no.'

68

Caleb stared at him. 'Who's the client here?'

'Exactly,' murmured Innocent. 'You are my clients. It is my job to keep you safe.'

'It's also your job to protect this place and the animals in it. If the poachers kill them all, you'll have no clients to look after. I'm doing you a favour here.'

Innocent screwed the lid back on his water bottle and carefully slid it into his webbing. 'Come on now, friends,' he said. 'Let's get back to camp.' But he didn't make a move to go.

Caleb put his hands on his hips. 'Every minute we stand here thinking about it, they're getting further away.'

'We're not thinking about it though,' said Innocent, adding, 'It's impossible!' Despite these protestations, his eyes were gleaming; I could tell he was tempted.

'You remember who my father is, yes?' said Caleb quietly.

Innocent looked away.

'This summer, according to him, is about me stepping up and taking responsibility. I wouldn't stand in my way.'

At the mention of Uncle Langdon, Innocent's resolve visibly weakened. He pursed his lips and shut his eyes.

'Well, I'm not going back there,' said Xander, trying in vain to bolster the guide. 'Amelia?'

I was relieved to see her shake her head, though I noted that what she said next didn't contradict Caleb's plan. 'All of us going doesn't seem logical: the bigger the group, the slower the progress, and the more likely they'll spot us.'

Deep down, thwarting the poachers mattered deeply to Innocent. He'd dedicated his life to protecting his country's wildlife, after all. He was torn, so tried for a compromise. 'OK, OK.' He smiled at Caleb, willing him to agree. 'I'll backtrack on my own, tail the poachers to their camp and inform the rangers. Marcel can take care of you.'

But Caleb was already shaking his head, chest puffed out, the big man. 'It was my idea,' he stated flatly. 'I'm going with you whether you like it or not.'

'Me too,' I said. It wasn't simply that I had to stand up to Caleb. Mum would want me to stay safe, but she'd sent me here to see the threatened wildlife and she would want me to do my bit.

The corners of Caleb's mouth twitched slyly. 'I suppose that makes sense. Split the group down the middle. Xander and Amelia head back with Marcel and little Patience, and we'll have three pairs of eyes on the poachers.'

Innocent's mouth was set in a grim, stubborn line, but Marcel, who had patiently endured this debate, had now had enough. He handed the rifle to Innocent, and said, 'I'll get these ones home. *A bientôt.*'

'Huh,' said Xander, trying not to show his annoyance. 'Whatever, I suppose.'

Of all of us, only one person was truly happy with this plan: Caleb. And even he was only really pleased because he'd imposed his will on the rest us. Though he was attempting to look businesslike, adjusting the straps on his pack, he wore the smile of someone who'd got his own way.

Marcel's group melted into the trees in seconds, Patience last, reluctant not to be coming with us. A jolt of fear went through me. Had Innocent sent her away because of the danger? I calmed myself with the thought that he probably just wanted her to stay with Amelia. If our little tracking mission had been that risky a prospect, he wouldn't have agreed to it at all, surely?

17.

As it turned out, retracing our steps through the jungle was easier than I'd expected. Innocent's tracking skills were unnecessary; even I could spot the signs of where we'd been: machete-hacked vines, stick-swiped stems and stomped vegetation. We made faster progress in reverse, mostly because we were following a sort of path, but also because we were in a different kind of hurry, racing against nightfall. The Democratic Republic of Congo is bang on the equator; unlike at home where the sun goes down slowly, here it sets fast. And what's more it sets at roughly the same time, 6 p.m., right through the year. There's no putting the clocks back for winter in the tropics.

We'd split up around mid-afternoon so had just a few hours left of daylight to catch up with the poachers. Without seeming to hurry, Innocent somehow set a pace that required Caleb and I to half-trot. Though we'd cleared a bit of a path, the ground was at best uneven, and not long after we started I caught my foot in a tangle of creeper and fell over. Caleb relished this; I'm sure I heard him laugh. When the same thing happened to him just minutes later, I made a show of checking he was all right; people like Caleb find sympathy harder to take than ridicule.

We soon reached the spot where we'd encountered Bingo's troupe. Innocent paused, but I would have recognised the forked tree with the ring of peeled bark anyway. The chimps were nowhere to be seen now. Innocent had told us to conserve our water. Now, from a packet he unexpectedly plucked out of his top pocket, he gave us each a boiled sweet. I hadn't realised how thirsty I was until the sugar hit my tongue. I've no idea what fruit it was supposed to taste like and I didn't care. It was the best sweet I'd ever eaten.

We were only stationary for a minute or so, and admittedly we'd turned to face each other, but when Innocent asked if we were ready to set off again Caleb said, 'Of course,' and started off back the way we'd come. I've always had a good sense of direction; his was apparently haywire. Innocent called him back. I didn't comment.

The going got tougher from there. Though the poachers had been a bigger group, they must have been moving through the rainforest more carefully, leaving less of a trail. I was tired. Everything ached. The boiled sweet had tamed my thirst for a while, but it had also triggered my hunger. A weakness pulsed in my belly. And yet Innocent kept up the fierce pace, and Caleb kept with him, and that meant I had to keep up too. It was a struggle.

Abruptly and mercifully, just when I thought I could take it no longer, Innocent stopped. In his lilting whisper he explained, 'Where we are, and the direction the poachers are going, they must also sleep out tonight. They'll make camp while they have light. Good progress. Tough boys.' Here he clenched his fist. 'I think we'll catch up soon. So quietly now – let's not run into their camp by accident.'

We moved on more slowly. The whooping, chattering hum of the jungle intensified around me as I tried to make less noise myself. In fact we had to endure another half-hour of this creeping progress before Innocent stopped again, and by this time the light was already failing. High above us, the canopy had turned a purplish black and all the green beneath it was grey. He motioned for us crouch lower, stay still and keep silent. We did, but it was hard; the mosquitoes, which had dogged us all day as we moved, clouded around us more thickly when we didn't. For many long minutes we sat there in the glowering dampness, waiting. I wondered whether Innocent had mistakenly stopped us too soon. Then the purple gloom deepened, and as night established itself I spotted the yellow dot of a flame in the darkness ahead. It danced and grew, a campfire taking hold.

'That's them?' I asked, my voice a whisper above the whining mosquitoes.

Innocent nodded. He took out his GPS and tapped its screen. Very quietly he explained, 'We know where they stopped us and we know now where they camp. Draw a line between two coordinates and extend it. We can predict where they head for tomorrow. *Et voilà*, rangers can intercept.'

Caleb looked pleased with himself. 'What did I tell you,' he said.

'Yes, that's the first part done. But now we must retreat as far as possible before making our own bed for the night.' Innocent's face was grim. 'No picnic.'

I turned from the distant firelight. The jungle we had to retreat through was now a dense black web. Beside me, cockiness gone, Caleb drew a nervous breath.

'Hand on my shoulder, and his on yours,' Innocent told him. We did as we were told, making a little human chain behind the guide. How he could see the way I've no idea. We didn't rush, that's for sure. At a glacial pace, step by step, doing everything we could to stay concealed, we inched away.

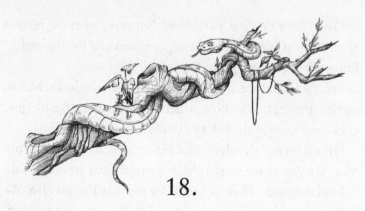

18.

When I was eleven I somehow caught chickenpox. That's quite late to have it, and everyone had assumed I was already immune. I only got a few spots, they didn't itch that badly, and aside from one high on my forehead they didn't scar. But for three days I had a blisteringly high temperature. I became delirious. At its worst I was convinced that my bedsheets, knotted about me, were an octopus's tentacles. Mum put a fan next to my bed: the sound of it was wave-roar. Apparently I started shouting all sorts of nonsense about drowning. That's because I thought I was! It was terrifying.

And yet it was nothing compared to the night we spent in the rainforest. Having crept along behind Innocent and Caleb for what seemed hours, with the more or less invisible jungle dragging at my ankles, thighs, face, I was relieved when we finally stopped in a tiny clearing. But that relief didn't last long. Innocent told us to put on our waterproofs, unfurled a poncho-type sheet of plastic from his own pack and tied it between two nearby trees. Then he told us to crawl under it with him and go to sleep.

This crude shelter was supposed to do two things: first, the obvious, keep us dry if it rained. Second, and more importantly, catch that rain so we could drink it. That's why he weighted down the middle of our roof with a stone. But – just our luck – it rained nothing but mosquitoes all night long. Their whining was a horrible white-noise accompaniment to all the other chirping, whooping, clicking, barking sounds that cut through it. Though the soundtrack had been a pleasant enough distraction in the day, its night-time counterpart was sinister.

What was out there?

What wasn't?

I imagined green mambas climbing the vines, warthogs rooting through the leaves, leopards in the trees. Innocent had said we would detour to a nearby river for water in the morning – but what if a crocodile was doing its own detouring towards us now? Even if nothing big got us, something small might have a go. Scuttling sounds nearby were undoubtedly hungry rats. And the constant drone of insects made my skin – where it wasn't already itching – crawl. We'd been issued malaria tablets in London, and I'd been taking them regularly, but right now they seemed a laughably weak defence. Enveloped in darkness, with the jungle alive around me and a plastic poncho for a roof, I'd never felt more exposed.

At one point, despite there being no rain, lightning split the sky. Everything jumped bright for a nanosecond. Then it happened again, and again, and again, each burst like an X-ray of the canopy, the twine Innocent had used to rig up the poncho, the dead leaves spread out around us, the swirling mosquitoes, and Caleb beside me, the thunder rolling through us, his eyes as wide and terrified as mine.

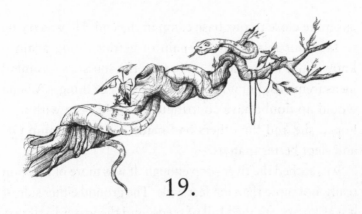

19.

I didn't sleep that night. Though I was exhausted beyond belief, the best I could manage was a flickering semi-consciousness. Every time I thought I was drifting off I was pricked awake again, either by something actually pricking me, or plain old fear. Innocent's stillness suggested he didn't have the same problem, but I'm pretty sure Caleb, like me, just lay there through the night, willing it to end. Dawn couldn't come too soon.

As it was, Innocent got up when it was still dark, just. I don't know how he judged it so well, but by the time we'd bustled ourselves ready, the first bluish hint of morning was filtering down to us. I was famished and parched and my feet were sore in my boots when we set off downhill in search of the river. Innocent explained as we walked that countless streams and rivers criss-cross the jungle, thousands of strands of water weaving into tributaries that eventually knit into the mighty Congo itself. We would pick one up nearby, drink, and follow it north; apparently this stream cut quite close to our base camp in the end. He was trying to take our minds off the pain of getting going again, I know. I did the same by imagining the statistics – rainfall measurements, humidity levels, that sort of thing – Amelia would no doubt have contributed if she'd been with us. I hoped she and the others had made it back to camp OK and slept better than us.

We reached the river soon enough. It was more of a stream really, not more than ten feet wide. The ground either side of it was boggy, stabbed full of reeds, and the water itself was brown as tea, but I was so thirsty I didn't care. Scrabbling for my empty water bottle, I started to wade in. Innocent stopped me.

'We need to purify it first.'

The thought of waiting while we built a fire – out of what? Damp sticks? – and boiled water – in what? We hadn't brought a pan – to purify it nearly made me snap, but he smilingly held up a hand, rooted in his pack, and produced a little plastic tube.

'Clever tablets,' he said.

Clever, but slow: added to our refilled water bottles the tablets took thirty agonising minutes to work, and that time spent waiting for the water to be safe to drink was an eternity. Being as parched as that made me realise I'd never actually experienced proper thirst before. Even when I'd thought I was thirsty, after sport, say, I wasn't really: my entire life, when I've wanted water to drink, I've been able to turn on a tap within minutes. I'd only gone about twelve hours without a drink now, but I'd been sweating in the humidity and the thirst I battled as I sat waiting for that tablet to work tasted like ash and headaches, sawdust and scabs. Innocent himself seemed perfectly content to wait, but I could tell Caleb was hurting too. Though he didn't say so, I saw him looking at his watch and he caught me looking at mine. Perversely, when the thirty minutes were up, I held back from taking the top off my bottle. So did Caleb. Innocent took a sip from his own flask but we both waited. I didn't fully understand why to begin with, though it was perfectly obvious. Neither of us wanted to crack first. As soon as I spelled that stupidity out to myself I said, 'Ridiculous,' unscrewed the lid, and drank half the bottle in one go. I'm pretty sure I caught Caleb smiling before he followed suit.

Purification tablets make water taste of chlorine, like a swimming pool, and there was grit in my bottle, and the water was lukewarm, but just as Innocent's boiled sweet had been the best I'd ever eaten, that was the most welcome drink of my life. Everything – even my sore feet – felt better after it. The water evidently rebooted Caleb too. 'Come on then, we should make tracks,' he said, bouncing on the balls of his feet. This show of readiness was unnecessary as Innocent and I were already primed to go. But Caleb obviously wanted to assert that he was in charge, so not content with having chivvied us pointlessly, he set off into the jungle, swinging his machete this way and that, a self-appointed expedition leader.

The only trouble was that he'd started out in the wrong direction again. It's hard to navigate in the jungle, I know, but we were supposed to follow the stream north, meaning the morning sun would be coming from our right, and Caleb had set off with the sun to our left. After he'd taken a few steps I glanced at Innocent. First to make sure I hadn't gone mad, and second because I didn't want to be the one to correct Caleb.

Innocent shot me a smile. 'Mr Caleb!' he sang.

Caleb, who was thirty metres upstream and already just about out of sight, shouted, 'What are you waiting for?'

Innocent took a deep breath to tell him, but before he could there was a rush of leaves and a yelp-scream and what we could see of Caleb through the foliage suddenly changed shape. Both of us sprinted towards him. On arrival, it seemed as if he'd collapsed mid-cartwheel. One of his green boots was wrenched awkwardly above his head, still firmly attached to his foot, beneath which the rest of him was writhing on the ground. He'd stepped in a snare. I was surprised to find myself genuinely worried he'd been hurt. But his 'Get me down!' was angry rather than agonised.

Caleb's machete was on the ground in front of me. The snare was made out of a loop of paracord rigged to a log, itself cantilevered over a bent tree. I couldn't quite work out the mechanics of the thing, but if *how to set Caleb free?* was the question, *sever the rope* had to be the answer. I fired off a quick photo for the record while Caleb was looking towards Innocent, then picked up the big knife and swung it at the knot. The log thumped to the ground, the treetop snapped upright and Caleb's leg joined the swearing rest of him on the floor.

'You OK?' Innocent sounded concerned: did he think Caleb was about to blame him?

'Of course I'm OK.' Caleb brushed himself down. 'I just . . .' He trailed off. For a half-beat I thought he might be about to laugh – since he wasn't injured, surely he could see the funny side? But his face hardened and aside from muttering a brusque 'thanks' as I handed him back his knife, it was pretty clear 'funny' wasn't on his radar.

'Dangerous, horrible,' said Innocent, holding up the snare. 'Many animals die this way. They do not have a friend to cut them down.'

'I'd have freed myself eventually,' Caleb muttered.

He might well have done so – the machete was probably within his reach – yet his lack of gratitude was irritating. I tried not to respond. But once he'd picked the leaves out of his hair and was ready to go again, I couldn't help pointing back downstream and saying, with a fake lightness in my voice, 'Right then, shall we head in the actual direction of the others this time?' I wish with all my heart that I'd held my tongue; if I'd stopped myself from goading him, we might have avoided the awfulness of what happened later.

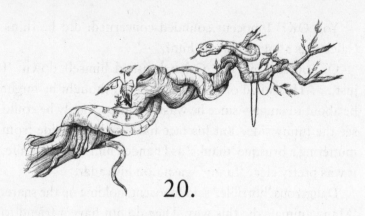

20.

As it was, we made it back to the others in good time. There was no chat on the way. Silent endurance felt both right and odd at the same time. When we'd reunited with Amelia and Xander, things were a little more normal. There was no way I could tell them about what had happened to Caleb though. Not out of solidarity, and not because I was in his thrall. It was more because his inability to take the joke meant that telling it would be cruel. However, the strange thing was that not taking the mick out of him, far from making him grateful, seemed to do the opposite. He bristled, ignored me, gave the others short shrift. The more nobody commented, the more het up he became. Mid-afternoon, when Xander, Amelia and I were on our camp beds playing cards, I heard a whacking, chopping sound outside and went to investigate. Caleb had cut a bough from a nearby tree with his machete and was hacking at the wood as if it was his mortal enemy. A relative of the tree used to spring the snare perhaps? I was about to leave him to it when Innocent also poked his head out of his tent to see what was going on.

'Are you OK, Mr Caleb?' he asked.

'Why wouldn't I be?' Caleb took another swing at the branch and a yellow bite mark appeared in it.

'Sharp knife,' said Innocent. 'Take care.'

'I know what I'm doing,' said Caleb, sending another chipping into the air.

Innocent smiled at him and was retreating, his arm affectionately around Patience's shoulders, when Caleb abruptly stopped chopping and said, 'Hang on a minute.'

'Yes.'

'What's with all this sitting around? When do we set off?'

'We rest here today and head home tomorrow.' Innocent's gentle voice made this sound more like a suggestion than a statement.

Caleb rounded on it immediately. 'I didn't mean when do we go home, I meant when do we see the gorillas?'

'The gorillas,' said Innocent.

'Yeah.'

'After the scare of yesterday and last night's difficulty, I think we take everyone back to Kinshasa, for safety. It's best,' Innocent said quietly.

'No chance!' There was an edge to Caleb's laughter. 'I didn't come all this way not to see gorillas, Innocent. Creep back home? You're going to have to do better than that.'

Hearing the commotion, Xander and Amelia joined us.

'Another time, maybe,' said Innocent. Smiling at Patience, he added, 'Everyone tired, I think.'

Xander nodded, but Amelia, failing to read the situation, said, 'Actually I slept very well, thank you.'

'Good girl,' said Caleb. 'I knew you'd be up for it.'

If I'd ever called Amelia a 'good girl', she'd have ripped my arm off and beaten me to death with the bloody end of it, but unbelievably she let this go with, 'All I meant was that I'm not sleepy.'

'And you want to see the gorillas, yes?' Caleb asked.

'Gorillas, yes. But not guerrillas. Primates not poachers.'

'Of course,' said Caleb. 'But we pinpointed yesterday's poachers for the rangers –' he made it sound like he'd done it himself – 'so they'll be out of the equation, and anyway the mountain gorillas are in a completely different part of the national park. The chances of coming across two sets of poachers in one trip has to be infinitesimal.'

'That's not actually the way statistics work in this context,' Amelia couldn't help explaining. That was more like it! But annoyingly she went on, 'It doesn't matter though. I'd still like to see them.'

A scraggy-necked chicken, which had been pecking at the dirt a few metres off, now wandered in among us. Caleb addressed Innocent: 'We signed up for chimpanzees *and* mountain gorillas. You're not going to let a minor scare like yesterday derail things, are you?'

While Innocent searched for a way to answer him Caleb waved at the chicken with the flat of his machete blade. Dust rose from the bird's wings as it skittered away.

'We could always come back,' said Xander, more to help Innocent out than because he believed it. Hearing the hollowness in his own words, he dug deeper. 'You know, later in the trip. We've got time.'

'*You* might have,' said Caleb. 'But not all of us are on holiday.' He drew himself tall. 'I have work to do, starting next week.'

Amelia couldn't help correcting them both. 'Work experience,' she said to Caleb. 'Though it's still work of course.' Turning to Xander she added, 'Logistics and costs-wise, travelling all the way to Kinshasa and back makes zero sense. It's not as if there'll be fewer poachers to run into a fortnight from now.'

It occurred to me that Amelia really did want to see the mountain gorillas. She'd researched everything about the trip in advance, chimpanzees included, but from what she'd already told me about the gorillas, I reckon she could write a book on them. And yet she hadn't spent the night without shelter in the jungle. That burning, tumbled sensation I get in my stomach when I'm exhausted was still there. The idea of heading back into the jungle feeling the way I was made me feel sick. Sensing my misgivings, Caleb upped the ante. 'Of course, I'm not suggesting we head out to look for them today. But first thing tomorrow, when everyone's had a decent night's sleep, you'll all be up for it then, yes?'

What was it with him? Why did I have to rise to it. I've no idea. I just know that my shoulders shrugged of their own accord and my voice, though it sounded distant in my ears, was clear enough.

'Why not?' I said.

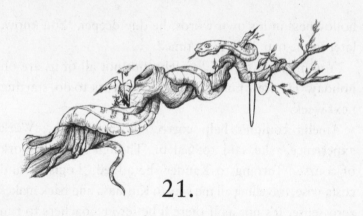

21.

A simple sleeping bag on a cot bed set beneath flapping canvas provided me with possibly the best sleep of my life that night. I didn't dream, just shut down as if under a spell and awoke ten hours later in daylight. Everyone else was already up, drinking sweetened tea out of tin mugs on benches set around the cooking fire in the clearing beyond our tents. I joined them and Patience handed me a cup. Marcel and Xander were talking together in French, while Amelia listened in. Xander is fluent in about six languages, and Amelia's general cleverness extends to French too, but I'm shamefully hopeless in anything other than English, so I had no idea what they were talking about. It seemed Xander was telling a joke or funny anecdote, because when he finished the big guide burst out laughing and cuffed him on the shoulder. A second later the penny dropped for Amelia, and she laughed as well. Her laugh is loud and infectious: Patience was grinning and I found myself smiling, too. It struck me that whereas the mission Caleb, Innocent and I had undertaken to locate the poachers, survive a night in the forest, escape snares and find our way home had served only to put more prickly distance between my cousin and me, Xander, Amelia, Patience and Marcel had obviously bonded on their return trip through the forest.

Though I'd slept well and felt rested, Innocent appeared tired that morning. His smile was still in place, but it was thinner, more brittle, and his face was tinged grey. After the pickup dropped us at the start point for the trek, he paused us, his singsong voice forced, for 'gorilla briefing'.

'What's there to brief?' said Caleb. 'Surely it's the same as for the chimpanzees.'

'Yes and no,' Innocent muttered. He'd had enough of Caleb now, for sure. With a sigh he told us that according to the rangers, the troop of gorillas we'd be visiting had spent the night some four hours' hike away, most of it uphill. The bulk of the walking would be easy enough, on existing paths, but the last stretch would be slow-going. When we found the gorillas we'd have one hour maximum in their presence. We weren't to approach within thirty feet of them, though they might come closer to us once we'd stopped. It was important that we keep quiet and still and avoid direct eye contact.

'Why's that?' asked Xander.

'It's confrontational,' said Amelia.

'They're very peaceful creatures,' Innocent said. 'But like any of us they don't like to be threatened.'

'Pretty obvious,' said Caleb. 'Shall we get on with it?'

As Innocent had predicted, the walking was fine to

begin with, but we were all subdued. Xander did his best to lighten the mood by teeing up questions for Amelia to answer (a silverback gorilla weighs about 200 kilograms, stands 1.8 metres tall, and has an arm-span of two metres; they construct a new nest of flattened branches and leaves each night as they move around their territory in search of plants to eat and are one of the only primates to sleep on the ground; there are fewer than one thousand mountain gorillas living in the wild, though that's an improvement on twenty years ago, and so on). Impressive as her mental factsheet was, it couldn't lift the heavy presence of Caleb. He wasn't outwardly angry, in fact he barely spoke, but everything about him put the rest of us, except Amelia possibly, on edge.

The fact of him, buzz-cut hair, stupid lime-green boots, brand-new machete and all, up front with his head down, pulsing with discontent, was maddening. Look at where we were and what we were doing: hiking through one of the most stunning landscapes on earth in search of one of the rarest and most impressive animals alive. How could he sour that experience? I forced myself to ignore him and take in the detail of the day.

It was cooler, but no less humid, as we climbed, and the clouds boiled up above us, unleashing lush curtains of rain that turned the path to mud. As we made our way higher into the mountains the glossy greenery of ferns and bamboo and gallium vines pressed in. Among them was something that managed to sting me through my trousers. Not knowing what it was made my heart race. Amelia put me at ease by saying, 'Ow!' almost immediately after I'd been stung. When I told her something had also bitten me, she laughed and said, 'The chances of two spider bites or snake strikes in ten seconds is infinitesimal. So it was a plant. I've not read about any deadly stinging vegetation in the jungle. Therefore we've probably just brushed against a pumped-up sort of nettle. We can relax.'

'Thanks,' I said. It came out more sarcastic than I meant. The truth was that the sting hurt, which made it hard for me not to think of what worse dangers might be lurking just out of sight.

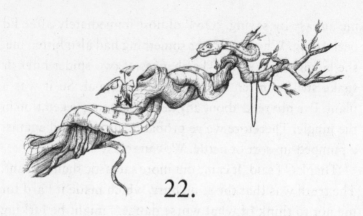

22.

The canopy above us thinned out a little from time to time, but the undergrowth, one or two welcome clearings aside, was pretty unrelenting. Innocent and Marcel – helped by Caleb, of course – had to use their machetes to cut us a pathway through it. The noise of the rainforest was unending, a constant drone-hum of insects punctured by rain-hiss and leaf-patter and the whooping and chattering of birds, monkeys, god-knows-what, overlain with our own hard breathing and the squelch of our boots and the snick of the machetes. It was music, of sorts: a soundtrack encouraging us to keep on walking. And that's what we did. We were all puffing harder than Patience, but managing to maintain a pace that I think impressed our guides. Innocent paused less often than he had en route to the chimpanzees. We took on water (I'd made sure to bring three times as much with me that day) without stopping for long. It was tough going, but either the troop had moved closer or we made better progress than Innocent had predicted. After just two and half hours

Marcel, who had been making the occasional soft grunting noise as we walked, heard something in response that made him kink left, push through some dripping ferns and kneel down next to a hefty pile of greeny-yellow droppings. '*Juste là-bas*,' he whispered.

Innocent handed out masks before allowing us to get closer, and not long after we'd begun moving forward again I glimpsed a tantalising hillock of black fur through the foliage. Moving stealthily, we emerged at the edge of a trampled clearing of sorts. I crouched low and quickly counted six, no, seven gorillas. The nearest one was stripping leaves from a long bent stalk. I was close enough to see the fibres in the stalk as she broke it, the shifting black of her fur and the tiny flies that rose in a cloud as she turned. Her eyes were a reddish brown. The creases around them looked like the laughter or worry lines you see in a human face. Immediately I realised I was doing the one thing we'd been told not to do, stare straight at her, but I couldn't help it. Her gaze was magnetic. It was all I could do to break from it and look to one side. Even then the imprint of what I'd seen didn't fade. To me the gorilla had the look of an elder, a judge, a prophet even; she seemed not only to know what I was thinking, but to be deciding it.

The rest of the group, as I looked around, camera clicking, reminded me of an extended family at Christmas, or on a picnic maybe. I felt as if I'd stumbled into somebody's front room or garden. A couple of the gorillas were grooming one another, one was dozing and others were absently stripping leaves to eat. The two young ones off to one side were rough-and-tumbling through the foliage. It appeared a scene of lounging contentment to me. So I was baffled when Innocent said, 'Something's strange.'

'Strange? They're magnificent!' insisted Amelia.

'But Spenser's not here,' said Patience.

'What? Who's Spenser?'

Innocent explained: 'The silverback. He's the head of this family. But I can't see him, or Annabel and her baby.'

Marcel, who had skirted the group, now came back with a worried look on his face and spoke hurriedly to Innocent in French. I caught one phrase I understood, *gravement malade*, and though I didn't know who he was referring to, I got the gist: somebody was badly sick. '*Agité, très agité!*' he went on.

Xander was about to explain what that meant when the situation became obvious. A female gorilla moved in among the troop carrying an infant. It was obviously sick, limp across her forearm, its head canted back. I wondered if it was in fact dead, until I saw its lolling head roll to one side. One of the baby's arms flopped forward. It was missing a hand, the stump still raw. Seeing the wound, I winced.

'Can we help it?' asked Amelia.

Innocent shook his head.

'Why not?' said Caleb.

A crashing sound cut off his answer. The foliage behind the troop shook and exploded. A huge gorilla, almost twice the size of the next biggest, shot headlong into the clearing. His back was a slab of muscle dusted in silver fur, which shimmered as he jockeyed sideways with the momentum of

94

a small car. He thumped the ground in front of him, then rocked back on his haunches and beat his chest, making an astonishing percussive sound like two coconut halves being whacked together. It echoed over the noise of the forest. This was Spenser. I couldn't believe the size of him. The other gorillas had seemed so solid and powerful, but this silverback dwarfed them. Without realising I'd done it, I'd copied Patience and shrunk low to the ground in the face of his display. Her head was bowed. I looked at my hands in my lap. They were quivering.

Yet Caleb was still standing beside me, arms folded across his chest. 'It's just for show,' he explained to Amelia, suddenly an expert, though his voice sounded a bit thin. 'Nothing to worry about.'

In a low murmur Innocent said, 'He's upset. We must be respectful.'

'Everyone knows they're nature's gentle giants,' Caleb said.

'Even so, he's protective of little Redmond, with the injury.'

The silverback, heavy on his knuckles, now crabbed sideways into a thicker patch of vegetation, which partly obscured him for a moment. I lifted my camera to my eye. Beside me, Caleb took a step forward. 'We've got to do something about that injured baby, you're right,' he said to Amelia.

'No, no, no,' insisted Innocent. 'Stay still.'

The bushes into which the silverback had retreated rattled, and staccato guttural alarm calls came from within them.

'It'll die if we don't intervene,' Caleb went on. 'Look at it. Poor thing.'

The injured baby gorilla, still limp over its mother's arm, wasn't moving. Of course I felt sorry for it. And for its parents too. But if we could have helped, Innocent would have said so. He was saying the opposite. Squatting next to Patience, I saw that the tendons in her father's neck were rigid with tension. If he'd had a leash on Caleb, he'd be drawing it in now. But there was no leash, and Caleb, shirtsleeves rolled and swinging that stupid machete of his, Caleb who I sincerely doubted would lose a moment's sleep over the baby gorilla, however things turned out, was taking yet another step towards the troop.

'Really?' muttered Xander. 'I mean, what's he trying to prove?'

It wasn't just *what* he was trying to prove that struck me in that moment, but *who* he was trying to prove it to.

Within the undergrowth concealing the silverback, the top of a large sapling bent sharply. A splitting, ripping sound accompanied the movement. The gorilla had torn down a tree three times his height. He rushed forward again, dragging it, and flung it aside without apparent effort, scattering some of the troop, most of whom were now noisy, restless and agitated. The silverback beat his chest again, veered off in a different direction, spun and faced us.

I could feel my pulse in my throat, hear my heart despite the din.

'Just showing off,' said Caleb.

'Perhaps we should give him some space?' said Xander.

'*Oui. Lentement, lentement . . .*' urged Marcel, smoothly stepping backwards.

'What's wrong with you?' said Caleb. 'The worst thing you can do in a situation like this is run away.'

Nobody was running. Quite the opposite. But having accused us of doing so, Caleb, looking straight at the silverback across the clearing, for some reason felt compelled to take two big strides towards him. He drew himself up tall, pointed his machete at the gorilla, and said, 'See? Harmless.'

The silverback charged. One second the whole scene was stock still, the next everything seemed to be in motion. The gorillas, the bushes, the grass and leaves, us; the whole tableau was a frenzy, with Spenser the prime mover, a whirlwind spinning forward. He came at us unstoppably fast. A vision overtook me in that moment; I saw light bouncing off car windscreens as the mini swerved behind me in the street, heard the squeal of tyres, felt the rush of something heavy moving wrongly through space. The crash was happening again, and this time I was in it, welded to the spot. As the gorilla closed in, Innocent jumped past me to pull Caleb clear, and Caleb swung both hands up to protect himself, and the gorilla thumped straight past them and kept going, running over Xander and bouncing me into the bushes as he swept beyond us and veered away.

The attack, if that's what you'd call it, was over in a flash. I jumped back to my feet before I knew it, desperate to see where Spenser had gone and if he was readying to charge again. He wasn't. He'd immediately retreated into the middle of his troop and was studiously ignoring us. Having witnessed the energy unleashed in that one charge, heard the heaviness of his feet as he'd pounded towards us, felt the massive blur of him knocking us aside, I knew that he'd barely tried to hurt us at all. If he'd wanted to do that, he'd have torn us limb from limb. I was still intact. And he'd not touched Amelia, Patience or Marcel. Caleb was also dusting himself down, apparently OK, if white in the face. But Xander was rolling from side to side, both hands gripping his left knee, clearly in pain. And Innocent was bent double, half groaning, half gasping, hugging himself hard. I leaned down and put an arm around him, thinking he was probably winded, since that's the same sort of noise I make if I hit the ground hard falling off my bike, and it was then that I noticed his fingers, pressed against his neck, were vivid with blood.

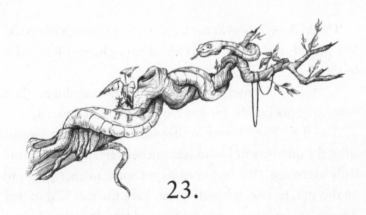

23.

Marcel immediately went to Xander's aid. As I knelt next to Innocent and pulled myself together to help him I heard them speaking in French – Xander through gritted teeth – about him being OK apart from his leg. In the aftermath of Mark's death Mum had made us all do a first-aid course. It wouldn't have saved him, of course, but I think in her paranoia – what if I got hurt too? – she wanted to take every possible step to equip us as best she could. In the shock of the moment I struggled to remember the detail of what to do, but I knew deep down that I knew, if that makes sense, and a sort of autopilot quickly kicked in.

'OK, Innocent,' I said, my voice as matter-of-fact as I could manage, 'let's have a look at this cut then.'

He was still on his haunches, fingers pressed against his neck, the blood flowing through them a shockingly bright red. He'd begun to shiver.

Patience was whimpering next to her father. I put a hand on her shoulder, but couldn't ease her away.

'Here.' Amelia was at my side, rooting through her pack. She pulled out a spare shirt she'd brought and handed it to me.

'It wasn't Spenser's fault,' Innocent mumbled. 'Just defending his family. He got me though. Bad scratch.'

'You'll be fine,' I said, trying to keep my voice steady, since the quantity of blood seeping between his fingers was truly alarming. 'We just need to get some proper pressure on this cut, to stop it bleeding, eh. Let's use this.' I'd folded Amelia's shirt into a pad and showed it to Innocent before easing his fingers away. The wound, a vicious, crimson cut at the base of his throat, ten centimetres long at least, was only briefly visible before it flooded with blood. I covered it instantly with the pad, grabbed Innocent's hand and pressed on the cut with him, very hard indeed.

'My God!' Amelia said.

'It's OK, it's OK,' I muttered, fighting the panic flooding my own stomach.

Innocent's shivering had become shuddering. He was going into shock. I didn't know whether to keep him upright, with the wound above his heart, or roll him onto his side into the recovery position. My first-aid course felt laughable now. I looked up for help and saw Marcel scrabbling frantically at the medical kit he'd brought. I was startled to see that his eyes were awash with tears. He found a roll of crepe bandage and held it out to me, Behind him, Caleb was walking in small circles, head down, as if looking for something. 'I can't believe that thing actually charged us,' he said, more to himself than anyone else.

'They're supposed to stop. It's a display. They're meant to be damned peaceful.'

Amelia's shirt, rolled and pressed against Innocent's terrible wound, was already sodden with blood. I couldn't press hard enough to staunch the flow. He flopped sideways against me. He was trembling and whispering, 'No, I'm sorry, no, no . . .' Marcel's response, in French, was high-pitched, borderline hysterical, and Patience was crying now too, echoing her father's '*Non, non, non . . .*' Between us we did our best to lever Innocent back onto all fours, but as he weakened he grew heavier, and though in that moment he seemed so young and frail in my arms, he was also becoming a dead weight.

'It's going to be OK,' I whispered again, but as I spoke Innocent lost consciousness and crumpled completely. I struggled to keep pressure on the wound but couldn't. He was too heavy for me. Everywhere was wet and sticky with blood. He slumped lower between me and Marcel, and for a moment my hand came away and another gout of blood pulsed hideously down the poor guide's neck.

Patience's whimpering turned into a moan of terror.

Amelia pulled the girl close, but couldn't help saying, 'It's bright red, meaning it's oxygenated, not venous. Cutting a vein is bad enough, but I think he's severed his carotid artery, meaning –'

'Shhh,' I said.

'*Mon dieu non,*' murmured Marcel.

The same bewildering numbness that I'd felt at the roadside with Mark overtook me now. Innocent was half

101

in my lap, half stretched out on the trampled ferns and leaves. I didn't know what to do. I just hugged him, keeping pressure on the wound, looking helplessly from his poor daughter Patience to Marcel to Amelia to Innocent again. None of us could speak.

Caleb was now crouched next to Xander.

'Mate, I hope you're not hurt. Just a sprain, right?'

'I'll be all right,' Xander hissed through gritted teeth.

'The speed of that thing, eh? The size of it. If they're as unpredictable as that, I'm surprised these visits are even allowed.'

'Sure, whatever.' Xander tried to adjust his position on the ground, winced and clutched his leg again. 'I think it's broken,' he said to me.

'No way,' said Caleb. 'Can't be. The pain will fade. Either way, I'm sorry, but this wasn't my fault. They should have . . .'

He dried up.

His fault? Did it matter? I couldn't focus, stared wildly around me. Some of the gorillas had already disappeared into the greenery. The wounded baby was nowhere to be seen, nor was the silverback, Spenser. Others were moving off, disappearing into the jungle in an unhurried, methodical procession.

With clumsy fingers Marcel was trying to wind the crepe bandage over the top of the blood-soaked pad of Amelia's shirt, but that quickly darkened with blood as well. So much blood. Poor Innocent's breathing, which had been laboured and broken, became shallower and shallower until he wasn't breathing at all.

102

'*Non, non, non,*' Marcel whispered. The tears were running down his cheeks now. '*Non!*'

Patience broke free of Amelia and pressed her face into her father's blood-soaked chest. '*Non, non, non!*' she wailed.

No.

No.

No.

The word made me suddenly furious.

Denying a fact doesn't change it.

Wounded by the charging silverback, our guide Innocent, now a still shape beside me on the blood-soaked jungle floor, was dead.

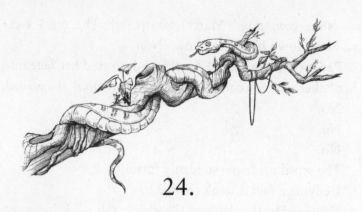

24.

An awful stillness descended. The gorillas had gone. Marcel, with his head bowed and eyes shut, was a statue beside me. Amelia stepped away and dropped to her knees next to Xander. Despite his own injury, Xander was in tune enough to know from the look on her face that the worst had happened. He fell back against the leaves. I was still cradling the dead guide's head. With my free hand I shut his eyes and stroked his daughter's shoulder. She wouldn't let go of her father. I laid the two of them down together, easing myself out from beneath them. What was going through Patience's mind? I couldn't bear to think of it, and backed a step or two away from them both, giving the girl some space. My trousers were sodden with his blood. I couldn't have cared less. Innocent looked even younger in death. That wispy beard, the relaxed line of his mouth. Marcel tried to comfort Patience now, taking hold of her wordlessly, lifting her away, the pair of them weeping silently together. I'm sure I was imagining it, but even the jungle seemed quieter, as if someone had turned its incessant pulsing soundtrack down a notch.

Caleb was the last to realise what had happened. He'd wandered off muttering to himself and now stood at a distance, scratching his head in a daze. After nobody else had spoken for what seemed ages but was probably only a minute, he looked up and said, 'What?'

None of us answered him.

'But what?' he repeated.

'*Il est mort,*' said Marcel.

Caleb came crashing back through the undergrowth. 'What do you mean? Don't be ridiculous!' was all that he could say. In that moment I hated him with all my heart. He was the screech of tyres on tarmac; he was pointed shoes and a trimmed beard; he was a reflection rushing across windscreens; he was stupid classical music swelling above the fumes; he was schoolbags slipping from my mother's shoulder as she ran; he was a low brick garden wall and a pool of blood. He was my fault, and a thing that could never be undone.

I jumped up to confront him, but when I saw the wild panic in his face something immediately shifted inside me. Across the clearing he'd been scratching his head in apparent confusion; now both hands were clawing at his crew cut, his cheeks, his throat. He jittered left and right in panicky circles, catching his feet, stumbling and swaying, and saying things like, 'ridiculous, impossible, no,' over and over again. A hole had opened up in me as Innocent bled out in my arms; the sight of Caleb's distress now filled it. I realised he was as close to the person I'd been at the roadside as anyone I'd ever seen, and though it's hard to explain why, my hatred for him morphed into a kind of guilt. Instead of punching him in the face, I tried to put an arm around him, but he flinched and lurched backwards.

I staggered after him, but my legs weren't working properly and I hadn't made it more than ten clumsy paces before I caught my foot on a vine and pitched headlong into the tangled vegetation. Caleb stopped and turned to see what had happened. As I pushed myself upright my left hand closed over something that felt wrong. Luckily I didn't grip it hard; if I had I might have cut myself. It was a machete. Caleb's, definitely: the handle had the same military-rubberised effect, and the blade, where it wasn't covered with mud, was that unmistakable newish blue. He must have dropped it as the gorilla charged. It was only as I held the knife up to Caleb that I saw the smear along its sharp edge wasn't dirt, but blood.

We both noticed it and we both understood what it meant. By disobeying Innocent, Caleb had provoked the silverback to charge. In doing so he'd created a danger from which our guide had tried to save him. Innocent had sacrificed himself, but the fatal injury he'd sustained hadn't come from the silverback's bared teeth, which would have caused a ragged slash. The deep clean cut to Innocent's neck had come from the honed blade Caleb had been brandishing.

Caleb, his face still a circus of guilt-stricken disbelief, blinked from the bloody knife to me and back again. He was in front of me, with Marcel and Patience and Amelia and Xander behind us. I wanted to turn and spell out what had happened, shout it beyond the rainforest canopy and all the way through Goma to Kinshasa. But instead, in silence, I carefully wiped the blade clean on the leg of my trousers and handed the knife over to Caleb.

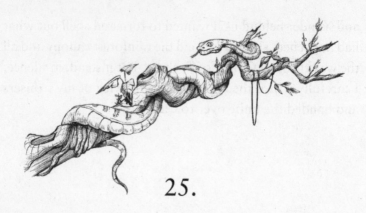

25.

After I gave Caleb back his machete he sat down in a heap with it, still a mess, and the sight of his fingers worrying at his buzz-cut made me want to deal with the horror of what had happened. Xander was hurt. Though he carried the first-aid kit, Marcel was trying to comfort a stricken Patience, so it was up to Amelia and me to fashion a splint and stretcher using the bandages in the kit, straight bamboo poles we cut from a nearby thicket and the roll of duct tape I'd brought – though I knew there was no end to what that stuff could fix, I'd never imagined I'd end up using it for this.

Droplets of sweat stood out on Xander's brow as we taped the makeshift splint to his leg. We'd already given him as many painkillers as the box said it was OK for him to take, and he claimed they were dulling the fierce ache in his leg, but when we rolled him onto the stretcher he couldn't stop himself shrieking. Amelia stood back once we had him settled in place.

'Caleb,' she said.

He snapped out of his reverie. 'Yes?'

'A stretcher has four handles. We each need to take one.'

In the dappled light that filtered through the trees, at that moment Caleb looked less substantial. 'Of course,' he agreed meekly.

'You're feeling guilty. It's understandable,' she went on. 'Yet this was an accident. You didn't intend for it to happen. None of us did.'

As ever there was logic in what Amelia was saying, but also as ever she was kind of missing the point: accidents happen when people are careless, stupid or so fixed on one outcome that they ignore other possible consequences of their actions. I know because I've had enough 'accidents' myself. Remembering that was possibly why I didn't press the point then.

Caleb's guilt, Xander's injury, none of it mattered, set against Innocent's death, and even that was somehow already history, thrown into relief by the horror of Patience's grief. She'd been so calm throughout the trip, gliding effortlessly through the jungle as we struggled to keep up. Now she was a jittery, distraught mess. Amelia tried to comfort her but Patience shrugged her off and wandered away and slumped to her knees. Then she stretched herself out flat on the earth next to her father's body, face down, moaning. I couldn't understand what she was saying, but perhaps she was begging the ground to swallow her up.

Marcel radioed base camp. Amelia summed up the conversation: he'd called for more men to retrieve Innocent's body, it being impossible for us to carry it back to camp as well as poor Xander. Marcel now covered the body with a foil blanket from the first-aid kit and attempted to lever Patience from the ground beside it. She wouldn't come. Though she was only a skinny ten-year-old girl, Marcel couldn't prise her away from her dead father. The thought of leaving her there alone was unbearable, but Xander needed medical attention. Marcel pleaded with Patience to come with us. So did Amelia. But she refused. She wanted to guard her father's body until the rangers arrived. The three of us stood together with her for a moment beside the covered form. I was mesmerised by the sight of the foil glittering in the gloom. Marcel took hold of poor Patience, hugged her wordlessly and kissed her forehead. My throat was a knot watching him. Once he'd finished this silent act of consolation and moved away I laid Innocent's machete, which I'd used to cut the branches for the stretcher, on the blood-soaked earth beside him. If and when the pathologist examined the body he might conclude Innocent was cut by his own knife when the gorilla charged. Why I wanted to protect Caleb in this way I cannot say.

Amelia, Marcel, Caleb and I each took a corner of the stretcher. I could not bring myself to look back at Patience as we left, and I hated myself for it. The weight of Xander split four ways wasn't too bad at first, but the awkwardness of manhandling a stretcher through the forest meant that the going was slow. Every time one of us missed our footing or had to adjust quickly, jerking the stretcher, Xander flinched with fear and pain. The thought of dropping him made me concentrate very hard indeed. Everyone else did too, and other than Marcel murmuring to Xander every now and then in French (I've no idea what he was saying but his tone was soothing) we barely spoke. During one of our many pauses Marcel cut some stems from a nearby tree and suggested Xander bite down on one against the pain. He told me afterwards that the wood tasted of aniseed and – whether it was just the distraction or some chemical property of the particular tree – that the chewing worked better than the pills we'd given him.

We fought our way back to a discernible path, but although the going got easier underfoot, by the time we reached it, Xander seemed to have trebled in weight. Amelia couldn't stop herself groaning with the effort every few steps, and more than once I was forced to call a halt to gather my strength. Caleb, stony-faced, wouldn't – or couldn't – stoop to admit such weakness, but he shut his eyes and shook out his arms in relief every time we put the stretcher down. Only Marcel seemed to take the ordeal in his stride. In fact, noticing Amelia groaning, he offered to take her handle as well as his. She refused.

'Might as well,' said Caleb. Turning to me, he added, 'If Marcel carries one end, I can take the other – give you a rest?'

'Guys, I'm so sorry about this,' muttered Xander.

'You should be. Your leg may be broken, but my arms are about to fall off.'

Xander's quick grin didn't show in his eyes.

'Wasn't your fault,' Caleb said, without looking at him.

'It wasn't anybody's fault,' said Amelia. 'Not even Spenser's. Especially not his, in fact. Let's make sure the rangers know that. It was a freak accident.'

Caleb looked at her and sighed. His shoulders fell. When he spoke it was gently. 'Come on, Jack. We're both tired. Let's try taking it in turns. I'll start.'

With this, Marcel lifted up both handles at the head end of the stretcher and Caleb moved to pick up those at the feet. Since something about him in that moment seemed less about proving a point and more about actual kindness, I let him do it.

As it happens, we'd only made it a hundred metres in this formation before we met the team of rangers deployed to pick up Innocent's body. There were a lot of them. They met us in virtual silence. Two of the rangers checked Xander's splint with deft fingers. Since they left it as it was, I assumed that Amelia and I had done an OK job. While they were doing that, Marcel took the only member of the team with grey hair to one side. I watched them closely. Sure enough, though I couldn't quite hear the French, much less understand it, Marcel shot a quick nod in Caleb's direction before pursing his lips and dropping his chin. The older guard snorted and his mouth set hard and something flickered in my chest. I was worried for my cousin. *There'd be repercussions*, the guard's face said. This wasn't over for Caleb.

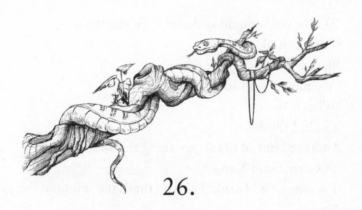

26.

Four of the rangers escorted us back to camp, carrying
Xander on the stretcher. They weren't big guys. One was
smaller than me in fact, with skinny little legs, but we
struggled to keep up with them. While I arrived on the
brink of collapse, those guys barely broke a sweat. They
managed to carry Xander dead level the entire way too.
We made it back to camp just as night fell. I don't know
whether Xander was exhausted by the pain, zonked by the
pills or out of it because of those twigs he kept chewing,
but he'd actually drifted off by the time we made it back.
Amelia went with Marcel to give an account of what had
happened to the head ranger. She had the French. I sat with
Xander while he slept. On his return, Marcel made it clear
we'd be setting off for Goma in the morning.

I slept badly and was awake before dawn. At first light I
saw Caleb emerge from his tent in a rush and stagger away
into the brush. Not quite out of sight, he bent double and
threw up. The sound of him retching woke Xander.

'Did he eat something dodgy?' he muttered.

'I don't think so.'

'Perhaps it's exhaustion.'

'My money's on something else.'

'What?'

'Guilt, I think.'

Another bout of heave-groaning reached us.

'Possibly,' said Xander.

'I'm sure of it,' I said. 'I reckon that's the sound of things sinking in.'

Xander didn't respond, just pushed himself up on his elbows, winced and looked forlornly at his immobilised leg.

'We'll get that sorted in no time,' I said.

'Course,' he replied. 'Marcel said there's a good little hospital in Goma.' He was trying to sound offhand, but I knew he was worried. Who wouldn't be? The state of the city – its poor roads and unfinished buildings – didn't exactly inspire confidence that it would harbour cutting-edge medical care. We returned to Goma in the back of the same pickup that had brought us out to the national park, driven by the same guy with the bloodshot eyes. But without Innocent or poor Patience. A sombre Marcel accompanied us instead. He sat up front with the driver while Amelia, Caleb and I tried to steady poor Xander and protect him from the worst of the bumps. We'd transferred him to a proper stretcher in camp, but though it was padded and had aluminium poles, it still had to sit on the pickup's unforgiving metal tray. We jacked it up on our backpacks to try and soften the juddering of the road. When I noticed that Caleb had wedged his legs under the stretcher too, using them to help absorb some of the jarring potholes, I did the same, but it didn't really help beyond giving us a share of Xander's discomfort. We'd not been going long when the pickup hit a particularly unforgiving rut which bounced all four of us into the air. Xander yelped at the blow.

Caleb banged hard on the cab window and shouted, 'Drive more carefully, will you?'

'Why wouldn't he drive as carefully as he can?' asked Amelia.

'I don't know,' muttered Caleb.

Amelia's question was genuine, and maybe Caleb really couldn't guess why the guy might not have been doing his best to drive steadily, but I thought I knew better. Catching sight of those red eyes in the mirror as we ploughed on, I saw them narrow with hostility. Marcel would have explained what had happened to Innocent. Was it any wonder that this driver might be at best indifferent to us feeling a bit of pain on the way back to Goma?

Amelia and I took Xander to the hospital with Marcel. I could tell Caleb wanted to come, too, but when Xander sighed that he didn't need an entourage my cousin's 'It's your call' was gentle. He'd mind our stuff, he said. Before we set off I overheard him tell Marcel to mention his father's name if he thought it would help. Though I bristled at the self-importance of this, I think he was genuine.

Xander and I had been wrong about the hospital. The building was small, but it looked recently whitewashed, and the little garden in front of it was full of bright ferns and carefully tended roses. The reassuring smell of disinfectant blotted out their perfume as Marcel and I stretchered Xander through the little lobby into a busy waiting room. The nurse who examined him wore the whitest uniform imaginable and had one of those little watches pinned to her top pocket. She told us there'd be a bit of a wait.

'That's fine,' sighed Xander.

'How long a wait?' asked Amelia.

'Maybe an hour and a half, two . . .' said the nurse apologetically.

'That's inside NHS targets,' Amelia replied.

The nurse had a warm smile but I could tell that she didn't know what Amelia was on about.

For once, so could Amelia. 'When I cracked my head on the side of the pool doing backstroke and needed twelve stitches, I had to wait in A & E at St Thomas's Hospital in London for three hours and forty-nine minutes,' she explained. This raised a smile in Xander, though the nurse remained none the wiser. A doctor would see Xander as promptly as possible, she confirmed as she left.

In fact, an orderly whisked him off for an X-ray pretty quickly, which was just as well because it meant he wasn't there when Amelia started thinking out loud about the trauma this hospital must have seen in recent years. Marcel appeared not to want to talk about it, but that rarely stops Amelia, and all it meant was that she delivered her monologue to me.

'Right here, the Eastern DRC, is the epicentre of the worst conflict on earth since the Second World War, in terms of casualties. Around six million people have been killed in these parts since 1996, and many more displaced.' Her eyes had that faraway look that I know so well; ever since we were little kids she's worn that expression while reeling off the facts about whatever she was interested in at that point in time, whether it be dog breeds or table-tennis bats. I did what I've always done, which is smile and let the detail wash over me, as she talked about a Rwandan genocide which prompted mass immigration, disputes with neighbouring Uganda and Rwanda in the wake of it, endemic corruption and the proliferation (her words, not mine, though I got what they meant more or less) of armed militia fighting for power and natural resources in the absence of government control.

'It's not just soldiers and militants who've been killed and hurt. Everyday civilians, women, the elderly and so many kids. It barely makes the news back home for some reason, but recent history here has been a tragic mess. The doctors in this hospital must have seen some horrific injuries. Not to belittle what's happened to Xander, but I imagine they'll make short work of a broken leg, if that's what it is.'

I would have felt awkward listening to this in front of Marcel. This 'tragic mess' was his country, but although we'd only been waiting ten minutes he'd already gone off, saying he was going to tell the nurse what Caleb had said about his father's name. All three of us told him that wasn't necessary, but he waved us away. It seemed almost as if he was worried that failure to do as Caleb had asked might cost him something.

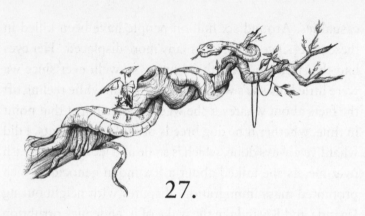

27.

As expected, the X-ray confirmed that Xander's leg was broken. He'd fractured his tibia, to be precise. It was a closed fracture, the doctor explained to us in the waiting room. When I asked her what that meant, Amelia butted in with, 'More serious than a hairline fracture, yet not misaligned or worse still poking through the skin, but then we knew that. At least it's unlikely to need surgery.'

The doctor had plump fingers with very pink cuticles. She did a little thumbs-up gesture and said, 'Impressive!'

'Thank you, but am I correct?' said Amelia.

'You are.'

It was a relief to hear they hadn't whisked Xander off to surgery. When I broke my wrist falling off my bike I had to have it pinned. Not pleasant. Neither is a plaster cast though, and that's what he was having fitted. When he emerged he was on crutches, his lower leg a solid orange boot.

'Do you like it? I got to choose the colour,' he said.

'Very . . . cheerful,' I replied.

'How long do you have it on for?' asked Amelia

'Six to eight weeks.'

'That's your trekking over and done with this summer then,' she pointed out matter-of-factly.

One of the best things about Xander is the way he looks on the bright side. 'At least I got to see the gorillas before it happened,' he said.

'Yeah, up pretty close,' I said.

'Too close,' Amelia pointed out.

The three of us dropped our heads at that. It seemed inconceivable that Innocent had lost his life trying to show us the best of his immense country, but it had happened, and athough I couldn't think of a way there and then, I knew I'd have to do something, however small, to make amends.

'Too close,' Amelia repeated.

Xander, risking a joke to break the tension, said, 'Really?'

'Yes, because . . .' Noticing Xander smiling at me, Amelia cottoned on and said, 'Oh,' instead of finishing her sentence.

It turned out that Uncle Langdon's private plane was occupied. Caleb looked crestfallen telling us this. Possibly he'd hoped to claw back some of his man-of-the-world status by spiriting us back to Kinshasa immediately, or maybe he was just disappointed at having failed in an honest attempt to be helpful. I'd charged my phone in the hospital waiting room, and as soon as it registered a signal I tried to contact Mum and Dad to tell them what had happened. Neither picked up. They were probably in meetings. I set the ringer to loud and waited for them to call me back, but neither did that day. It didn't matter – I'd fill them in soon enough.

Whatever painkillers they'd given Xander, combined with the relief of knowing his leg had been properly seen to, gave him the energy to use his French to organise tickets on a commercial flight back to the capital. Amelia went with him to sort this. Later he told me it was a good job she had, since although it was only a domestic flight they'd needed our passport details, and apparently she'd memorised them in a moment of boredom. 'When I asked if she was sure they were right, she didn't even answer,' he explained later. 'She just started reeling off other random numbers she knew, like the serial number for her laptop, her parents' TV licence, the ISBN numbers of her favourite books, et cetera. She's properly weird, you know.'

'Yeah,' I said, and I laughed with him, feeling oddly proud at the same time.

Caleb didn't object to the risk of taking a normal Congo Airways flight this time. He knew it wasn't as foolhardy as provoking a silverback, I suppose. Still, he got antsy with the flight attendant supervising the boarding when she said it might not be possible to swap Xander into a seat with extra legroom to accommodate his cast.

'Course it's possible. What you're saying is that you're not prepared to do it,' he said.

'I'll do my best.'

'And if your best isn't good enough, you'll regret it,' Caleb insisted.

Amelia tried to help, pointing out, 'She hasn't said it's *im*possible,' as the flight attendant retreated.

120

'I'll cope, either way. It's not like I can't bend my knee,' said Xander.

'That's good, but not the point. These people –'

Xander cut him off kindly, saying, 'Listen, thanks anyway.'

Caleb had to make do with carrying all Xander's luggage as well as his own. I would have helped, but Amelia beat me to it, and of course my cousin told her the extra weight was no bother to him. There were no free trolleys in the airport. Although we didn't have to walk far to drop our stuff off, it was a hot day, and by the time we made the plane Caleb was bright red with effort. They put Xander in a standard seat. He was fine with it and mercifully Caleb didn't argue. He just sat there, next to Amelia, stewing. My cousin had drawn in his spikes for now, but I couldn't help feeling he was likely to do a different kind of damage when he eventually lashed out again.

28.

When booking plane tickets Xander had got a message through to the hotel, so I was hopeful Mum or Dad – possibly both of them – might be at the airport in Kinshasa to meet us. I was surprised to see Uncle Langdon there instead. He was wearing a yellow Hawaiian number today, and somebody in the bustling airport crowd had just bumped his takeaway coffee cup, slopping some of its contents down his shirtfront. He was annoyed by that, seeming more bothered by the stain – he kept dabbing at it with a handkerchief – than he was concerned to see how we were. I imagined that meant he hadn't heard about the gorilla attack, Xander's leg or the death of Innocent, but when he finally gave up with the coffee spot, his offhand 'Bad luck' to Xander suggested that he knew exactly how it had happened.

I watched carefully, and he didn't so much as shoot Caleb a look, which seemed strange. My uncle has always been tough on my cousin when he's messed up, punishing even the smallest mistakes hard. One of my earliest Langdon memories is of him locking Caleb out in the garden, in the rain, because he'd failed to take his shoes off coming into the house and had tracked mud across the kitchen floor. Caleb had been about seven, and Langdon refused to let him back inside until Mark and I had finished our dinner. I remember what we ate, sausages and mash, because the sausages were incredibly hot and when Mark told me to eat up quickly I'd burned the roof of my mouth.

Was he waiting today until he had Caleb alone before tearing into him? Apparently not. Once we'd made our way – slowly, Xander wasn't that good on his crutches yet – to where his driver had parked up his big, blacked-out SUV, and all climbed in, he turned from the front seat and, addressing Caleb, said, 'Terrible shame about young Innocent. First guide to be killed in a gorilla attack for years apparently.'

When Caleb didn't reply I said, 'It was absolutely awful.' The words sounded ridiculously hollow, and I didn't improve things by adding, 'A complete tragedy.'

Langdon glanced at me, sniffed and said, 'Must have been. Still, I suppose it's a valuable lesson. Nature's unpredictable, no matter how experienced you are. Big animals like that can always turn.' Nodding at Xander he went on, 'Not something you'll forget in a hurry, eh . . . boy.'

Two things were clear: first, that he couldn't remember Xander's name, and second, equally obviously, that he wasn't bothered about Innocent. If Caleb was a self-regarding idiot, here was a reminder of where he got it from.

'It's not really something any of us are likely to forget,' said Amelia. 'Unless we develop amnesia.'

Langdon looked her up and down before conceding, 'S'pose not.' Seemingly out of a sense of duty, he went on, 'No, it's an awful tragedy for Innocent's nearest and dearest, you're right. We should just be grateful that – your leg aside, sonny – none of you were hurt or worse. I've made arrangements to compensate the family.' Then he turned to face the road again, gripping the handle above the door to steady himself as we swerved to avoid a woman cycling on an ancient bike with a basket balanced on her head. This little speech seemed to have drained the goodwill from my uncle. As the driver pulled back into our lane Langdon turned to him and snapped, 'Take it easy. It's not a race!'

We rode on in silence. So Langdon knew about the accident, but not apparently Caleb's role in it? I wasn't about to change that. One thing was for sure – Caleb didn't need his dad to make him feel he'd done something wrong. Though the signs were subtle – he'd stared out of the plane window the entire flight home, rather than looking for the usual excuses to big himself up, and more than once I'd caught him shaking his head, as if in disbelief – he was clearly struggling guilt-wise. The longer we drove without speaking, the more our silence seemed to come from him, or be his fault at least. If Amelia, Xander or I had started talking about what we'd witnessed, we might have dropped him in it.

But that didn't explain Langdon's apparent lack of curiosity. By the time we arrived at our hotel the passive, stare-straight-ahead stuff was really bothering me. What was going on?

I found out soon enough. Caleb tagged along while Langdon got us checked back in to the hotel. To his credit, he made sure the concierge gave Xander a room on the ground floor. But there was something strange about his attentiveness, as if, like Caleb, he was only stepping up because he felt guilty. I wanted to get away from him, so I said, 'I'll be back down in a minute. Mum and Dad are probably out lobbying or something, but I just want to see if they're in their room.'

'Ah, yes, Jack,' said Langdon. 'I need to talk to you about that. Let's take a seat, shall we?'

He put a hand on my back and steered me, with Amelia and Xander following, through to the bar area by the pool. A hollowness ran through me as he made a show of ordering us all Cokes (his had Jack Daniels in it) and sitting us down and asking the waitress to bring some bar snacks to go with our drinks.

'You must be hungry,' he said to us. 'I know I am!'

'Not particularly,' said Amelia.

'What do you mean, you need to talk to me?' I asked.

'It's nothing serious,' he said, in a way that made me think the opposite was true. 'Just that your mum and dad didn't imagine you'd be back here so soon, obviously, and they've gone on a little research trip. Out east, as it happens, not a million miles from where you've just been. Only they're still out there, and you're back here, and I've got a hundred and one work things to do, as has Caleb now, so you guys will have to stay put in the hotel, do a bit of recuperating, just until they return.'

'Researching what?' I asked.

'It's no hardship hanging out here though, is it? Games room, pool – not that sonny here can use it, but still – good food.'

'He's called Xander,' said Amelia.

'Course he is. Xander, with the duff leg. This is as good a place as any for it to mend, don't you think?'

'Where exactly have they gone, and what are they doing?' I said.

'Eh? Research, as I say. Into mining. They wanted to see how a responsible outfit like ours can contribute both economically and environmentally. I wasn't really in favour of them taking the risk since our operation reaches into some quite . . . spicy . . . territories, but you know what they're like.'

One half of me was reassured by this, since it made sense of why neither of them had called me back. If they were somewhere remote there was probably no signal. But I didn't like Langdon's use of the word *spicy*, and the fact that neither of my parents had left me a message before they set off was odd. Perhaps there'd be a note in my room. I must have looked worried.

Amelia, no doubt trying to help, said, 'You're concerned. But you yourself suggested they go and take a look at your uncle's mines.'

'Did I?'

'Yes. At dinner on our first night. You were sitting at that table over there, in the seat on the corner. The one with a red back. You were drinking a –'

126

'I get it, Amelia.' To Langdon I said, 'When are they due back?'

'Ah, here we are,' said Langdon, as our order arrived.

The waiter seemed nervous. He set everything down very gingerly, comically concerned he might spill something. It took ages.

Langdon didn't hurry him though. When the man had finally finished, and retreated with a little bow, my uncle still didn't answer my question, preferring to sit back in his chair and take an appreciative sip of his drink instead.

'When are they due back?' I repeated.

'Well . . .' he said reluctantly, 'travel plans in the DRC can be difficult to pin down.'

'I know. But when were they aiming for?'

'They didn't intend to stay long.'

'That doesn't answer the question,' Amelia said for me.

Langdon shot her a look. 'There's no cause for alarm. We would have expected them to have been in touch by now, but they've probably taken the opportunity to go exploring. You know how wilful your mother can be. Communications out east are patchy. It's nothing unusual.'

'You're not telling me everything you know,' I said. The statement came out more forcefully than I intended, and Caleb, who'd seemed uninterested in the conversation until that point, glanced up sharply to see how his father would take it.

Langdon put down his drink. 'I beg your pardon,' he said levelly.

'All I mean is, please don't keep anything from me.'

'I wouldn't, Jack.' His smile revealed his teeth. 'I'm a little concerned my people haven't given me an update. I'll admit that. But it's probably nothing. I certainly don't want to alarm you with guesswork at this stage.'

His reassurances were making the hollow feeling in my stomach twist in on itself with nervous dread.

'What can we do to track Jack's parents down?' asked Amelia. 'Who do we contact for help?'

'I've made all the appropriate enquiries,' Langdon said firmly. 'Right now we just sit tight. I'm sure we'll hear from them very shortly.' He drained his glass. 'Like I say, make the most of the facilities here in the meantime,' he went on, waving vaguely towards the pool and games room. It was a muggy day and his shirt had sweat rings under his yellow-patterned armpits. In that moment I hated Hawaiian shirts more than anything in the world.

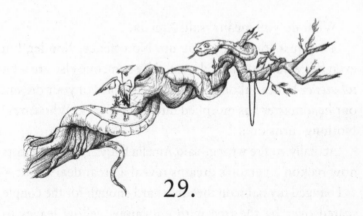

29.

I had no choice but to do as my uncle said and wait for news. It was hard. I turned the hotel suite upside down in search of a note or any other clue that might have put my mind at rest, but found none. All I could do after that was keep my phone fully charged with the ringer on in case anyone called. Though I tried not to, I must have checked it every other minute, but it stayed infuriatingly silent and message-less. By the end of that first day waiting, I felt like chucking the phone in the pool. I didn't though – I'm not a complete idiot.

At breakfast the following morning, after an awful night's half-sleep, I guess I looked pretty ragged. Xander tried to take my mind off things by telling me about a dream he'd had in which our school had been relocated to the rainforest, but right now I wasn't interested. Though I knew he meant well, I couldn't help cutting him off, saying, 'The funny thing about other people's dreams is that even at the best of times they're pretty boring.'

'What do you mean?' said Amelia.

'They just sound so made up. No offence, Xander, but even the wildest dreams dreamed by someone else are a bit *whatever* to hear about. In the unreal world of your dream, our headmaster has morphed into a silverback. Who cares? Nothing turns on it.'

'Actually you're wrong,' said Amelia flatly. 'Neuroscientists now reckon a person's dreams reveal a great deal about –'

I banged my palm on the table hard enough for the couple seated over by the tree with enormous yellow leaves to look up.

'Sorry,' I said to Amelia. 'But . . .'

'But what?'

Xander answered for me. 'Jack's right, Amelia. Now's possibly not the time for an update on cutting-edge neuroscience or my stupid dreams. I'm sorry.'

I felt guilty after that. Xander was the one with the broken leg; the painkillers he was on had probably prompted his dream. I should have been gracious enough to listen to it at least. But I was worried out of my head. I didn't know where to put myself, so stood up and walked out into the hotel lobby, did a tour of the stupid pool area, and was surprised, stomping back into the restaurant, to find that Uncle Langdon and Caleb had turned up in my two-minute absence. My heartbeat sped up. I jogged over to the table and asked, 'Any news?'

Langdon smiled weakly and said, 'Yes and no.'

'Is it good? Bad? What?!'

'A bit of both, I suppose. I've finally got through to my

people. That's good, in that it means we have a proper channel of communication again . . .'

There was a *but* coming. I said it ahead of him. 'But what?'

'It's not that Nicholas and Janine took a detour *after* visiting the mines, as I imagined.' He shook his head in apparent wonder. 'It turns out they went off-piste from the get-go and never showed up there.'

Amelia muttered, 'He said he had good and bad news. In fact the good news seems to have been that he managed to speak to someone who gave him bad news. It doesn't add up.'

Caleb, who had some sort of gel in his hair this morning, shrugged in agreement, as if Amelia was addressing this thinking-out-loud to him.

'Unless of course he's relying on the no-news-is-good-news adage, which would be ridiculous, given that we're talking about a missing-persons case here.'

'Never showed up?' I repeated.

Langdon softened. 'Apparently not,' he said, pulling out a chair for me. 'But look, you know your mother better than anyone. If she says a thing, she does it. She said she wanted to do her own research; as good as told me she wouldn't just be taking my word – and the example of my company – as gospel. I admire that, in a way. I'll bet they're just doing their own digging. It's a nuisance that they've gone AWOL for now, and a worry, I'll admit it, but let's not overreact.'

Amelia's words – *missing persons case* – were rattling round my head unhelpfully. They sounded ominously official. But if Mum and Dad hadn't arrived at Langdon's mining operation it meant they'd been out of contact for nearly a week, without apparently having told anyone where exactly they were going. That meant they were indeed missing.

To make matters worse, Amelia was still doing her thinking-out-loud thing: 'Janine and Nicholas were due to meet some pretty important people in the run-up to the vote. By important, I mean powerful, and by that I mean ruthless. We've discussed the endemic corruption in the DRC, its lawlessness. They could have crossed some proper villains, people prepared to go to any lengths –'

I cut her off. 'We need to tell someone, raise the alarm,' I said.

Langdon shifted in his seat.

'They wouldn't just go silent like this. Not if everything was OK. Even if their own phones weren't working, after this long they'd have found a way of getting a message through.' I bolstered myself with this, unable to look directly at Langdon as I built up to say, 'I want go to the police. Right now.'

'I understand,' he said.

Caleb's chin dropped and his head bobbed backwards, as if to say, *Come again?*

Ignoring Caleb, I said, 'Good,' before Langdon could change his mind.

It seemed he wasn't about to do that. Instead he gave his best impression of a sympathetic smile, saying, 'I'm not sure they'll be able to help, but if it will help put your mind at rest, Jack, that's what we should do.'

It might just have been that I noticed Langdon was wearing

a relatively sober, blue-on-blue patterned shirt that morning, but he sounded measured and sincere, and when he answered Amelia's 'Unless reporting them missing to the police makes the situation worse, we should do it even if the likely gain is minimal' with, 'You're right, Amelia. It can't hurt, can it?' I realised I'd been holding my breath, and let it out. He patted me on the shoulder then, before leading us out to his SUV, parked across the street with its engine running, and even followed up with an offer to oversee the process.

Langdon's truck was some sort of Hummer, I think, with three rows of seats. Caleb and I climbed into the back, leaving Amelia and Xander – struggling with his crutches – to the middle two seats. Caleb sat beside me with his head bowed. He seemed to have shrunk. Langdon rode up front next to the driver. He checked his watch before turning to explain that we'd head straight to the police station just as soon as we'd dropped off Caleb.

'That's not "straight" then, is it?' said Amelia.

Langdon chuckled. 'I suppose not, but you know what I mean. He'll miss his plane though, if we don't take him first. Not a good start to the world of work.'

'Why did he come to the hotel with you in the first place?' Amelia asked Langdon, though Caleb was right there with us.

Craning to see his son, Langdon smiled. 'Something to do with wanting to say goodbye to his newfound friends in person. That was it, wasn't it, Caleb?'

Xander turned to me and muttered, 'That's touching,' as Amelia, apparently intent on changing the conversation, said, 'When I was small I had an ammonite collection. I used to go looking for them on the beach in Lyme Regis with my uncle. Fossicking, it's called.'

Caleb has small ears. The one nearest me was definitely turning red, as was the side of his neck. I'd not seen where Amelia was going with her strange fossil anecdote, but perhaps he had. She brought it round to his impending work experience, with, 'What I mean is that rocks can be very interesting. I hope you have as good a time down the mine as I did on the beach.'

'Thanks,' he grunted.

Amelia generally talks with the certainty of a newscaster, but now she was almost stuttering. 'I'd certainly b-b-be interested in seeing a mine myself, one day.'

'I'm sure Caleb will report back,' said Langdon slyly. 'No doubt you've got each other's numbers.'

It seemed Amelia might nod her head off in front of me. My mouth tasted stale all of a sudden. I'd brought my camera with me and raised it to my eye now, wanting to distract myself. On the kerb opposite, a man was selling long loaves of French bread from a plastic crate between his knees. He had this slick way of flipping the sticks out of the crate and into a long thin plastic bag in one movement: it was mesmerising to watch. We worked our way into a district full of taller buildings, and within a few minutes pulled up in front of an office block. It had mirrored windows and sat behind railings. To one side of the entrance stood an SUV identical to the one we were sitting in. 'There's your ride, boy. Better get going, if you can tear yourself away,' said Langdon.

In order for Caleb to climb out of the SUV Amelia had to scoot her seat forward and shift sideways so he could reach the door. In the end she stepped down to the tarmac with him and waited there while he retrieved his luggage, a sort of camouflage-patterned military kitbag. Ridiculous. Willing him to be gone, I was surprised when he reached back into the truck and thrust his hand at Xander and me in turn.

'Thanks,' he said, shaking mine.

I gave him a *whatever* shrug.

'And . . . sorry.' Saying the word seemed trickier for him than coughing up a lump of concrete would have been.

'Sure.'

'I mean it. I apologise, and I'm grateful,' he said more emphatically, before turning away.

He'd stopped short of saying he owed me one, but it felt as if that's what he meant, and for a second I thought he might actually have come along simply to admit he'd been at fault and to show he was grateful I hadn't mentioned his bloody machete to anyone. But did he have an ulterior motive? Something about the bashful look on Amelia's face made me suspect so. All her life she's stared straight at anyone she's talking to, but today, saying goodbye to Caleb, she was fixated by the SUV's aerial. Caleb's ears were pretty much purple now. In what seemed to me slow motion, he leaned towards Amelia and kissed her on the cheek before swinging his stupid kitbag up onto his shoulder and walking away.

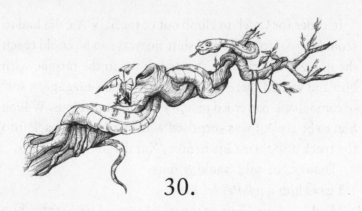

30.

I imagined Langdon would take charge at the police station, that the whole conversation would be in French and that I'd have to rely on Xander to translate, but I was wrong on all counts. Langdon led us into the breeze-block building and asked the sergeant on the desk if he could find someone who spoke English. When, some minutes later, a Detective Hubert arrived on the scene with a very clear, 'How can I help you?' Langdon flipped his thumb in my direction and said, 'This poor boy has lost his parents and wants to report them missing.'

Detective Hubert's sympathetic face made something well up inside me. I struggled to hold it together; the last thing Dad would want me to do in this situation is blub like a baby. But Langdon saying out loud that I'd 'lost' my parents brought it all home. It stoked my fear, clouding my head with panicky sparks. I tried to stay focused. The policeman picked up a laptop from a nearby desk awash with papers, snapped it shut, tucked it under his arm and took us to an interview room. Somebody in the station evidently liked spider plants. The one shelf in the room, high on the back wall, was a forest of them. Spider plants spread by growing new miniature versions of themselves at the end of long thin droopy stalks. All those spider-plant offspring searching for soil in mid-air made the panic roar up inside me again. My face grew red with it. Detective Hubert offered me a glass of water before we began.

I liked him. He let me explain who I was, who my parents were, what they were doing here in Kinshasa and why they had decided to head east, without interrupting me, despite the fact that not everything I said was relevant. I could tell that by watching his fingers. They tapped away at the keyboard when the detail was useful, and sat calmly on the tabletop when it wasn't. To his credit, Langdon didn't interrupt me either. Not until I petered out with a vague, 'They didn't leave me a message and I don't know exactly where they were going.'

Then Langdon said, 'They left a message through me, Jack.' To the policeman he said, 'I offered to organise their transport, but my sister-in-law had already made arrangements. She's a formidable woman and her husband – my brother – a most capable man. They had the address of my business operation. I understood that's where they were headed. But either voluntarily or otherwise, they've clearly been . . . waylaid.'

Detective Hubert said, 'Most worrying for you, Jack. I'm sorry.' His voice was deep, and smooth as treacle, at odds with his thin frame and scrawny neck. Yet the *sorry* was sincere, no doubt about it, and his, 'We'll do our utmost to help end the uncertainty for you, I promise,' was reassuring. I hadn't realised it, but I'd been gripping the desk hard as I said my piece. Now I let go. It wasn't long before I was clamping the thing tight again however, thanks to Amelia.

'Excuse me,' she piped up, 'but I have to point this out –'

'You're sure about that?' muttered Xander.

'Yes. You two –' she nodded from Langdon to the police detective and back again – 'are using deliberately wishy-washy words. *Voluntarily or otherwise waylaid* and *end the uncertainty* skirt round Jack's real concerns. He's worried someone has got hold of his parents and hurt them, or worse. What he wants is for you to find them and bring them back to him, not pretend everything's OK.

Amelia was totally right – as usual – and totally wrong at the same time. Of course I wanted my parents found. But a bit of reassurance in the meantime from the policeman had actually made me feel better. I wouldn't have minded the 'better' bit carrying on for a while. She meant well though, so I shot her a grateful smile and asked Detective Hubert, who was actually scratching his head while looking at Amelia askance, what would happen next.

'I need photographs of them,' he said. 'For identification purposes.'

I'd thought of that and had two good headshot portraits I'd taken ready on my phone. The policeman gave me an email address to send them to, but it turned out that either his laptop or the police station's Wi-Fi was on a go-slow; though the email showed as sent on my phone, for ages it didn't show up in the relevant inbox on his screen. I counted the spider plants – parents and sprouting offspring – while we waited. There were fifty-nine in total.

'Not exactly confidence-inspiring,' Amelia stated after the detective had apologised a second time for the continuing delay.

'These things happen. It'll work eventually.'

'Do you want me to have a look at the router configuration, help pinpoint the problem?' Amelia offered.

'Thank you, but no,' said Hubert with a smile.

'Why not?'

'It's a police computer, Amelia,' Xander said patiently. 'As a rule they're not just handed over to the public.'

'I suppose not,' she conceded. 'But at least he should turn everything on and off at the wall.'

'I suppose *he* should,' said the detective. 'In the meantime *he* could also ask Jack to text the photographs, or share them on WhatsApp.'

'You do know I'm talking about you, don't you?' asked Amelia.

'Amelia's smart in a particular way,' I told the policeman. 'What's your number? I'll text them through.'

I'd just pressed send when the Wi-Fi kicked back in, so now detective Hubert had the photographs twice. Why that made me feel better I don't know. In his smooth, deep voice he said he'd share them with the authorities in Goma and beyond, and he tried again to reassure me that, in his experience, communications difficulties were generally just that in the DRC. While he and his colleagues would launch an urgent search, he'd fully expect, on the balance of probabilities, that Mum and Dad would call me or turn up of their own accord soon.

'What are you basing your probability-balancing on?' asked Amelia.

Without missing a beat, the policeman, who seemed now to have figured her out, said, 'Twenty-two years of experience.' To me he wrapped things up with, 'Rest assured, Jack, we'll leave no stone unturned.'

'Is that a joke?' asked Amelia.

She was sincere, but sincere for her sometimes comes out as hostile. The policeman bristled. Seeing his friendly face tighten, Amelia tried to right the situation. 'Because, as Jack said, his parents were off to visit a bunch of mines. Lots of stones to look under there. I just thought –'

Xander said, 'There's a real joke here about digging yourself out of a hole, but in the circumstances I won't make it,' which was funny, because as always happens when a person says, 'There's a joke here but . . .' he'd basically made it anyway.

I managed to laugh somehow.

Detective Hubert did too. 'We'll do everything we can,' he told us all. 'I'll initiate our missing-persons protocol. As soon as I have any news, however small, I'll be in touch.' He handed me a card with his contact details written on it in a startlingly green font. 'And you do the same for me, OK?'

The words *missing-persons protocol* sounded so official. My gaze fell to the floor as he said them. I fought back the fear, tried to put some steel in my voice and failed. 'Sounds like a fair deal,' I whispered.

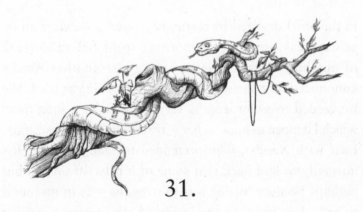

31.

Langdon ran us back to the hotel. En route he made it clear that he'd intended to fly east with Caleb that morning but would be staying in Kinshasa to help deal with what he called 'the situation'. He said he was pleased I'd persuaded him to go to the police. It felt like he was on my side, genuinely trying to be helpful, and there was no hint that he resented the inconvenience of my absent parents, but I still felt the need to apologise for mucking up his schedule.

He waved the apology away. 'I've got bags of things to be getting on with here,' he said. 'And anyway, it'll be good for Caleb to make a start without me breathing down his neck.'

'Thanks,' I said, meaning it.

'That's OK. You have my number. Use it if you need to. I know it'll be tough waiting here, but try not to worry. Think how much they'll owe you when they show up again!'

With that he was off, leaving us on the steps of the luxury hotel I'd grown to hate more than boarding school. At least the days pass quickly there. That afternoon and evening

141

in the hotel dragged by tortuously slowly. We were all up at daybreak, and after a morning spent failing to think of anything constructive to say to one another Amelia announced that she was going to cool off in the pool. She proceeded to swim lengths very quickly for a long time, which I happen to know is her way of venting her frustration. I sat with Xander, who pretended to read a book. He's normally so laid back that some of it rubs off on me, but perhaps because his leg was hurting, he was in no mood to talk. I gnawed on the inside of my lower lip until it bled, trying to make myself believe in what Langdon and Detective Hubert had insisted: that Mum and Dad would stroll through the lobby doors any moment, or at least that the phone on my lap would light up with one of their numbers. But of course neither of those things happened and I could not will away my fears.

Eventually – and it took a while – Amelia wore herself out and joined us. She was red in the face with exertion. Her hair dripped on the stone floor. She didn't bother drying it, just wrapped her towel around her middle and slumped into a seat next to Xander, who went on 'reading' for an awful long time without turning a page.

'Good book?' I asked him when the quiet – which had a wrong feeling about it – had gone on too long.

'Riveting.'

The silence between us descended again, punctuated by a bit of traffic noise which filtered in over the hotel's high walls.

'I'm going to order some food,' Amelia said.

'I'm not hungry,' I replied.

'Me neither,' said Xander without looking up.

'Nor am I,' said Amelia. 'But we can't live on air. Waiting on an empty stomach is worse than just waiting: fact. I'll order.'

She called over a waitress who can't have been much older than us. There were bright beads at the end of her cornrows and her fingernails were all painted a different colour, which you'd think might mean she was a playful person, but as Amelia established that the hotel served cheeseburgers and ordered three, clarifying that they weren't all for her, the girl's face stayed absolutely set, as if it was carved from marble. None of us said anything after she left, and we sat in that heavy silence for the fifteen or so minutes it took for her to bring us our order, which she set down solemnly on the glass tabletop, her face as expressionless as before. Even the cheeseburgers looked leaden in that atmosphere. None of us made a move towards them after the waitress had gone.

'Who's going to say it?' said Xander.

'Say what?'

'Not you evidently, Jack. That's understandable.'

Not knowing what he meant, I turned to Amelia.

'I'm always saying the wrong thing these days,' she said. 'So not me.'

'What are you guys talking about?'

Xander took a deep breath. 'You obviously bought into that little stunt of your uncle's.'

'Stunt?'

'Him finding a tame policeman who'd pretend to take you seriously.'

'He did take me seriously!'

'You'd want to believe that,' said Amelia. 'Wish fulfilment is a thing.'

'He did enough to make you agree to park yourself here and wait it out. I'll give him that,' said Xander.

Amelia cut back in. 'You have to admit his plan of action – spread some photos about among his policeman mates and hope – sounded pretty weak.'

'Precisely,' said Xander. 'The first thing he should have done, if he wasn't in Langdon's pocket, is interview him properly, since your uncle is pretty much the last person to have seen your parents before they disappeared.'

Now that he pointed it out, it seemed obvious, but I'd liked Detective Hubert and didn't want to think he was somehow in my uncle's thrall. 'Langdon's cancelled his plans to be here helping,' I said lamely. 'Maybe he's giving the police the detail now.'

'You think?' said Amelia.

'Langdon says there's no problem,' said Xander. 'Your mum and dad will turn up eventually, he thinks, and that's that. Somehow he got Detective Hubert to agree.'

I'd taken the policeman's agreement as a positive thing, but according to my friends I was deluded. I felt my hackles rising, even as I saw the sense of what they were saying.

'We all want them simply to show up,' said Xander. 'Of course we do. But there has to be more we can do than just hanging around here, waiting.' He reached towards the cheeseburgers, took the fork from beside the nearest plate instead of the burger on it, jammed the fork handle down the inside of his plaster cast, and wiggled it about.

'Nice,' said Amelia.

'My shin is so itchy,' he explained.

'Scratching itches makes them worse.'

'You're wrong about one thing at least,' he said, scratching harder. To me he went on, 'If we could piece together their movements before they left, find out who they met with and what they talked about, we might come up with a lead. As I understand it, they were pitting themselves against some pretty powerful people who – I hate to say it, but there's no point in pretending – might well have had good reason to want them out of the picture. Do you know the detail of this summit they're attending in the run-up to the vote?'

'Not really.'

Amelia said, 'It's called the Inaugural DRC Conference on Sustainable Development, and basically it's an opportunity for environmental activists from around the world to persuade the Congolese government to regulate mining in and around the national parks. A lot of unscrupulous businesses, not to mention armed militia, want the opposite. There's a big vote on a bit of legislation called Article 16B – which sets out what's allowed and what's not – coming up the week after next, and the summit is an attempt to influence the outcome.'

'Where does she get the detail from?' Xander asked me.

'Here and there,' I said.

'Actually, I googled it while we were in the police station,' said Amelia.

'Why?'

'Because the one thing we know for sure is that Nicholas and Janine will want to be here to witness that vote. They'd also like to be around to meet with officials, ministers, businessmen, et cetera, in the run-up period, but knowing when the actual vote is happening gives us their absolute deadline. That's when they have to be back.'

Having informed us of this, Amelia made a start on one of the cheeseburgers. She's always had a good appetite, probably as a result of all the swim training. Watching her eat stirred up my own hunger. Unexpectedly the burger itself was slathered in some sort of chilli sauce and the cheese was also pretty punchy; the food tasted better than it looked.

Between mouthfuls I said, 'You guys are right. We should do something. I can't just sit here waiting anyway; I'll go mad. But I think you've got Detective Hubert wrong. Let's pay him a visit without Langdon, tell him to investigate any enemies Mum and Dad might have made over this Article 16B thing and ask him what that missing-persons protocol he mentioned is all about.' I know Amelia had already called me out for 'wish fulfilment', but as I took another bite of burger I felt genuinely optimistic. I gulped the mouthful down and said, 'Who knows, he might already have turned up a lead.'

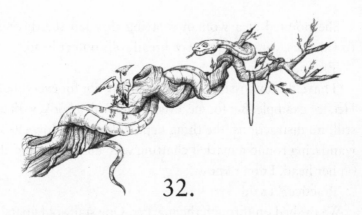

32.

Since Xander's leg was aching I suggested he wait in the hotel. If Langdon or anyone else turned up with news, he'd be there to field them. I'd paid close attention as we'd driven to and from the police station and was confident I could find my way there on foot. It wasn't that far anyway. At one point the car had dog-legged around a big market. Now we cut straight through it. Everything about the market was a screamingly bright colour. There were stacks of fluorescent flip-flops alongside trays of oranges, mangos and cherries, and pink buckets full of blue plastic straws set out on bright green plastic tablecloths next to trestle tables piled with dark red gobbets of meat. To keep the sun off everything, the stallholders had stuck striped beach umbrellas at jaunty angles everywhere, and the light pouring through was like one of those crazy Snapchat filters that makes everything look unrealistic.

'Have you ever actually tried to do that?' Amelia asked.
'What?'

She pointed at a woman weaving through the throng towards us, carrying a tray of bread rolls on her head.

'Er, no.'

'I have. It's impossible. Well, obviously not for everyone. Her, for example. But for me, even trying with a book, sitting still, no distractions, the thing kept sliding off. How she's wandering round a market chatting with all that balanced on her head, I don't know.'

'Practice?' I said.

We pushed on through the market. One stall sold goats' hoofs, the next wire mesh, the one after that fake Nike trainers. This one here, beneath a pink-and-yellow umbrella, had nothing but battered old motorcycle helmets; that one there sold seeds. In among the general scruffiness, one person stood out. He was tall, he walked towards us like he was stepping onstage to sing a song, and he was dressed in an immaculate purple corduroy three-piece suit and bowler hat. In that heat! He was also wearing a monocle and carrying a cane. As he passed us he twirled it and gave me a nod. I realised my mouth was hanging open.

'I've read about that,' said Amelia. 'It's a thing.'

'What do you mean?'

'A fashion thing here, known as *Sapeurs*, which means "Society of Ambience-Makers and Elegant People", in French. It's a sort of competitive bling spiffiness. Dates back to the Second World War, when the men who had fought for France came back to Brazzaville, across the river, with bits and pieces of posh clothing to wear or sell. It spread to Kinshasa later. The Sapeur attitude is no-matter-how-hard-life-gets-I'm-going-to-look-the-bomb. Those guys spend masses on clothes, even though some of them barely have enough left over to buy food. Stay cheerful and look-like-a-god-at-all-costs – that's their motto.'

I took the guy's photograph. He gave a little bow. We watched him swagger away. Pretty much everyone else was in shorts and a T-shirt, or a simple dress. He must have been boiling! But he got a lot of appreciation – high fives, whoops, fist bumps – for his efforts, and there was something about his attitude I liked.

Once we made it through the market the police station was round the corner, as I knew it would be. I walked into it with my shoulders back and head high, hoping that some of the Sapeur's confidence might have rubbed off on me. I even managed to talk to the desk sergeant in French. Obviously it wasn't very good French as he replied in English, saying that Detective Hubert was on his lunch break but would be back soon. He invited us to take a seat. We did so, but not before I'd noticed that he was playing chess on his mobile phone.

The desk sergeant put the game aside a few minutes later when the door banged open and two of his colleagues hauled a young guy inside. His T-shirt had a huge rip down the back and his skin was cut beneath it. Blood had soaked into the waistband of his jeans. He was unsteady on his feet, mumbling in French. I don't know what he was saying, but it evidently annoyed the bigger of the two officers manhandling him, and out of nowhere the policeman hit the guy in the stomach so hard that he left the floor before crumpling to the ground. I was flabbergasted. But the officer looked almost bored. He followed up the blow by rolling the guy over with a kick. When he didn't get back up the two policeman dragged him away down the corridor by his feet!

'Wow,' breathed Amelia.

The casual brutality of what had happened was underscored by the fact that the desk sergeant went back to his chess game as soon as the commotion in the corridor was over. Not long after that, Detective Hubert appeared, his sympathetic smile already in place.

'You got my message?' he said as he approached.

This threw me. 'No?' I said.

'It was just to say that we've tracked down the guy who helped your parents arrange their trip out east.'

Immediately my scepticism evaporated. I checked my phone. Sure enough, there was a text. It must have landed just now when I was distracted. The detective had even given me the travel fixer's name. I showed my phone to Amelia, who read it aloud: 'Yannick Mugalia'.

'If you didn't get the message, what are you here for?' he asked gently. 'Do you have some information to tell me?'

I didn't know how to answer. Amelia did however. 'There were things we wanted to know about your missing-persons protocol, but since it's already turning up results it sounds as if it's fit for purpose.'

Detective Hubert smiled. 'I'm glad if you think so.'

'We also wanted to suggest you trace anyone Nicholas and Janine might have rubbed up the wrong way with their environmental activism. They were meeting with businessmen, other activists, government officials, and –'

The policeman cut her off. 'We're well aware of all of that,' he said emphatically. More gently, he added, 'We've drawn up a list and we're working through it. True: they were due to meet with some . . . unsavoury people. But I still think the most likely explanation for their lack of communication is a lack of signal wherever they've gone exploring. Let's not lose sight of that.'

'Of course,' I heard myself say.

'Have faith,' the detective said with a smile. 'Our country gets a bad press, but many – most – among us are trying to make things work.'

He had such pride in what he said that I could not disbelieve him. In fact, I felt borderline sleazy for having doubted him in the first place.

'We're doing our best to get hold of this Yannick Mugalia, and when we've talked to him I'll be sure to update you. How about that?'

'Thank you,' I said.

Detective Hubert had been steering us towards the exit with these last words. Amelia drew up short of the door, swivelled on the heel of her trainer, and asked point blank, 'How long have you known Langdon Courtney?'

The detective's head bobbed back on his thin neck, but his smile stayed in place. 'I was introduced to him yesterday. You were there.'

'And before then you'd never heard of him?'

'I'm afraid not, no. Should I have?'

'That's not the point,' said Amelia bluntly. I fought back a shudder at her rudeness. Perhaps she noticed, since she backtracked lamely with, 'For what it's worth, I believe you.'

Detective Hubert's smile thinned to a sarcastic line. 'Well, that's a relief,' he said.

I was worried that he'd taken offence and wished I could rewind Amelia's little interrogative outburst. But I had to make do with, 'Thanks for all you're doing. I'll be sure to keep a closer eye on my phone from now,' as I reached for the door. When my fingers closed on the handle – a silver bar running the length of the door – I recoiled. It felt sticky. Glancing at my hand I saw that it was stained red. The cut-up guy whom the two officers had shovelled through the door earlier must have rubbed up against handle, bloodying it. For some reason I didn't want Detective Hubert to feel bad about that. Not that he should have done, it wasn't his fault. Either way, I pretended it hadn't happened, held the door open for Amelia with my foot and said goodbye to the detective over my shoulder as I followed her out onto the street.

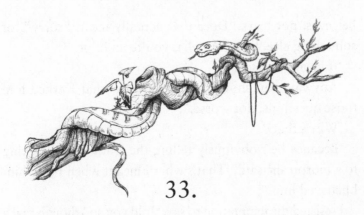

33.

'I can't believe you accused him of that!' I said to Amelia when we'd rounded the first corner.

'I didn't accuse him of anything,' she said, taken aback.

'As good as. All that "How long have you actually known Langdon?" stuff. You might as well have called him a liar to his face!'

'I don't recall using the word *actually*.'

'You don't get it, do you?' I said. 'You don't have to say a thing explicitly to give the impression that's what you mean.'

'You might not, but I do,' said Amelia quietly. She'd turned her face from me. For a horrible moment I thought her shoulders had begun to quiver. Had I hurt her feelings? Was she actually crying? I immediately felt bad; Amelia's straight-talking cleverness is what I like most about her, after all. The stress of not knowing where my parents were was obviously getting to me.

I reached out to pat her upper arm and said, 'Sorry.'

She turned back to me and I was relieved to see anger in

her eyes, not tears. 'Does that actually mean "sorry", or something else, like: "Amelia, you're an idiot."'

'It means I'm sorry.'

'Anyway, you should feel better now that I asked him those questions, not worse.'

'Why's that?'

'Because he's obviously telling the truth.' As if talking to a moron she said, 'That's what I meant when I told him I believed him.'

I resisted the temptation to say, 'Told you so,' though that's what I wanted to do as we cut back through the market. One of the stallholders recognised us, or Amelia at least, and offered her a mango. When she accepted, he sliced it in half and filleted it, his knife a blur, before offering her the result turned inside out, a sort of spiky mango hedgehog. Amelia tried to pay him but he waved her money away.

'Weird business model,' she said with her mouth full.

The guy heard and understood her. '*Tu seras de retour*,' he said with a smile.

'Possibly,' Amelia agreed, and we walked on.

This exchange, and what had felt like a mini-breakthrough at the police station, meant that I returned to the hotel with a spring in my step. It was a surprise to find Xander in the lobby, doing the man-on-crutches equivalent of pacing about. Careful not to fall into the told-you-so trap with him either, I quickly filled him in on our conversation with the detective. He read between the lines though – as he always does – and said, 'So you were right all along. I'm glad to hear it.'

'Right, wrong, it doesn't matter,' said Amelia. 'The point is the police appear actually to be on the case.'

'What are you doing hobbling about, anyway?' I asked him. 'The whole point of leaving you here was to give you a chance to rest your leg.'

'I know,' he said. 'But I got bored. And there was something going on out here so I came to see what was happening.'

'What was it?'

'I'm not exactly sure. Some delivery guy in a motorcycle helmet causing a fuss. The receptionists called security on him.'

'Not many people here bother to wear them. They were probably just curious,' I said.

'Well, this bloke was so proud of his he refused to take it off. They escorted him out at gunpoint with his hands above his head. I don't know what they were so bothered about. He didn't hassle anyone or try to take anything, and he rode off peacefully enough.'

'Weird,' I said.

'Seriously?' said Amelia. 'Now who's being slow? It's obvious!' She turned to Xander. 'You said it yourself, he was a delivery guy. Did you get a look at the front of his helmet?'

'Yeah.'

'And was the visor down, and possibly tinted.'

'I think so, yes.'

'With me now?' she said, looking from Xander to me and back again.

'He didn't want to be seen,' I said, dread blooming in my chest. 'Meaning he didn't want to be linked to whatever he was delivering.'

'I wonder what it was. Did you see?' asked Amelia.

I don't know how Xander responded as I was already on my way to the reception desk. That horrible instinct I have for knowing something bad is about to happen just before it does had kicked in. The concierge was filling out a form as I approached. His handwriting was extraordinary, regular as type, and very slow to execute. When he finally looked up I said, 'My name's Jack Courtney. Has anything been delivered for me?'

He checked the pigeonholes in the little room behind his desk, and sure enough came back to me with a brown envelope. My name and room number were printed on the front.

'The guy in the motorcycle helmet delivered this, didn't he?'

The concierge raised an eyebrow. 'You know him?'

'No, but I'm sorry to have caused a problem.'

'There's no problem,' the concierge insisted kindly.

But I knew he was wrong. The problem was pulsing in my hands.

Xander had hobbled over with Amelia beside him. The three of us looked down at the envelope.

'Aren't you going to open it?' asked Amelia.

'Yes, Amelia,' I said, sliding a finger beneath the flap, 'I am.'

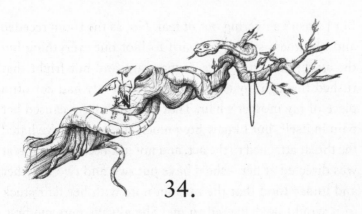

34.

The envelope contained a single sheet of A4 paper. It was blank on one side with a typewritten message on the other. The message wasn't long, just a few lines in fact, but I didn't read them immediately because my eyes were drawn first to the bottom of the page, where the sender had taped a lock of hair, a single auburn curl, the exact colour and texture of my mother's. I steeled myself before reading the note.

To Jack Courtney, son of Nicholas and Janine Courtney. We have your parents. We are holding them hostage and will release them when we receive US$75,000, paid in banknotes directly to our representative. Call the number below immediately for further instructions. Do not contact the police again. If you do, the next envelope will contain a body part.

I looked again at the lock of hair. It was trembling, as was the whole piece of paper, as was my hand, arm, all of me.

But I wasn't shivering out of fear. No, as the room receded and blackness surged forward to blot out everything but the awful quivering note, it was rage and not fright that rushed through my entire being. Somebody had cut off a piece of my mother's hair. That wouldn't have caused her pain in itself, but I knew how much she would have hated the threat attached to the act, and not just because the threat was directed at her – she'd have put two and two together and understood that the ransom note with her hair stuck to it would be delivered to me. She always puts me first, so she'd have been most worried about the effect the note would have on me. Dad, too, would be beside himself. He hates losing control. Being held hostage would be his worst nightmare come true.

I fought the shivering, forced the page to stay still.

Amelia had read the note upside down. That didn't surprise me. If you stare at your phone long enough she's likely read that over your shoulder too. I didn't object today.

Xander understands that reading another person's mail is inappropriate. Gently he asked, 'Well, what does it say?'

'Some creep claiming he's taken Jack's parents hostage, and demanding money – $75,000, weirdly – in exchange for their release,' said Amelia. 'Plus a bit of Janine's hair. Allegedly. I mean, it does look like hers but . . .'

She petered out as I passed the note to Xander. 'See for yourself,' I said through gritted teeth.

I watched his face, my mind leapfrogging itself. After I'd found and freed my parents from the scum who had sent me this note, what would I do to them in revenge? Turn them in to the authorities ultimately of course, but – my blood really did feel like it was boiling in my veins – only after I'd personally made them pay. I realised I was bouncing on the balls of my feet, my face tight with anger.

By contrast Xander remained calm. 'Wow. I'm sorry, Jack,' he said, handing the piece of paper back to me. 'But listen, at least there's a way to get your folks to safety. I know $75,000 is a lot of money, but your mum and dad could pay more than that if they had to. And Langdon can put up the money now. Call him.'

'Why that amount though?' said Amelia. 'I mean, it doesn't even divide neatly in two. Are they saying your dad's worth more than your mum? Or maybe it's the other way around.'

'Possibly that's not the point,' said Xander kindly.

'The note says to call the number straight away, meaning before calling anyone else,' I said.

'It's a ransom note, Jack, threatening to hurt your mother,' said Xander. 'The first thing we need is adult advice.'

This made good sense, yet something in me resisted. '*Immediately* is a pretty clear instruction,' I said. 'What if they're monitoring me somehow. If they think I'm disobeying them and take offence –'

'Xander's right,' said Amelia firmly. 'This is Langdon's brother and sister-in-law we're talking about. He'll want to know they're in danger right away. There's no evidence anyone's "monitoring" you anyway.'

Amelia's fingertips made air quotes around the word *monitoring*. It annoyed me. While she was right that I had no concrete evidence I was being observed, that didn't necessarily make me wrong. Either way, I *felt* wary. Amelia knows a lot and thinks logically, but I'd trust my gut instinct over hers any day.

I read the note again slowly. It told me not to contact the police again, but didn't say anything about anyone else. Amelia and Xander were obviously sensible to suggest I call Langdon, and I would. But the note was addressed to me. It concerned my parents. And it said to call the number at the foot of the page immediately.

'Thanks, guys, but this is my decision,' I said evenly, and pulled out my mobile phone.

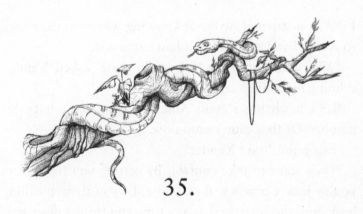

35.

Nobody picked up.

I'd entered the number carefully and double-checked it before pressing call. I was expecting whoever was on the other end to answer immediately, but they didn't. The phone rang for what seemed like ages. Sometimes, if I glance at a clock with a second hand, anticipating seeing it move, the second it should take to tick seems to take forever, precisely because I'm waiting for it. Waiting for the kidnapper to answer my call felt a bit like that that, with the waiting stretching time improbably, so much so that I almost hung up. But in reality the delay was probably just the normal length of time it takes for voicemail to kick in, and just as I was about to take the phone away from my ear to end the call, that's what happened. An automated, satnav-type woman's voice said the following:

After the beep, please say your name. We will contact you with further directions shortly.

I did as instructed, without knowing why, and explained to Xander and Amelia what had happened.

'Why would they get you to do that?' asked Xander, echoing my bafflement.

'Isn't it obvious?' said Amelia. 'They don't have his number. Or they didn't until now.'

'Fair point,' said Xander.

'They want to take control. By getting you to confirm you're Jack Courtney, they know it's you they're calling back, and they can do that at a time and from a place that they choose.'

'Makes sense,' I said.

Amelia gave me a 'course it does' look, then said, '*Now* will you call your uncle?'

I was already scrolling to find his number. He answered after the first ring. I realised, as I began to tell him about the letter, that I didn't want to sound panicked by it. Was I fighting to keep calm to stop my imagination from running away with itself, or because I wanted to protect Langdon (this was his brother in danger after all) from jumping to his own terrible conclusions? I don't know. I do remember that I went so far as to suggest to my uncle that the note was partly good news: we knew my parents were alive and well and considered valuable by their kidnappers. All we had to do was follow their demands and Mum and Dad would be set free unharmed, surely?

'Stay put in the hotel. I'm on my way,' Langdon said.

He arrived within minutes. I waited just inside reception with a view past the potted palms out onto the street. His big SUV slewed to the kerb in front of the hotel with the passenger's door opening before the car had quite stopped. Langdon jumped down and walked briskly up the steps, put a hand on my shoulder and steered me in silence, his face grim, through to a corner table on the far side of the bar. Amelia stuck with us, but I'd already handed my uncle the ransom note by the time Xander, clicking on his crutches, caught up. I noticed a sheen on Langdon's forehead as he read the note, and saw that his Hawaiian shirt was pasted to his sides. Was it the dash across town or fear making him sweat like that? He inspected the note carefully, turned it over, folded and unfolded it again, and took a deep breath.

'What do you think?' said Amelia, just as he was obviously about to speak.

I gritted my teeth.

'Your parents understood the risks of coming to the DRC with their . . . agenda,' he began. 'We discussed it at length in advance. This is a volatile country at the best of times, and the battle between conservationists and those seeking to develop the country through mining and other industries is fraught. Add poaching into the mix, as you've seen for yourselves, and the national parks your parents are here to protect can be very dangerous. On top of that, most of the police are corrupt, in the pockets of politicians and businessmen who are more corrupt still. Given the general lawlessness, organised crime is rife.'

'We know all this,' said Amelia bluntly.

Langdon gave her a sharp look. 'I'm explaining it again

to emphasise the array of people who could be responsible for this . . . outrageous demand.' He tapped the ransom note. 'If your parents made it to one of the parks, they could have been captured by poachers linked to criminals here in Kinshasa. Or your mother's insistence on visiting cowboy mining operations very different to mine could have put them in the way of any number of mercenary crooks. In addition they could quite simply have been targeted by opportunists on the lookout for Westerners to kidnap for the cash. Lastly, there's an outside chance that the whole thing is a hoax; someone who has never even met Nicholas or Janine could have got wind that they might have gone missing and be trying to make a quick buck out of the situation before they show up again. One thing's certain: whoever is demanding the ransom can't have worked out exactly what your parents are worth, since the sum they're asking for is comparatively modest.'

I was pleased he thought $75,000 was a small price to pay for Mum and Dad's release, but something in his stony expression worried me. 'I don't suppose it matters that much exactly who has them, in a way,' I said. 'All the groups you've mentioned have one thing in common. They want money. Once we've paid them and they've freed Mum and Dad, we can track them down and bring them to justice with the help of the police.'

Langdon snorted dismissively through flared nostrils. 'If only it were that simple,' he said.

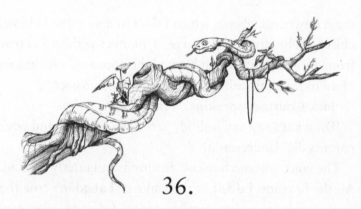

36.

'What's not simple about it?' I said, trying to keep the heat out of my voice.

'First up, it's a matter of principle. As a businessman here, and more importantly as a member of the Courtney family, I simply cannot give in to demands of this type. If we pay once, we send a message that we're prepared to pay again.'

'That's a sound train of thought in the abstract,' said Amelia loudly. Her voice rose further still: 'But, *hello* – these are Jack's parents we're talking about, one of whom happens to be your own brother.'

Langdon replied in a steely whisper, 'Precisely. And he'd never forgive me for bowing down before such a threat. What he – and your mother – would want is for us to track down these crooks and make them rue the day they heard the Courtney name.'

Langdon's ire was actually pretty rousing. The flush of anger I'd felt on first reading the note rose within me again. But just as I was about to ask him how he planned to track them down, my phone, which I'd set to maximum volume, chirruped loudly. The screen read 'number withheld'. I rose from my seat, walked out beyond the pool area – somehow I had to take this call alone – and pressed answer.

'Jack Courtney speaking,' I said.

'Do what I say and nobody gets hurt. Disobey and your parents die. Understand?'

The voice was mechanical, distorted, and utterly chilling. All the bravado I'd felt in the wake of Langdon's 'rue the day' speech drained from me instantly. I shut my eyes, saw my mother's face, and the thought that I'd been holding at bay since discovering that they were missing crashed in. I'd lost my brother. If I lost Mum and Dad too, I'd be alone in the world. I gulped air.

'Hello, you're still there?'

'Yes, yes, I understand,' I stammered.

'You have visited the national museum and seen the statue of the tyrant criminal Leopold.'

'Yes, but how –'

'Your mother gave us this information.'

I was standing next to a gardener's hosepipe that was wound in a coil and bolted to the wall. It made me think of a noose, a coiled whip, a poisonous snake. How had they got Mum to reveal this bland fact about our visit? 'Tell me they're OK,' I blurted out.

'They can tell you themselves,' said the voice. My ear filled with random noise as whoever was holding the phone manhandled it, and my eyes filled with tears at what I heard next.

166

It was my father's voice, shaky with fear but unmistakable.

'Jack, listen. Do exactly what these guys say. We're fine for now. It's just money. Your uncle Langdon will put it up. He knows I'll repay him. This isn't a time for heroics. I love you.'

'You will find your mother's headscarf at the foot of Leopold the butcher's statue this Friday at 4 p.m.,' said the mechanical voice, after another bout of phone-shuffling. 'Place the money beneath it in an envelope and leave the museum immediately. Your parents will be at your hotel, safe and unharmed, on your return. If you fail to deposit the money, or attempt to follow the representative we send to retrieve it, we'll kill them both. Understood?'

Still blinking back tears, I nodded, only thinking to add a weak, 'Yes,' after a pause. 'I understand,' I said more firmly. 'Four o'clock on Friday, under the headscarf at Leopold's feet. Yes.'

'Good boy,' the voice replied. 'Very good.'

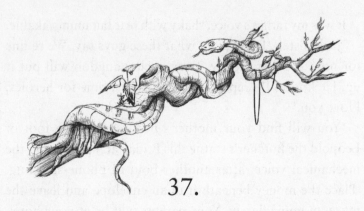

37.

I turned to see Langdon, flanked by Amelia and Xander, standing in the entrance to the restaurant on the other side of the pool. He had his hands on his hips. There was no way that he could have heard my half of the conversation from over there, but he looked angry with me. Possibly he'd read my body language. I tried to walk tall as I returned to him.

'That was the kidnapper, I take it,' Langdon said.

'One of them. They keep referring to "we", so I guess there's a team,' I said.

'That's not a bad thing,' said Xander, trying as ever to look on the bright side. 'The more people are involved, the harder it will be for them to keep what they're doing a secret.'

Langdon looked Xander up and down and said, 'Good point. And with my connections, once I've put the word out for people to keep an ear to the ground, I'm sure we'll turn up a lead.'

'What do you mean by *connections*?' asked Amelia.

Langdon ignored her. 'So?' he said to me. 'What did they say?'

I told him what the kidnapper had said, relaying the unthinkable threat word for word. When I say *unthinkable*, I mean it; hearing myself repeat out loud what the kidnappers were threatening to do to my parents, my brain put up a kind of shield that stopped me connecting the horror to them. Instead it gave me two random memories in quick succession. The first was an image of Dad with his hands on his hips in a very Langdon-style way. They're brothers after all. Dad was in the downstairs hall at home and I was viewing him from the top of the stairs. His hands were on his hips because I'd made myself some toast and left everything out with the lids off. He wasn't particularly angry, just annoyed in an everyday sort of way. The second memory that came to me was equally standard issue. It was just me glancing across at Mum as she steered the car through traffic at night. Headlights swept across her and I saw she had her concentrating face on, lips pursed, eyes alert and glistening. That was it, two normal memories of my parents to blot out the horrible unknown of wherever they were now, and how I'd be unable to cope without them, in the aftermath of the kidnapper's call.

'They put Dad on,' I whispered, once I'd lain the full horror of the threat at Langdon's feet.

'Bang goes your last theory,' Amelia said to him. 'It's not a hoax.'

'She doesn't mean it triumphantly,' I felt I had to tell Langdon.

'Of course I don't!' said Amelia, confused. 'I'm just ruling things out.' As if my uncle wasn't standing right beside her, she went on: 'Langdon said the kidnappers might not in fact have your parents, but we can discount that possibility now. The kidnapping is real.' Seeing me wince, she was kind enough to add, 'Sadly.'

'I've never heard Dad sound so scared,' I told my uncle.

Langdon smiled sympathetically and said, 'Your dad's no fool. He'll want to make the kidnappers think he's cowed by them, but really he'll just be feeling the same anger we all do, and weighing up his next move. He won't want to provoke them by showing his steely side, though.'

'It's hard to think of what his "next move" might be if he's being held captive,' said Xander, adding, 'Just putting that out there.'

'He's a Courtney,' Langdon replied. 'Whatever the situation, he'll work to take control of it.'

'He said to pay the ransom,' I said quietly.

'Of course he did,' said Langdon. 'For the same reason. He's got to look as if he's cooperating.' Deliberately, like a man laying bricks, he went on, 'The last thing your father would want is for us to actually pay a ransom. He wouldn't forgive us for doing that.'

I couldn't bring myself to reply. Langdon hadn't heard my father's voice, I had – and the fear in it wasn't made up, it was real. My fists balled up at my sides. Luckily, before I had a chance to threaten Langdon with them, Amelia spoke for me.

'Hold on.' She looked askance at my uncle. 'You're

claiming that when Nicholas said "pay the ransom" what he actually meant was "don't pay the ransom"?' To me she added, 'I know all about how people don't say exactly what they mean, but your dad tends to be fairly straight-talking and in this instance it seems, how can I put it, *unlikely*.'

Xander under his breath, chimed in: 'What she said!'

Langdon puffed himself up. 'Now then,' he said, 'one of us here is an adult with fifteen years' experience negotiating the complexities of the Democratic Republic of Congo. The others are children, none of whom, with the utmost respect, has fifteen years' experience of anything!' He gave me what passed for a kind smile, put an arm around my shoulders and added, 'Trust me, Jack. I know how best to handle this.'

The anger that had built within me withered as he said these words. I felt lost and deflated and I realised, however reluctantly, that I wanted him to be right. 'But Friday is the day after tomorrow,' I said lamely, 'and I said –'

Langdon waved away my attempt to tell him that I'd already agreed to pay the ransom. 'That's time enough for me to put out the word. Tell you what – let's agree the following: we'll decide upon a course of action on Friday at noon, in the light of what I can find out between now and then. In the meantime, sit tight and have faith. I know what I'm doing.'

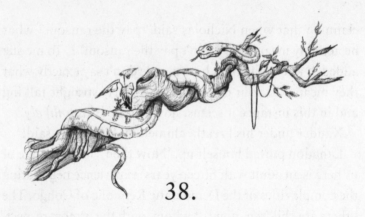

38.

Langdon swept back to his SUV, confident we'd do as he said, but there was no way on earth I could just sit back and wait for news. Now I knew the truth of my parents' situation, and could no longer blindly pray that they'd waltz back into the hotel any minute, 'waiting for news' was its own special kind of torture. I paced to and fro, my mind ablaze. Perhaps Langdon's 'connections' would enable him to track down the kidnappers between now and Friday. I hoped so, obviously. But if they didn't, I would go to the museum drop, and I had no intention of going empty-handed.

Where could I get hold of $75,000 though? The only people I knew who could access Mum's and Dad's money were, well, Mum and Dad. If I'd been at home I could perhaps have sold some stuff, Mum's jewellery, some of Dad's fancy paintings, but home was nearly ten thousand kilometres away. Even if I'd already organised flights, I could barely get there and back in two days, and anyway, I knew that there are rules about the amount of cash you can take to certain countries. I was stuck in a luxury hotel with my spending money for the trip and my parents' restaurant tab. Though the place had a swanky pool and armed guards, there was no way they'd advance me $75,000 on the off-chance my dad would turn up and pay it back. Could I steal the money somehow? I'd risk ending up in jail myself if I did that. Which only left forcing Langdon to give me the cash. But how on earth could I do that?

'You realise you're actually walking round in circles,' said Amelia as I passed her lounger for a third time. 'Or rectangles at least, it being a rectangular pool.'

'I can't help it. My head's on fire.'

'You're better off jumping into the water than walking round it if that's the case.'

'He doesn't mean it literally,' sighed Xander.

'I know that. I do though. Swimming always helps me untangle my thoughts. You should give it a try, Jack.'

'Swimming up and down the pool is no more likely to produce $75,000 than walking round and round it,' I said.

'Is that what you're worried about?' said Amelia.

'Er, yes!'

'But surely you can find a friend to lend it to you, someone with a rich family,' she said, looking around offhandedly.

For a second I thought she was referring to herself, but we both know that her mother has struggled to make ends meet since her dad left ten years ago. My parents have helped out Amelia and her mum over the years, not the other way around. They'd quietly paid for her to come on this disastrous trip, for example. But on double-checking I realised that Amelia's eyes had settled on Xander, who'd already sat up in his seat.

'Of course,' he said. 'What an idiot! I should have thought of it and offered to call home myself.'

Xander's rich. He never goes on about it, but he always seems to have access to cash. He'd brought a fair bit on this trip. Not $75,000 obviously, but might his dad be able to come up with the money? I knew he had something to do with oil fields, but I had no idea if he'd be able to lay his hands on that kind of sum at such short notice, let alone get it to us in time. Neither did Xander. He took out his phone from his pocket and hobbled off somewhere quiet to make the call to Nigeria nonetheless.

'I had another thought,' said Amelia, while he was gone. 'The ransom note says not to speak to the police again, but it doesn't say anything about anyone else.'

'Who else do you mean?'

'Well, Detective Hubert said he'd be back in touch when he'd got hold of the travel-fixer guy, didn't he?'

'I haven't missed a call, if that's what you thinking,' I said. 'I've been checking five times a minute. Anyway, strictly speaking, I shouldn't even answer him.'

Amelia cocked her head on one side, bridling at the exaggeration, but chose to let it pass. In her spelling-it-out-slowly voice, she explained, 'My point is that the police have already given you the name of the guy they're trying to track down. Yannick Mugalia.'

Unsurprised that she'd remembered the name, I saw where

she was going with this train of thought and completed it for her: 'And there's nothing to stop us looking for him ourselves, you're saying?'

'Exactly.'

Fighting my frustration I said, 'I have the name of a man the police haven't yet been able to trace, who is one of eighty-two million inhabitants in a country roughly the size of western Europe. Not to mention forty-eight hours to raise $75,000!'

Sometimes, when Amelia is a step ahead of you, which I'll admit is quite often, she can't help doing this compressed smile with the left side of her mouth. She was doing it now. 'You do know Google works here, don't you? The man's a travel agent, not a secret agent. I found out where his office is while you were wearing out the pool decking with your pointless pacing.'

'Did you call him?' I said, trying not to get my hopes up.

'Yes, but there was no reply,' she said. 'I looked on Maps though, and the office isn't far away. We should check it out.'

Xander clomped back through the archway at this point. When he caught my eye he tried to look cheerful, but the words coming out of his mouth didn't lift my spirits. 'I got hold of Dad,' he said, 'and he's really upset for you, and wants to help of course. But he thinks we should report the kidnapping to the police straight away, and I'm afraid he wasn't optimistic about coming up with that sort of money in cash himself at such short notice. Though he's going to try,' he added lamely.

'At least he didn't spout Langdon's *never-pay-a-hostage-taker* line,' said Amelia.

'Sure.' Xander gave a little shrug of agreement, but I could tell from the way he avoided my eye that his father must have said something pretty similar to Langdon.

The same helpless feeling I have when I'm alone at night and fall into a Mark-shaped hole swept over me. It tastes of exhaust fumes, sounds like bottles flung into a recycling truck and is as blinding as sun bouncing off windscreens. I thought of Patience crouched over her father's body. She'd lost him. I'd lost my parents too, for now. The prospect of making do without them, as Patience would have to make do without Innocent, *forever*, was too frightening to consider. I shut my eyes and tried to pull myself together, grasping for the only straw I had. 'This Mugalia guy's office is walkable from here?' I asked Amelia.

'People have walked across entire continents.'

'You know what I mean.'

'I do. You mean is it close. And yes, the app says it's a half-hour walk. But it's calibrated for dawdlers. It'll take us twenty-five minutes tops.'

'Right then,' I said. 'Let's pay the place a visit.'

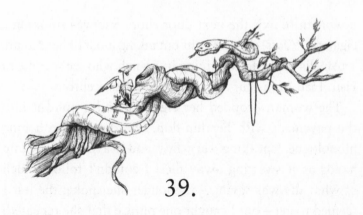

39.

In fact it took Amelia and me an hour to reach the travel fixer's office. There was a protest against the government going on that day, and our route took us straight into it, or it would have if we'd carried on blindly. Amelia wanted to cut through the crowd. But the chanting and jumping up and down had an electric, unpredictable feel to it, and the silent police chaperoning the march, with their sunglasses, batons and Perspex shields, made the whole atmosphere seem more rather than less volatile. We doubled back, cut across a dual carriageway baking in the sun and eventually made it to the scraggy street the office was on.

Sadly, the metal grille fronting the little building was pulled down, the window behind it opaque with dust. The letter box in the front door was choked with flyers, some of which it had spat back out into the street. Never mind shut, it didn't look as if anyone had been here for days. I wouldn't have bothered, but Amelia, apparently oblivious to the signs, pressed the door buzzer. Surprisingly, this prompted a woman to exit the next-door shop. She was smoking a cigarette. '*Oui?*' she said, without taking it out of her mouth.

Amelia replied, explaining in French who we'd come to visit. Had Monsieur Mugalia been here recently?

The woman dropped her cigarette and ground it into the pavement with her flip-flop. She then began a long monologue, speaking very fast and waving her plump hands as if swatting away flies. I couldn't follow much of what she was saying – the longer she spoke, the less I seemed to get – but I caught one phrase that she repeated: '*tragédie familiale*'. She looked agitated, angry almost. Why hadn't I concentrated in French lessons! I was desperate to understand her. Was the woman somehow talking about a family tragedy for me? It couldn't be possible. I turned to Amelia for help, but she was listening with her head cocked on one side, concentrating. The woman went on and on. When she finally stopped speaking, Amelia was ready with a question: '*Ce guide, est-ce qu'il s'appelle Innocent?*'

'*Oui! C'est Innocent, le pauvre.*'

With that the woman turned heavily on her heel and banged back through her shop's front door. Looking at the display in the window, it seemed she sold second-hand electrical goods, mostly ancient TVs.

'Innocent?'

'He is – was – Yannick Mugalia's brother,' said Amelia quietly. 'They ran their travel company together. It makes sense. Your parents organised the safari. Why wouldn't they turn to the same outfit for help with their own trip?'

'But where is he? Did she know?'

'The last she heard he'd gone to Goma.'

I tried to piece together the timeline. Mum and Dad had set off on their own research trip – with Yannick, presumably – before we got back. He might have heard about his brother's tragic death en route, or when he arrived in the east of the country. Could he have abandoned Mum and Dad in his grief, or even blamed them for what happened? Might he have handed them over to the kidnappers on purpose? There had been nothing about Innocent in the ransom note or on the phone, but that didn't mean there wasn't a link. The police hadn't been able to find Yannick yet. If he'd been taken hostage too, the note would have mentioned it, surely. And if he'd been released, wouldn't he have raised the alarm? I smelled a rat! Standing on the dusty step in front of the Mugalia brothers' office, I spelled my thoughts out to Amelia, only pausing when a cement mixer with the loudest exhaust pipe I've ever heard trundled past, blotting out what I was saying.

She brought me down to earth with a bump when it rounded the corner: 'That racket made more sense than you were making,' she said.

'What do you mean?'

'You've no evidence Yannick was involved in the kidnapping. His brother died. He's gone missing. Your parents employed both brothers and they're missing too. That's it – the facts.'

'Yes,' I admitted, 'but until we find him we can't rule it out.'

'How are you going to do that?'

179

'Marcel,' I said. 'He worked with Innocent. So he'll know Yannick too. He may be able to give us a steer.'

'Good point,' said Amelia, and followed it up with something I've rarely heard her say. 'I hadn't thought of that.'

'What's his number?' I said, pulling out my phone.

'He gave his card to you, not me,' she said.

'Didn't you see it?'

Looking sheepish, she said, 'No.'

I couldn't help grinding my teeth. The one time Amelia's photographic memory would have been useful, it turned out she hadn't looked at Marcel's contact details when he handed them over. 'Never mind,' I said. 'His card is with my stuff at the hotel. Let's get back there.'

We set off more or less at a run, headed straight for the hotel. But the demo was still going on. Maybe the crowd was quieter now, or didn't look as intimidating, or perhaps I just thought the risk worth taking to avoid another delay; either way, this time I ignored my better instincts, grabbed Amelia's hand and ploughed straight into it.

Big mistake.

We had indeed arrived during a lull. I didn't realise how tightly packed the crowd was, or even that it was virtually all men, young and strong and facing the same way, waiting for somebody important to start speaking at the head of the square. We'd sidestepped ten or fifteen people into the throng before the speaker emerged on the platform. The crowd erupted. It became one pulsing, cacophonous animal, with Amelia and me caught in its throat. A surge from behind pulled us apart. I heard her scream, saw her stumbling sideways, her orange top immediately blotted out by a rush of protestors pushing forward. I dived after her, but I was pushing against a current of jumping, shouting people. I glimpsed Amelia's pale skin, and her brown hair swishing between dark heads, and I yelled out to her, but she either didn't hear me or couldn't turn around. Desperately ramming my way against the flow to reach her, I was knocked to one knee by another crowd surge. For a terrifying moment I thought I was about to be trampled, but strong hands gripped me under the armpits and hauled to my feet.

'*Attention!*' yelled the smiling face in front of me, and the hands holding me actually lifted me from the ground. I was bouncing with the crowd, swept along with it. With my second or third jump I caught one last glimpse of Amelia heading the other way, and then she was gone.

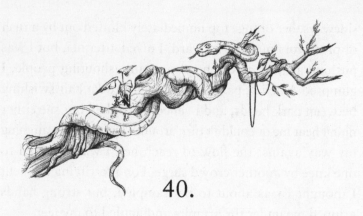

40.

The quarter of an hour it took me to fight my way through that crowd felt like forever. Gnawing worry about my parents knotted into panic, not for myself, but for Amelia. The heat and the yelling and the smell of sweat and fumes swelled with the protestors, a moving mesh of limbs and backs and chests. What had I been thinking, leading her into such danger? Despite the kind hands that had stopped me from hitting the ground, the crowd felt unpredictable to the point of menacing, a pent-up force about to blow. She was pretty much the only girl here, and it was all my fault. I'm not religious but I found myself murmuring, 'Keep her safe, keep her safe . . .' in time with the crowd's chanting, and it felt like a kind of prayer.

When I reached the far side of the square I saw that the protestors were hemmed in by a wall of riot police. Their shields were braced low and their truncheons were either folded across their chests or down at their sides. Every now and then though, if one of the demonstrators got too close, a policemen might casually poke him back with the end of his baton, or even lash out with it properly. I saw a guy take one of these blows to the side of his head, and another nearer to me already had blood pouring from his mouth.

As the only white boy in the crowd, I obviously stood out. I could think of nothing better to do than to try and use that to my advantage. I'm tall for fourteen, but I crouched as I reached the edge of the crowd, and I did my best to look young and petrified – it wasn't hard – in the hope that one of the officers would take pity on me and let me pass.

My pathetic plan worked, but not how I'd expected it might. A protestor, not a policeman, helped me escape. He grabbed the scruff of my T-shirt and thrust me towards the shield wall, yelling, 'Ce garçon n'a pas de place ici!'

I got the gist of that, and nodding, wide-eyed, I pushed forward. At first it seemed the policemen either hadn't noticed or didn't care. But then a crack between two of the shields widened just enough for me – with the help of a kick up the backside – to stagger through.

Once behind the police line I ran up and down it searching for Amelia in vain. I tried calling her number but she didn't pick up. Huddles of reinforcement police were clumped along this side of the human barrier, waiting to take their turn in it. I asked one group if they'd seen a white girl my age come through, but a combination of my terrible French and the noise of the crowd meant they just stared at me blankly. Should I wait and hope Amelia would be spat through a gap soon, or race back to the hotel to raise the alarm? Shaking all over and feeling like I was about to throw up, I decided on the latter, turned and ran.

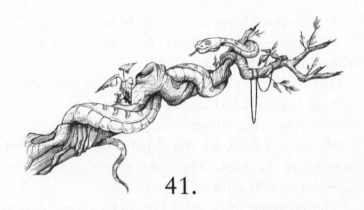

41.

By the time I reached the hotel my face was slick with sweat and my T-shirt was sodden. I thundered through the lobby to the pool area and stopped dead. This was probably wise, since the security guard had already swung his gun in my direction. But that wasn't what drew me up short. The sight of Amelia sitting on the edge of the pool did that. Relief flooded through me like iced water. My burning lungs emptied entirely. I thought I might collapse. The image of her there, unharmed, was as welcome a sight as I'd ever seen.

She spotted me, stood up and said, 'You took your time.'

'I couldn't get across the square. It took ages. The cordon . . .' I petered out.

'You carried on? Well, that makes zero sense.'

'Why?'

Infuriatingly patient, she replied, 'If you were swimming the Channel and got cramp a quarter of the way across, you'd swim back to England rather than continue to France, wouldn't you?'

'The Channel? What are you on about?'

'When we got split up, I went back the way we'd come without too much trouble.'

I felt like an idiot but didn't care. We were both here.

'Then I caught a taxi, also easily enough.'

'Why didn't you call me?'

'My phone's dead. Or was. I put it on charge before jumping in the pool. The maps app is a nightmare battery-wise. GPS software always –'

'Shut up about software!' I said and – I couldn't stop myself – I grabbed her wet shoulders with both hands and pulled her to me.

She smelled of sunscreen and chlorine. Quietly, into my ear, she said, 'Pretty sketchy afternoon. But hey, we're OK.'

Over her shoulder Xander hobbled out to the poolside. He didn't smirk or wink or say anything, but the fact of him brought me to my senses.

'I'll fetch Marcel's number,' I said, stepping back from Amelia.

'Possibly have a shower while you're at it, or a swim?' she said.

Reaching us, Xander said, 'Before you head off, you might want to hear my news.'

'What news?' I asked him.

'Don't look so worried,' he said. 'It's good, possibly, no . . . probably, I'd say.'

'Has your dad come up with a way –'

'Nothing to do with him, no,' he said.

He appeared quietly pleased with himself, much like I've

seen him look at school when he's effortlessly persuaded a teacher to extend a homework deadline, or smooth-talked his way out of a detention.

'Who then?' I asked, trying to keep a lid on the hope bubbling within me.

'I've just had a little chat with your uncle, and I think I may have persuaded him to change his mind,' he said.

'How?!'

'After you two went off I had a bit of time to think, and I realised we'd missed a trick. No disrespect to Langdon, but the most important thing in his world is his precious mining business, yes?'

I nodded.

'And he's not keen on the environmental protections your parents are lobbying for, is he?'

'Not particularly.'

'Red tape – that's what he called it.'

'The phrase rings a bell.'

'Well, I pointed out that realistically the only way to stop your parents becoming martyrs to the environmental cause – and drawing massive attention to it – is to secure their release. If we don't pay and the kidnappers do what they've said they will, which I'm sure is an empty threat, but still, the eco-warriors will say Nicholas and Janine were silenced because of what they were trying to achieve. The publicity for their cause would blow up globally, making it far more likely to succeed. But if they're released, the story goes away.'

'You told him that?'

'More or less. I wrapped it up nicely by suggesting we're far more likely to catch the kidnappers if we engage with them. '

'True. Probably,' said Amelia.

Xander shrugged. 'And of course I made the whole thing seem like it was probably what he'd planned to do anyway. People love it when they think they've come up with a good idea themselves.'

'Amazing.'

'It seemed to work, as I say, but there's no guarantee.'

Xander was trying to be understated, but I could tell he was optimistic. I know first-hand how persuasive he can be. Particularly with adults. He has this knack of making them feel good about themselves. I've mentioned it before, the way he is with my parents, asking them questions and listening to the answers, looking like he's really interested. They'd do anything for him. Langdon's a tough nut to crack though. Making him think selfishly was a stroke of genius by Xander. It could definitely have changed his mind.

'How did you leave it?' I asked.

'He agreed it would be wise to have the money ready just in case. If the situation hasn't changed between now and the deadline, at least then we can choose whether or not to pay off the kidnappers; without the money we won't have that option. Again, I made it clear he'd no doubt thought of that and sourced the cash already, making it easy for him to say of course he had.'

'He could have,' said Amelia.

'Sure,' said Xander, suppressing a smile.

Realising I was bouncing on the balls of my feet, I let out a long breath and steadied myself. 'We'll see,' I said.

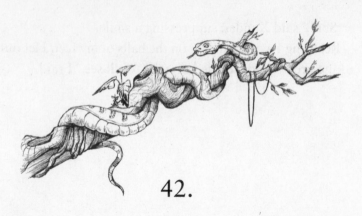

42.

Though I called again and again that evening and throughout the following day, I couldn't get through to Marcel. Xander and Amelia tried too. We all left messages. But neither Marcel the guide nor Yannick the travel operator answered our calls. With each hour that passed it seemed somehow less likely we'd ever manage to contact them.

Would Langdon bring the ransom money? As the deadline loomed ever larger I started to lose hope. By the next day even Xander's quiet confidence seemed to have evaporated. Our conversation withered and died. My uncle had promised to be at the hotel at midday on Friday. Half an hour before then Amelia, Xander and I were waiting together in the bar area. We ordered club sandwiches at Amelia's insistence, but I couldn't eat mine. The minute hand swept past twelve o'clock, and Langdon didn't show up. At half past twelve he still wasn't there. One o'clock: ditto. I watched the ice melt in my untouched Coke as the corners of my sandwich curled.

Just as I was about to crack, call my uncle and demand

an explanation, he strode through reception. He was wearing sunglasses, so I couldn't read his expression as he approached. He was also wearing a plain white shirt today. That unnerved me. I'd never have expected it, but I missed the reassurance of his usual Hawaiian swirls. I noticed that he took the seat next to Xander, instead of the nearer one beside me. He made himself comfortable. I couldn't help checking my watch.

'Ah, yes, sorry I'm a little late.' He sounded more frustrated than sorry. 'I was hoping for a breakthrough before I set off, but sadly it turned out to be a red herring.'

Xander leaned forward, made an expectant steeple of his fingers, and asked, 'Does that mean you're switching to plan B?'

Langdon looked at the three of us in turn, taking what seemed an eternity before replying. 'I thought, on reflection, I would,' he said at last, and drummed his fingers on the leather flap of his briefcase.

The sign seemed obvious enough, but I needed confirmation. 'You've brought the money?' I said.

'I'm not happy about it, but . . . yes. Thanks to your friend here.' He nodded a smile in Xander's direction. 'It makes sense given the . . . err . . . context.'

Amelia drew breath – to interrogate this vagueness, I was sure – but I cut across her with, 'Thank you. Dad said he'd pay you back straight away.'

'The money's not the point, Jack,' Langdon explained, as if to an idiot. 'It's the principle. When all's said and done, I don't want either of us to have paid a single dollar's ransom.'

For one awful moment I thought he might be about to reverse his decision, but Xander said, 'Your idea of using marked banknotes is a good one though. It increases our chances of catching the kidnappers. In a way the money is just a lure.'

Langdon was nodding along with this, but Amelia interjected. 'I imagine they'll have thought about that. Money-laundering is a thing.'

I shot her a what-the-hell look, but Xander immediately said, 'That's harder to do than you'd think, isn't it, Langdon?' and mercifully my uncle ignored her interruption in favour of more nodding in Xander's direction. Realising she'd misspoken, Amelia stood up abruptly, stripped to her swimming costume, dived into the pool and started swimming laps: her way of saying sorry, I suppose.

She tore up and down that pool for ages. By the time she'd finished, got changed and returned, it was almost time for me to leave. The museum wasn't far away, but I wanted to head off the chance of being delayed en route. Langdon kept checking his phone while we waited, no doubt hoping for last-minute news that would protect his precious $75,000, but none came. Reluctantly he said his driver would take us to the museum.

'Nobody but me is allowed in to drop off the money though,' I said. 'I'm to put it under my mother's scarf at the foot of the statue for four o'clock, on my own, and leave. The guy was very clear about that.'

'We know,' Langdon replied through gritted teeth.

'Shall we get going then?' I said.

Every step Langdon took towards the SUV hurt, I could tell. And the short trip to the museum, his phone still silent, was agony for him. I just wanted the drop-off over and done with so that we could return to the hotel. Mum and Dad would be there then, because that's what the kidnapper had promised. I had to believe him. We pulled up outside the museum with twenty-five minutes to spare. They ticked away horribly slowly. With five to go, Langdon finally pulled a brown envelope from his briefcase and handed it over. I could have hugged him. But he's not the hugging type at the best of times, and at that moment I think he'd have punched me if I'd so much as touched him. So I simply took the envelope from him and let myself out of the car. I bought a ticket for the museum with my own money and worked my way through the grounds to the statue of Leopold sitting on his towering horse. The last time I'd visited, the museum had been deserted. Today a group of sweating tourists were having a guided tour. I had to wait for them to clear off before I could approach the statue, with just seconds to go before 4 p.m. Something twisted inside me at the sight of my mother's grey-and-pink headscarf, balled up next to one of the horse's front feet. It looked like it had been trampled. But I recognised it as hers – more proof the kidnapper had told the truth. If I did my bit, they would do theirs. The tour guide's chatter faded as the group disappeared from view. I darted between the horse's front legs, slid the envelope beneath the scarf and left without looking back.

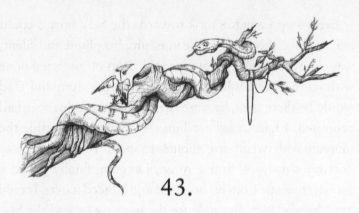

43.

Langdon and I made the return trip in silence. I assumed he was angry at having paid off the kidnappers. There was no point in apologising. Dad would sort him out soon. Dad and Mum. I couldn't wait to see them. From the back seat I willed the driver to put his foot down, but inevitably we hit traffic. Some guy on a motorbike had apparently taken out a fruit stand. They were loading him into an ambulance while the cars failed to swerve around pulped melons spread across the road. I was surprised I wasn't more annoyed by the delay and realised that I was as nervous of reaching the hotel as I was desperate to get there. The fact I was nervous made me more worried still. My gut was telling me to brace for bad news. I didn't want to trust my instincts, but I knew they were usually right.

The delay was torture. I decided to call Amelia; she might be able to put me out of my misery. I hit call, then wished I hadn't, but she answered almost immediately so I had no chance to end the call before it had begun.

'Any news?' I asked.

'Yes,' she said.

I bit my tongue, then, when she didn't offer any more, said, 'Amelia, is it good or bad?'

'Good,' she replied, and my heart, which I now realised had been hammering away in my chest, skipped a beat entirely.

'Great!' I said. 'Tell me they're both OK?'

'Ah, no. I mean, I don't know. Not yet, but Xander received a call.'

'Xander? What about? From who? Put him on!'

Xander had evidently heard Amelia's end of the conversation and reverse-engineered mine. He was quick to apologise, though he needn't have: my literal genius friend wasn't his fault. 'It's goodish news, in a limited sort of way,' he said. 'Marcel called. He picked up our messages and said that he's been in touch with Yannick, who did indeed organise your parents' trip east. But he didn't accompany them himself. He took them to the airport, but he had business to attend to in Kinshasa so arranged for an associate to chaperone them from Goma. Marcel doesn't know who that associate was, and Yannick's been out of contact since Innocent died. Marcel heard he was dealing with the funeral arrangements. It'd be understandable if monitoring your folks' whereabouts hasn't been top of his to-do list. But it looks like they did set off for Goma, en route to the mines.'

Langdon was regarding me closely as I listened to Xander. His eyebrows were up, expectant, to start with. Then they dropped with his shoulders when he realised Mum and Dad hadn't been released. Had I been hard on him? Perhaps his silence had been more anxious than angry. He wanted good news too, obviously.

'But look,' Xander was saying, 'all this is probably beside the point. If you've made the drop, then we can expect to see them any minute. Where are you?'

'Stuck in traffic, or we were.'

'You'll be here soon?'

'Yeah,' I said sadly, as the hotel swung into view.

'So don't worry – they're probably stuck in traffic too.'

'Sure,' I said. We rocked to a stop. The driver pulled up the handbrake with a finality that made my skin shiver.

Langdon and I climbed down from the truck slowly. We were astronauts wading through treacle; neither of us wanted to arrive in that hotel and find my parents weren't there. But I knew they wouldn't be. I'd known before I called Amelia. To his credit Langdon didn't make a meal of it. He sat with us that evening as the minutes ticked into hours without his brother and sister-in-law arriving, and he didn't utter a word of told-you-so. In fact he tried to comfort me. First he said the kidnappers might be waiting to release Mum and Dad after dark, and when that didn't happen he said, 'Look, it may not have worked, but making the payment can't have made your mum and dad's situation worse.'

I supposed not.

'No doubt the kidnappers will be back in touch soon,' he said.

'If only to ask for more money,' added Amelia unhelpfully.

'We'll cross that bridge when we get to it,' Langdon said,

giving my shoulder a squeeze as he rose. 'In the meantime, let me check with my people to see if they've turned up any leads. Stay put, keep your chin up and I guarantee we'll get to the bottom of this soon.'

He headed for his car. As soon as he was out of sight I stood up and started pacing around the pool. God, I hated that pool. Pacing was pointless too. But blind hope plus sitting still? That was the very last thing I could do.

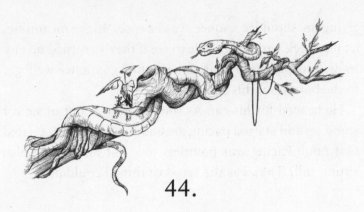

44.

I'd been marching around the hotel grounds for some time before they turned the pool lights off. Now I had a black hole to circle instead of bright blueness. It suited my mood better, I suppose. The blackness couldn't be trusted. It was a hole my parents had been sucked into. Orbiting it, I felt so alone. Without my parents I was a rock tumbling through empty space. I made a decision. Mum and Dad had last been seen heading east. Come what may, and ignoring Langdon, I'd make the same journey. With Marcel's help I'd track down whoever had chaperoned them to the mines. I'd retrace their steps. I'd find them.

Possibly because I stayed up so late, both Xander and Amelia both beat me down to breakfast. I was hungry so ordered a full English. I'll say one thing for the hotel: it had a very international menu. While waiting for my breakfast to arrive, I filled my friends in on my plan. They exchanged a knowing glance before I finished talking.

'I thought you might say that,' said Xander when I shut up.

'Knew it actually,' Amelia agreed. 'Or at least thought it so obviously likely we've already started getting organised.'

'How?!'

'Remember Joseph, the pilot who flew us here after we were diverted?'

'Of course.'

'Me too. Unlike you though, I also remember the number he had written on the back of his clipboard. I called him. He's flying you and me back to Goma.' Amelia checked her watch. 'In an hour and half's time.'

'And Marcel is going to meet you at the airport,' Xander added. 'He reckons he's worked out who Yannick would have lined up to look after your folks. Or at least he's narrowed it down.'

'But how –'

Xander cut me off, spinning a credit card next to his coffee cup. 'The ransom money was beyond my reach, but this worked to pay Joseph. I'll hold the fort here, smooth things over with Langdon when he turns up.' He tapped the card on his plaster cast and said, 'I'd break a leg to come with you, but it seems I already have.'

I was gobsmacked they'd done all this before I'd even got up. 'Am I that predictable?' was all I said.

'Pretty much,' said Amelia. 'Waiting, and being bossed around by people – named Langdon or otherwise – has never been your thing.' She put her hand on my arm as she said this, then swiftly took it away again. A warm shiver went through me nevertheless.

I immediately turned to Xander. 'Thanks guys,' I said.

'Better eat up and gather your stuff,' Amelia said. 'The cab will be here soon.'

I wolfed that breakfast down in about three mouthfuls and was out on the kerb with my kitbag in under ten minutes. Langdon could turn up at any time: I wanted us to be gone before he did. And we were. The cab Xander had organised turned up promptly, we made it to the airport without a hitch, and Joseph was exactly where he'd promised Amelia he'd be, waiting outside the departures terminal. The sight of him with his ironed jeans and his pens in his top pocket and that crisp line cut into his hair threw me back to the start of the trip, before anything had gone seriously wrong. I'd just saved Dad's briefcase from the incompetent thieves on their clapped-out motorcycle when we met him. Dad had been pleased with me. He'd be more grateful still when I found him and Mum. Something about Joseph's face, its open smile of recognition when he spotted us, made me feel light on my feet, ready and optimistic. He spirited us through the airport to his charter plane. From where I was sitting in the seat behind him, I could see him running through his preflight checks: toggling levers, setting dials, jotting down readings and flipping switches with precise and confident fingers. That buoyed me up too. This guy knew what he was doing. I had a problem to solve, but somehow, with Amelia's help, I'd work it out.

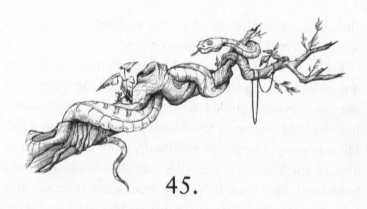

45.

Marcel picked us up in the same battered pickup we'd used for our safari. I winced at the memory of Innocent's cheerful face in the cracked wing mirror. Without him, there was room up front for both Amelia and me, a comfier ride than sitting on our packs in the dusty open tray, but I paused before climbing in. It didn't seem right. Amelia had no such qualms; she jumped up next to Marcel without hesitating.

The guide seemed genuinely pleased to see us. The fact we were without Caleb might have had something to do with it. He chatted away with Amelia as we churned through the traffic. They spoke in French but I got the gist of what they were saying. Marcel wanted to know how Xander was doing. Amelia told him. Then she asked whether anything bad had happened to the silverback in the wake of the tragedy. No, Marcel said. All the rangers knew Innocent would never have wanted that. Everyone understood the accident wasn't the gorilla's fault. As far as I could tell, the guide stopped short of saying whether everyone also knew who had actually been to blame.

I'd worked out how to ask Marcel whether his lead had any news of my parents, but Amelia got there ahead of me. My optimism stalled in the pause before he answered her, the light feeling in my stomach hardening into a fist. He was sorry, but no, he eventually said. He'd not been able to track down the guy he was sure Yannick would have used. However, he'd also done some research into Langdon's mining interests. They were spread far and wide, but the biggest project was a flagship modern operation, called the Canonhead Complex, just to the west of the national park.

'Modern?' I asked Amelia as much as him. 'Surely all mines are pretty modern these days.'

Marcel understood my question but his lengthy reply went over my head. Amelia could see I was lost. 'He says not at all. The vast majority of mining in the DRC, whether it's for tantalum, cobalt, or any precious metal, even gold, is done by hand with picks and shovels. It's incredibly dangerous, brutally hard work, and the miners who do it are paid a pittance. At least half of their work feeds a government-backed black market. They sell what they mine for virtually nothing to traders who sell it on to bigger companies who export it to the West and China. So a modern, mechanised, well-regulated mine is an exception.'

'And that's what Langdon's doing?' I said. 'If so, it's pretty impressive.'

Marcel snorted, hearing that. '*Toute en face*,' he said.

'That means *on the face of it*,' Amelia said, though I'd kind of guessed that.

The truck was rattling along a potholed road now: I realised I had no idea where we were going. It seemed sensible to ask. Marcel again replied at length. I tried to follow but he talked quite fast. I caught the words *rivière* and *oblique*, but couldn't piece his meaning together.

Amelia translated: 'Marcel here has done some digging,' she said. 'No pun intended. Apparently your mum and dad were headed to this Canonhead place a few days ago. So it makes sense to start the search there. It's where Caleb is working too. Trouble is, to get anywhere in among the mines requires a whole load of paperwork, permits, vehicle checks and so on. Langdon cut through the red tape for Caleb, but we're going to have to be a bit more cunning.'

'Cunning, how?'

'Marcel's thought it through. We need to take an oblique route. That means indirect.'

Sometimes Amelia takes me for an idiot. I dug my elbow into her side and said, 'You don't say!'

'Sorry,' she said, returning the prod with her own elbow just below my ribcage. 'Just trying to be clear. Anyway, he's lined up motorbikes.'

I looked across Amelia at Marcel. He was leaning forward in his seat, squinting as he wove the pickup through a chicane of potholes filled with water the colour of mustard. 'It's very kind of Marcel to help,' I said. And more quietly, to Amelia, 'What's in it for him exactly?'

'You've lost your parents. He wants to help find them.

He's one of the good guys,' she said, adding, to Marcel, 'I'm right, aren't I?'

'*Peut-être*,' he answered, smiling sideways at her.

'Also money,' Amelia said matter-of-factly. 'I offered him double his normal day rate.'

We drove for a good couple of hours down that appalling dirt road without making it particularly far, and finally wound up in a village – just a few huts really – beyond which the truck couldn't go. This was where Marcel had arranged to pick up the motorbikes: two old scramblers. All I saw at first glance was dented fuel tanks, a bent brake lever and half a front mudguard. The guy who owned the bikes was tinkering with the more beaten-up of the two, though the distinction was marginal. I didn't know whether it was a good or a bad sign that he was working on the bike right before handing it over, but he gave the keys to Marcel confidently enough.

Marcel immediately tossed one of the sets of keys to me. '*Amelia dit que tu montes*,' he said.

Amelia, deadpan: 'You do, right, ride something like this?'

'A mountain bike, yes, but not one of these,' I said quietly.

'You'll get the hang of it, I'm sure,' she said, climbing onto the back of Marcel's bike.

'Mine has pedals,' I muttered under my breath.

Mercifully the motorbikes came with helmets. I took my time adjusting the straps and putting mine on. It looked like I was being safety conscious, but in reality I was simply trying to remember everything I'd learned the one time I'd ridden my friend Justin's scrambler, on his parents' farm in Wales. That was over a year ago. I knew how to work the clutch and gears at least. This meant I didn't make a complete fool of myself as Marcel set off, expecting me to follow. But I wasn't that smooth: I nearly came off, swerving to avoid a small, stark-naked child who wandered across the track as we headed out of the village, and I pulled an unintentional wheelie accelerating too hard when Marcel opened up the throttle in front of me. I got into the riding though. The smell of the exhaust fumes from Marcel and Amelia's bike was instantly the same as the smell of the bike on the farm, and weirdly the scenery rushing past, all green and gold and full of flying mud, though thousands of miles distant, felt pretty similar, too. I had to concentrate. The bike squirreled and squirmed in the rutted muck. Marcel didn't hold back: we had ground to cover. I kept an eye on the line he was taking, gritted my teeth, fought the handlebars and by doing my damnedest I just about managed to keep up.

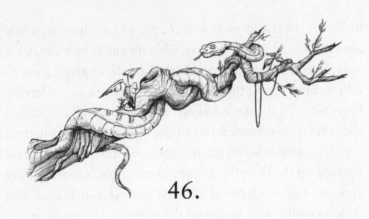

46.

We rode for six hours straight. It was tough: my shoulders seized up with the effort of hauling the bike left and right, and the rattling, bucking bike frame, shot through with vibrations, made my feet, hands and bum so numb I could barely feel them. The burden of my pack didn't make it any easier to keep the bike upright. And the ancient helmet was heavier than I'm used to as well. My head felt like it was about to come off. We kept having to slow down to cross tiny streams, either through the water itself or across crude bridges made of little more than branches. I got wet. Ahead of me, I could see Amelia struggling to stay balanced on the back of Marcel's bike. Every now and then she'd tense up rigid, the tendons standing out in her neck, and on more than one occasion I saw her bump helmets with Marcel. But she didn't call a halt, and Marcel didn't either, obviously. So neither did I. I battled on, though before long every part of me seemed to be screaming, *I need a rest!*

Just as I was about to give in and admit I had to stop,

we rounded a bend in the track and came upon a sizeable river. It was one of the thousands of tributaries to the mighty Congo, about a football pitch wide and the colour of milky tea. The water seemed so still that to begin with I couldn't tell which way it was flowing. Though we'd barely seen anyone as we'd fought our way to this point, there was a man waiting next to the river. He was skeletally thin and leaning on an old bicycle hung with big, heavy-looking plastic containers. Amelia immediately jumped down and started talking to him with Marcel. Apparently he was transporting palm oil. His bike, I noticed, had no pedals; he was using it as a means of lugging his wares. It struck me that if it had taken us all those hours to motorbike here, he must have been pushing his incredibly heavy load down that miserable track for days. Immediately I felt less sorry for myself.

'He's waiting for the ferry,' Amelia explained. 'Apparently there's one due today.'

'Just "today"?'

'That's what he says.'

'What do we do until it gets here?' I asked.

It was a stupid question and it got the answer it deserved from Marcel. '*Nous attendons*,' he said, adding the translation himself: 'We wait.'

A cloud of mosquitoes had already gathered, whining around us, but since we were here on account of me I couldn't complain, and as it was we didn't have long to wait. Marcel had just broken out some water for us to drink, and we were passing it round, when the 'ferry' drifted into view. I don't know what I'd been expecting, but not this. The boat was

207

a hollowed-out tree trunk. In the distance it looked like the black husk of a seed pod. Up close it was actually pretty big.

'What do you call that?' I said to myself as much as anyone.

'The French name is *pirogue*, but you can call it a dugout canoe,' Amelia replied.

'Right.'

'Think about it: no seams. It's all one piece. Properly watertight. This design hasn't changed for hundreds of years.'

Two men were piloting the ferry, one at the front and one at the back. They swung it into the bank gently and three women climbed out. All of them were carrying plastic drums that looked as heavy as the cycle-pusher's. One woman had a package on her head, wrapped in yellow leaves and tied up with actual vines. She smiled at me as she passed us, and the kindness in her eyes was so like Mum's I had to look away. Where was my mum now? Was this attempt to track her and Dad down a fool's errand? I couldn't allow myself to think that. But here we were, in the middle of nowhere. The landscape around me stretched infinitely in that moment. I fought back a sudden, stabbing hopelessness by manhandling my motorbike to the edge of the river bank.

The dugout was surprisingly deep: the tree it was cut from must have been massive. Even so, I didn't expect the ferryman to load both our bikes, our packs and the bicycle laden with palm oil into it in one go. But that's what he did, and with all of us passengers loaded in as well we sat low in the water, the surface less than a handspan from the gunwales.

I stayed very still in the bottom of that canoe. We all did. If the oarsmen had caught a crab and rocked the boat more than a little one way or the other, it would have filled with water and sunk instantly. But having presumably made the trip thousands of times, the pilots moved as gently as the river and we were soon safely on the other side.

Marcel had in mind a village he wanted us to reach before nightfall. I didn't much fancy sleeping out in the open, so readied myself to set off again quickly. Amelia asked if she could ride with me this time. It felt like a compliment. I had to wear my pack on my front to make room for her, and handling the bike with the two of us on it was doubly hard to start with, but the track was better defined this side of the river and she'd learned to ride pillion well with Marcel. I quickly grew used to the weight of her pressing against my back. We forged on. At dusk Marcel turned on his bike's headlamp. I did the same. The two beams scissored wildly ahead of us, full of insects. I couldn't have gone on much longer, but just as the river had saved me earlier in the day, we arrived in the village abruptly. There were no electric lights here. After a quick meal of heavily salted vegetable mush, Marcel negotiated us floor space in what seemed little more than a shack. I didn't care. Curled in my sleeping bag, with Amelia already breathing deeply next to me, I shut my eyes and fell into a weird half-sleep, the muddy track still unspooling ahead of me, the bike's engine still loud in my ears.

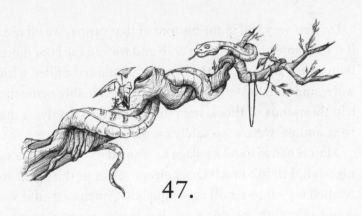

47.

We made it to Langdon's flagship mine, Canonhead, the following afternoon. The landscape we were biking through had opened up by then. Marcel crested a low hill ahead of me and as I drew up alongside him the operation was laid out beneath us, an open wound cut into the brush, reaching into the distance. It was big, a proper sprawl of prefab huts to one side of a cavernous, tiered, open pit, swarming with men and stabbed full of heavy machinery, diggers, trucks. The day was a muggy one. Standing on that ridge, the heat seemed to come from the mine, spread out down there beneath a dirty yellow haze.

We'd taken a cross-country route to avoid the checkpoints dotted along what passed for main roads. Without the right paperwork, Marcel had explained, the government officials – or vigilantes – who manned those posts wouldn't let us pass. I hoped that by dropping my uncle's name hard enough at the mine itself I'd be able to get a meeting with the head guy or those close to him, anyone who might know something about my parents' visit. But I hoped wrong. We hadn't even made it to the perimeter fence that ran round the southern edge of the settlement – which on approach seemed actually the size of a small town – to the main entrance, when a guy with a gun materialised on the path ahead of us and started yelling in French. We were wheeling the bikes at this point, though the clanking, grinding noise of machinery in the mine would have masked the sound of them. Marcel kicked down his stand and put his hands above his head. I didn't need Amelia to interpret, just followed suit. Marcel started to say something in his most soothing voice, but he stopped pretty quickly when the guy yelled '*Ferme ta gueule!*' and swung his rifle onto his hip.

The end of the gun's muzzle was as unblinking as the guard's eyes. He waved it at us lazily, motioning us on with the bikes. Something wasn't right with him. Was he drunk, or high on something? I don't know, but everything about him unnerved me. He ushered us along the fence-line. I tried to remain calm by focusing on the track ahead of us, overgrown with weeds, but couldn't stop myself glancing sideways every now and then. I noticed that although the guard had a uniform – of sorts, it was filthy and his shirt and trousers were different shades of khaki – he wore no shoes. Marcel tried talking to him again; I heard the words *Monsieur Langdon Courtney* more than once, but the guard didn't reply. Presumably he was taking us to his boss. That would make sense. We could explain ourselves to him and get back on track, surely?

Sadly not. The guard spoke only to make it clear we had

to leave the bikes at the entrance to the compound. Then he marched us straight through the big gates, past a gaggle of men who barely looked up as he led us along a dirt track lined with huts. The track led to a row of shipping containers plonked on breeze blocks in the mud. One had its door open. The guard stood back from this and, though Amelia and Marcel were both pleading with him for a chance to explain ourselves, he didn't listen. Instead he told us to get in the container. There was something completely unarguable-with about this guy. He was a robot with a screw loose, not exactly threatening to shoot us, but apparently unhinged enough for it to be a possibility if we annoyed him. 'It's OK,' I found myself whispering to Amelia. 'He's probably just parking us here while he goes to fetch someone.' I wasn't convinced by this myself, but she was shaking beside me and it was all I could think of to persuade her that we should comply and step inside.

As soon as we did, he slammed the door with a metallic clang. A rusty screech followed as he locked it. Mercifully we weren't plunged into complete darkness. Though there were no windows, somebody had drilled a few holes through the sides and top of the container. Pencils of light speared through these in all directions, more than enough beams for us to see by, but menacing, somehow; it was as if we were pinned down by snipers. That imaginary horror wasn't as bad as the real problem though. It was muggy outside and hotter in the container. If the sun came out properly, we'd bake to death.

'What do we do now?' said Amelia.

It was a fair question.

Dust motes swam in the beams while I thought.

'I'll try Langdon,' I replied eventually, pulling out my phone. Though we'd gone behind his back to come here, he was the only solution I could think of, the only person who might be able to get us out of the mess we – by which I mean I – had created. 'This is his mine after all.'

I ignited my phone with a sense of dread, doubting there'd be a signal somewhere this remote, let alone one strong enough to penetrate the metal box we'd managed to get ourselves shut in. But there was. A solid three bars at that. I breathed out and hit Langdon's number with a different sense of trepidation. How angry would he be that I'd cut him out of the loop and set off to find my folks myself?

I needn't have worried. Not, sadly, because he instantly forgave me, but because although the phone rang straight away, it went on ringing and ringing and ringing, all the way to his ridiculous 'Langdon Courtney, speak to me!' voicemail greeting. I didn't have it in me to leave a message admitting what I'd done. I learned long ago that bad news is always best delivered directly. He'd see I'd tried to contact him anyway, and would no doubt call me back.

'No answer,' I said pointlessly, once I'd hung up.

Amelia had an eye pressed to one of the holes. Her, 'Don't worry, you can try him again later,' sounded weird, and I hoped that was because her mouth was up against the metal of the container, rather than because she was panicking. I felt horribly responsible in that moment, and looked to

Marcel. But he'd simply sat down with his elbows on his knees and his head bowed, apparently prepared to wait it out. He looked so resigned, suffering patiently, but I couldn't do the same.

'What can you see?' I asked Amelia, and peered through a hole near hers.

'Not much,' she muttered.

She wasn't wrong. Along that side of the container the pinhole view outside was of nothing at all, or at least just the griddled flank of another metal box about two feet away. Why was she staring at that? I knew better than to ask. We all cope with stress in different ways, and if Amelia wanted to focus on the box next door, so be it. I wasn't about to do the same though, and instead worked my way round the container, reaching and stooping and even lying down to see whatever I could out of all the various holes. It turned out, unsurprisingly, that we were hemmed in on both sides by the neighbouring containers and the holes all showed close-up nothingness. Fewer had been drilled through the front door, and all that I could glimpse through them was a stretch of the dusty track we'd been marched down, flanked by a boring section of the perimeter fence. I waited a while, but nothing moved along it. The holes in the rear of the container were a little more promising. Two to the right were obscured by scrubby bushes, but the ones on the left showed a wedge of sky above a slice of prefab hut with its door hanging open, and some grey scree beyond it, sloping away in the direction of the open-cast mine. I couldn't see any of the mine itself, but trucks crossed that slope from

214

time to time, and I didn't have to wait long before two guys in hard hats ambled up it and into the hut.

As I watched, the sun cut through the clouds. It may have been my mind playing tricks, but I swear I could feel the container heating up in real time. Amelia, who'd swapped positions to look out of a hole with a view, either felt it too or read my mind. 'Alternate between looking out of the hole and breathing through it,' she said. 'The air's cooler outside.'

There were still hours to go before the sun went down. What little water we had left we divided as equally as we could, careful not to spill any. The temperature in our prison rose and rose. Every now and then one of us banged on the metal wall, trying to attract attention, but although the noise was horribly loud inside the box, it had to compete with the background rumble of the mine, and nobody came. The nearest people, going in and out of that hut every now and then, didn't even look up. Had we been put in here to die?

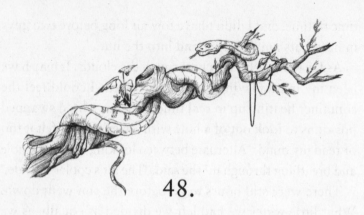

48.

About a year after Mark was killed, Mum bought us a dog. I say 'bought', but he came from a rescue home. Still, the donation she made to the charity that ran the home was bigger than they were expecting, so in a way she bought him. The dog was a nine-month-old mixed breed – part whippet, part sheepdog – called Chester. When Mum arrived home with him she made the mistake of saying he might help cheer us up. Dad put his coffee down and walked out of the kitchen when she said that. To be honest, I felt the same way. A dog, instead of my dead brother – what was she thinking? I knew she didn't mean it that way, but when I looked at Chester that morning, I hated him.

Although Dad has never really warmed to Chester – it's nothing personal, he says, he's just not really a dog person – I couldn't help it. A week or so after we'd got him I realised it was pointless blaming an accident I'd caused on a dog who hadn't even been born when it happened. Also, he had this way of following us around with his head low and a worried look in eyes, as if apologising for wanting to be with us, which was both pathetic and impossible to ignore. I took him out running beside my bike. He loved that immediately and still does, keeps up effortlessly and has an amazing knack of staying dead close without getting in the way. So Mum was right, he did cheer me up, I suppose. What really made me want to take care of him properly though was when I heard how he'd ended up in that home. His previous owners were done for neglect. They'd left Chester and their two other dogs in the back of a car while they went to the cinema. In the daytime. In June. They'd opened the windows a crack and parked in the shade, but – surprise – the sun moved. The dogs got overheated and the other two died. Chester only just survived.

Locked in that container, I couldn't get his ordeal out of my mind. Amelia kept asking Marcel if he knew what was happening, but he clearly knew no more than us, and the meditative trance he'd decided to go into didn't reassure me much. He sat as fixed as a tree stump, the occasional bead of sweat dripping from his nose.

I called Langdon again and left a message this time, trying to convey the seriousness of the situation but keep the panic from my voice so as not to alarm Amelia. Then, for want of anything else to do, I put my eye to the best peephole and left it there. Nothing had changed about the scene, and nothing much did. It got marginally worse at one point, when a flatbed truck carrying concrete tubes parked up near the Portakabin thing, blocking out the grey scree. I was passing the time counting the concrete tubes when something beneath the truck, or on the other side of it, rather, made me switch eyes: a flicker of lime green, jerking along beneath some legs, supporting a person I couldn't see because of the damned truck, moving from left to right. I whipped out my camera and zoomed in as far as the telephoto lens would go.

'Really? You're still thinking about your photo-journalism thing? Now?' said Amelia.

'I can't believe it. That has to be him,' I said, and banged on the wall of the container as hard as I could with my free hand.

The shoes kept walking. Just before they disappeared from view, I clicked the shutter. They were still only tiny on the display screen, but I knew Amelia would recognise Caleb's stupid boots. As soon as I tilted the screen her way, she did.

'Why didn't I think of him earlier?' she said.

'It's no use,' I muttered. 'He can't hear us.'

She looked at me with a spark of the usual are-you-actually-an-idiot glinting in her eye. I was genuinely relieved to see it, as it generally means she's thought of some clever idea. This solution was actually simple enough to make me feel stupid. Amelia pulled out her phone and called Caleb's number.

It's idiotic, but the fact that he was already stored in her contacts made me shiver, despite the ridiculous heat.

'Hey, Caleb,' she said beside me. If there had been panic in her voice a moment ago, she now sounded ridiculously matter-of-fact. 'Are you wearing your very green boots?'

I was still pressed up against the drill hole with my camera, so couldn't hear his reply.

'Cool. And are you at work,' she went on, 'doing whatever they've got you doing at your father's mine?'

The truck hadn't moved, and neither had anything beneath or beyond it.

'Cool,' she said again. 'Because we're here too and we could sort of use some help.'

Cool? Sort of? She wasn't just trying to be matter-of-fact, I realised. She was trying to sound offhand! 'If you give that to me, I'll talk him to us,' I said as levelly as I could, reaching for the phone. I pretty much had to prise the thing from her fingers.

'Yeah, hi, Caleb, it's me. We're locked in a container. It's the third one of four in a row along the inside of the northern perimeter fence, on the left as you come through the main entrance to this mine-complex place. I just saw you, through a tiny hole in the metal wall. You were walking away from us, behind that truck with all the concrete tubes on it, heading east. If you could –'

'You're locked where?' he cut in.

As patiently as I could, I said, 'Just retrace your steps, quickly, please. We're melting in here, seriously.'

I was still looking through the hole. When his shoes appeared again, tiny ticks of lime-green hope, I let out a breath. 'Stop,' I said. The shoes stopped. 'Turn left, towards the main entrance.' Astonishingly the shoes turned right, heading for the hut. 'Left!' I said. 'Round the back of the truck.' The whole of him, phone held out like a little tray in front of his chin, the way idiots use them in the street sometimes, came into view. 'That's it. Now look to the north. You'll see the containers.'

To be fair to him, he broke into a trot once he got himself orientated up the hill, and although I lost sight of him he was quickly outside the door, fighting to open it. The lock defeated him at first, but having shouted that he'd be back immediately with help, he summoned a key quickly too, and I could hear him giving whoever he'd got hold of a hard time: 'Quick, you moron. When my father hears about this, the fool who thought it was a good idea will regret it.'

Marcel didn't break from his statue-like trance until the key turned in the lock. I've never been so happy to see a door open. The rush of air felt positively cool compared to our little oven. The first thing I saw was Caleb pushing the security guy away, hard. That was surprising enough, but nothing compared to the expression on his face when he turned back to greet us. In the few days we'd been apart, it seemed the stuffing had been sucked out of my cousin. He looked gaunt, bloodlessly pale. Also, the shape of him had changed. Gone was the puffed-out chest and high chin; in its place was a stooped, rounded thing. He couldn't meet my eye.

'Guys,' he said, inspecting the dirt between our feet. 'I'm so sorry.'

'Why?' said Amelia. 'You didn't lock us in here. You got us out.'

'I know but . . .' he petered out.

'Without you we'd probably have cooked in fact,' Amelia went on, desperate to cheer him up. 'So you've literally saved our lives.'

'Someone else would have come eventually,' he said.

'Maybe, but nobody had until now. I'm not sure how much longer we'd have lasted.'

Caleb was shaking his head, eyes still fixed on the floor. The penny dropped for Amelia. She changed tack. 'Oh, so the sorry isn't about your father's security detail locking us in here. Well, at least that makes sense. But what else do you have to apologise for?'

Did he know something about Mum and Dad? I opened my mouth to ask, but before I could get the question out, Caleb glanced up at Marcel, shook his head and said, 'For Innocent.'

I'm ashamed to say it, but instead of sadness in that moment I felt relief. If this new hollowed-out version of Caleb meant that he actually felt guilty about Innocent's death, then good. It was what he deserved.

'But that was an accident!' Amelia said, a bit too loudly. She meant to reassure him, but the false brightness in her voice made it obvious she knew the 'accident' could have been prevented. Nevertheless, she stepped forward and put an arm around Caleb's hunched shoulders to comfort him.

It seemed to work; his mouth twitched in a pitiful half-smile. 'What are you doing here anyway?' he said.

I told him why we'd come. I so wanted him to give me news about my parents that I couldn't bring myself to ask him for it directly. To his credit, as I was rambling on about our motorbike journey he cut in. 'I'm sorry, Jack,' he said. 'If they were here, I'd know. Either they'd have arrived with a fanfare, or security would have picked them up; the place is pretty much a fortress, as you guys found out.' He paused, then went on, tentatively, 'I can help you look for them though. If they're touring the . . . er . . . less professional mines in the area, someone here is bound to know.'

'What do you mean by "less professional"?' Amelia asked.

'Let's get you some water,' he replied, 'and I'll explain.'

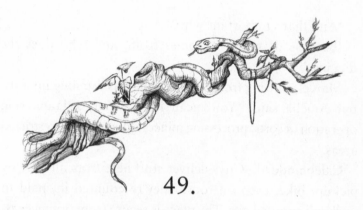

49.

Caleb led us to a standpipe set on the other side of the very Portakabin I'd spent so long watching through my peephole. Though Marcel hung back, I insisted he and Amelia drink before me. It was my fault they'd nearly been cooked alive after all. Once I'd drunk my own fill I ducked my whole head under the tap and let the blissful coolness run down the inside of my T-shirt. Then I looked around. From here we could see right into the huge open-cast mine, criss-crossed by diggers and trucks, plumes of dust in their wake. Caleb was banging on about the size of the operation, its efficiency and profitability, but not in a boastful way. He seemed to want to get something off his chest.

To help him, I cut to the chase: 'It's a big mine. So what?'

'It looks like a big mine, you're right. But it's a bigger processing plant.'

I looked at him blankly.

'A lot more tantalum gets brought here from outside than is dug up mechanically onsite.'

'And that's important why?'

'Because of where it comes from, and who does the digging.'

Marcel, shifting from foot to foot, was listening intently, but Amelia said, 'You mean it's a front, a laundering operation of sorts, processing minerals dug up from restricted areas.'

Caleb nodded. 'Guys deliver stuff here from all over by pickup, bike, even on foot. They're counted in, paid in cash and counted out. The place is secure from prying eyes, but on the inside it's an open secret: we take black-market precious minerals, process them and sell on the good stuff. Nobody here tries to hide it.'

'Why are you telling us this?' I asked.

'Isn't it obvious?' said Amelia.

'Not to me.'

'Your mum and dad's suspicions about Langdon's business are true,' she said flatly. 'He's corrupt.'

'Yes, but –'

'Caleb said he wanted to help,' said Amelia, a note of indignation in her voice. 'What's hard to get about it?'

For me, everything! Why would Caleb rat on his dad like this? When I searched his face for an answer he looked at his feet again, so I asked him outright: 'What's in this for you?'

'Since I arrived here, I've talked to people,' he muttered. 'I'm the boss's son, the heir to the empire, so to speak. Naturally they think I'm on his side. Also, they're kind of scared of me. So they have to tell me the truth. They've admitted that a lot of these smaller mines we get stuff from

224

are inside the national park. Sooner or later the government will let people mine there anyway, they think, so all they're doing is getting ahead of the game. They're proud of it! But I'm not.' Though his chin was still low, he met my eye for the first time and went on quietly, 'I can't undo what happened to Innocent. We all know it was my fault. The best I can do is honour his memory. He was all about protecting Congo's wildlife. I don't want any part in destroying –'

A metal-on-metal shriek rose up from the mine to slice the end off Caleb's sentence, but it didn't matter. Everything about him in that moment – his slumped shoulders, the way his fingers were gnawing at one another, his quick-blinking eyes – told me he was sincere. I trust my instincts. Marcel seemed to have to come to the same conclusion. He put a hand on Caleb's shoulder, left it there for a moment, then patted his upper arm twice. If he could offer Caleb this forgiveness, how could I not do the same? I wanted to. Amelia, as so often happens, beat me to it.

'Satisfied?' she said.

Sometimes an apology can be hard to take. You have to climb down off your own high horse to accept it. Amelia's clunky, obvious rightness, swept the awkwardness away. It made me smile at Caleb. Only briefly, but enough to prompt a nanosecond-long half-smile back. This was enough.

'Let's get on with it then,' he said.

'With what?' asked Amelia.

'Finding Jack's parents,' he said, holding his hands out, palms up. 'So we can help them clean up this mess.'

50.

With the air between us cleared, Caleb sprang into action.
Though he'd shrunk with shame in the time we'd been apart,
he inflated again as we approached his father's foreman, who
was among a group of workers squatting beside a digger
with a broken caterpillar track.

'Butcher!' Caleb hollered as soon as we were within
earshot.

A fat white guy in a hard hat jumped up.

'I need Francis, provisions, a Land Cruiser with a full
tank of diesel, a working GPS and the coordinates of our
five biggest below-the-line suppliers. Text the coordinates
to my phone. Right away. As in, we leave in ten minutes.'

This Butcher fellow scratched the two-day-old stubble on his
double chin with one hand and cupped his belly protectively
with the other. It was obvious he wanted to ask who we were
and what Caleb had in mind, but thought better of it. Instead
he scuttled off and returned riding up front in an enormous,
dusty Toyota 4x4, evidently expecting to come with us.

'Get out,' said Caleb.

'But shouldn't I –'

'Do as I say? Yes,' Caleb said simply. 'You're in charge here at the moment, are you not? My father will want to tell you when to hand over the reins in person.' More kindly, his voice lowering conspiratorially, he went on. 'Mind the fort, there's a good chap. Jack here's family and Dad has asked me to show them what's what.'

Before Butcher had a chance to object, Caleb opened the passenger door, and ushered him out, motioning for Marcel to take his place. The three of us promptly climbed into the air-conditioned rear. Caleb's boss-like sense of entitlement was contagious. None of us so much as glanced at Butcher as Francis, the driver, did as Caleb ordered and slewed the truck round in a three-point turn, raising a cloud of dust that blotted out the foreman as we sped off towards the setting sun and chain-link boundary fence.

'Take us to Bleu-Neuf-Cinq first,' Caleb instructed Francis. With less certainty he continued, 'You know where that is, right?'

The driver had lines of scar tissue bisecting both cheeks. They creased up with the quick smile of relief that accompanied his nodding. Clearly he wanted to please Caleb. 'Of course, sir,' he said, flipping down the mirrored sunglasses perched on his head.

'Very good,' said Caleb. 'Quick as possible, please.' He sat back and started fiddling with the handheld GPS Butcher had given him. Last time I'd travelled with him he'd have cut off a finger before admitting he didn't know

227

how to read it, but today he simply handed the device to Amelia and said, 'You'll probably work this thing out quicker than me.'

As it happened, *I* got the device working. Simple stuff like on-off buttons aren't Amelia's strong point. But I admit she took over after that, programming in the coordinates Butcher had dutifully texted to Caleb. Having done this, she spent a while fiddling with her phone, cross-checking maps she'd downloaded with information she pulled off the GPS. At length she sat back.

'The coordinates of two of these five suppliers place them within protected areas. The mine we're heading for is one of them.'

'You're sure?' I stupidly asked.

'No, I'm guessing at random. What do you think!'

With Amelia's help, I monitored our progress towards the first secret mine. It wasn't quick. As in, we were barely one-third of the way there when the orange sunset we were driving towards dropped like a guillotine through purple to black. Francis sped on into the cone of our headlights. He didn't even take off his sunglasses. Caleb's 'quick as possible' clearly meant something to him.

I have to admit that despite the bumps and twists and turns, I drifted off. I woke when we stopped and peered out. 'Bleu-Neuf-Cinq' seemed to be a deserted fork in the dirt road. The headlights lit up scrub and nothingness – anyone Caleb might have expected to see there had apparently gone to bed. It seemed we had no choice but to do the same. Francis – job done: he'd got us there – turned his head to one side and began snoring immediately. Marcel did the same. The rest of us slept one way or another on the big back seat. At some point I came to with Amelia's head on my chest. Her mouth was open. My arm was numb behind her back, but I didn't have the heart to move it. There are worse things than a numb arm anyway.

My dreams that night were Mark-shaped.

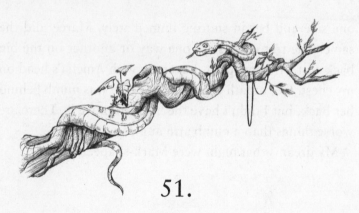

51.

Caleb was already out of the Land Cruiser when I woke up properly, morning having broken. He was sitting on the truck's running board opposite Francis, who was squatting in the dirt. The driver had already boiled a pan of water over a little propane stove. He passed me a cup of tea so full of sugar you could have stood up a spoon in it, and in case that wasn't sweet enough his idea of provisions for this trip was plastic-wrapped chocolate biscuits. Lots of them. He'd brought a big box and, as far as I could see, nothing else. I was so hungry I ate about ten and shoved more in my pockets.

'Francis knows people here,' Caleb told me as I munched. 'If your parents have been through, they'll tell us.'

As if on cue, a group of men and women appeared up the track, walking unhurriedly towards us. Each of them was carrying something. The guy in the lead had a spade over his shoulder, the one next to him was lugging a load of hessian sacks rolled up under his arm, and the skinny woman bringing up the rear of this first team was carrying a pickaxe. Another couple of shovels followed in the next knot of men. Also, a crowbar slung from a rope. More bags on the back of a guy with torn, dirt-smeared shorts. Everyone's clothes were filthy in fact. Holey T-shirts, mismatched gumboots, bare feet. A boy there who looked not much older than me had a Make America Great Again cap on, its stained brim angled comically to the sky. Where had he got that from? None of these guys were wasting breath talking to one another, and they didn't say anything to us either. They already looked exhausted. When they reached the junction we'd parked at, they simply turned downhill, one or two of them eyeing the Land Cruiser uncertainly. I took a photograph of the group before a bend in the track folded them out of sight. As the last of the men rounded it, I had an absurd urge to whistle the tune the seven dwarfs sing when they say goodbye to Snow White and head off to work. If Xander had been there, I'd probably have followed through. He would have understood.

'What do we do now?' I said instead.

'*Nous les suivons*,' said Marcel, dusting himself down.

'How far is it?' asked Amelia.

As another gaggle of men appeared up the track, Caleb said, 'The mine's close, a short walk. Some of these guys will have trekked for a couple of hours in the dark to get here this morning.'

We fell in behind this group. The path was well worn, steep in places, a yellow scar cut through the undergrowth. It wasn't the only route down to the mine. We'd been walking just fifteen minutes when another path joined ours, and

231

when the great gash of the mine opened up ahead of us it was obvious you could come in from the other side too.

The place was alive with activity. A swarm of men and women, more than a hundred of them, were already hard at work on the tiered, filthy plateau cut away beneath us. The expanse of raw dirt was at least ten times the size of the football pitch at school; ragged edged, multi-levelled, a great scab picked off the face of the earth. When I say men and women hard at work, I mean exactly that: everywhere I looked men were wielding shovels and picks and filling bags with dirt and hefting those bags this way and that, heaping them in little pyramids down below for other men to lug up to that lip, while yet more men hacked rock from the wall over there for others to shovel into heaps to be picked through by . . . my eyes snagged on the four little guys at work not fifty metres away.

They weren't little men; they were children.

And in fact, looking harder at the scene, there were other children, kids way younger than me, at work among the adults. Instinctively I stepped forward, camera raised, to take a closer look, but I hadn't taken many shots or steps before a man with his back to me cradling his shovel in his arms turned round to reveal that the shovel was in fact a rifle. Seeing me advancing, with Caleb and Amelia just a few metres behind me, as pinkly out of place as I was, he shouted something unintelligible in French. It didn't matter that I couldn't understand him, because he brought his gun up onto his hip at the same time, making it very clear that if I took another step he'd shoot.

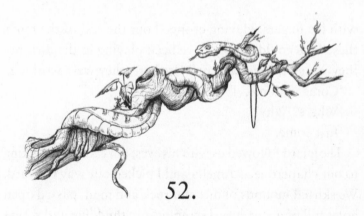

52.

I stayed where I was, welded to the spot.

Caleb, however, was undeterred by the man's gun. 'Francis!' he said. 'Tell this idiot who we are.'

I was gobsmacked by my cousin's acting abilities. Knowing how cut up about Innocent he was, deep down, made all this 'I'm in charge' stuff impressive. Backed by his father's name, it worked too. Francis, with Marcel in tow, only had to have the briefest of chats with the gun-toting guard to make him sling his rifle onto his back and spread out his hands in a 'my bad, please let it go!' way. He didn't even object when I raised my camera to my eye again. I took a few wide-angle shots to start with, trying to capture the great spread of ramshackle activity before me, before switching lenses and zooming in on the detail. The big lens sucked the children in the distance full-frame. They were even younger than I'd thought. One was filling a sack with what looked like grit, using his bare hands, while the littler of the two squatted next to the pile, picking out bits of whatever it was with his fingers. Having cropped out the rest of the mine, these kids could simply have been playing in the dirt, but they weren't. Like everyone else here, they were working.

'Come with me,' I said to Amelia.

'Where? Why?'

'Just come.'

The guard followed us with his eyes, but carried on talking to our chaperone as Amelia and I picked our way forward. We skirted mounds of dirt and rock and mud, passed open holes full of water, heard scraping and thudding and sifting and grunting, a cough here and a gasp there, sounds so puny and human, completely unlike the mechanised rumble at Langdon's mining HQ, it was hard to imagine those tools had been invented. The most high-tech things they had here were bicycles. People were using them to wheel sacks of whatever it was they'd dug up to a set of filthy-looking interconnected puddles, where more men, women and children were busy sluicing the muck, picking through it with their fingers. I made a beeline towards the littlest kid I could see. He was so absorbed in what he was doing that he didn't notice us approaching, but when he did clock us he was all eye-whites, so surprised by my 'Hi', that I thought he might burst into tears.

I squatted next to his pile of dirt. It was the colour of ash, as were the boy's hands and feet. 'What's your name?' I asked.

He blinked at me as Amelia translated the question, and replied so quietly I barely caught what he said.

'Beno.'

'*Et quel âge as-tu?*' I managed.

'*Six*,' he whispered. It sounded like *seess*.

'Unbelievable,' I said, as much to myself as to Amelia.

'Not really,' she replied.

I glanced up at her sharply.

'I mean, it's common knowledge that child labour is a thing here.'

'That doesn't make it right!' I said.

'I didn't say it did,' she said, and I immediately felt bad for snapping at her, because on closer inspection it was obvious from her compressed lips and deliberate breathing that she was as shocked as I was. '"Artisanal mining", it's called,' she went on quietly. 'Huge un-mechanised pits like this employ whole families for next to nothing, making even the youngest kids work in these terrible conditions, chemicals everywhere, breathing in poison, with middle men selling on the fruits of their labours at a handsome profit.'

In French she asked Beno if his parents also worked at the mine.

'*Non.*'

When she asked why, I understood his answer easily enough. '*Ils sont morts.*'

I winced when she immediately asked him what killed them, but her directness didn't seem to bother Beno, who explained that both his mother and father had been sick before they died.

In response to Amelia's follow-up 'What with?' the boy just shrugged.

'*Qui vis-tu avec maintenant?*' Amelia asked him.

The boy flicked his eyes at a group shovelling dirt into sacks fifty or so metres away. '*Mon oncle*,' he said.

Looking more closely, I saw that not all of the men and women in the group were working. One guy, wearing jeans whose legs had for some reason been ripped off at different heights, one above the knee the other below it, had his hands on his hips and was watching us. When my eyes met his he called out in French, but not to us, it turned out. He was yelling at Beno. The little boy squatted down in the dirt and started picking through it again. When I looked back to the man – his uncle, presumably – I saw he'd also returned to his sack-filling. We'd interrupted Beno's work, and when told to get back to it that's what he'd done, immediately.

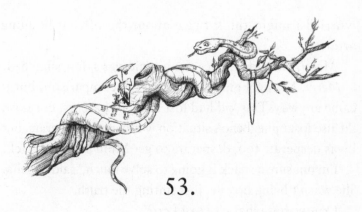

53.

Amelia was still asking Beno questions. When had he last eaten? How many days a week did he spend here? What time did he start and stop? But although I also wanted to know more about his life, I sensed what she didn't: if we stopped him working again, he'd probably pay for it. I shushed her and we both took a step back. But I couldn't quite bring myself to just walk away. As I watched, a fly landed on the boy's thin neck and crawled up towards his hairline. He didn't bother to wave it off.

'How can we help him?' I said.

'It's not just him though, is it?' said Amelia.

Of course it wasn't. Beyond Beno, another slightly bigger boy was also sifting muck, and dotted around us there were other boys and girls mixed in with the adults.

Without consciously knowing why, I'd been digging around in my pockets. My hand emerged clutching one of Francis's chocolate biscuits. I knelt down next to the boy and offered it to him. He took it very quickly, as if worried I might think twice about the offer if he hung around.

'*Merci*,' he added, once the biscuit was safely snatched.

Merci. Mercy. I gulped, fighting the comparison, but it came anyway. This kid had lost both his parents. For now, I'd also lost mine. Beno's situation was beyond desperate, but I was desperate too, desperate to get Mum and Dad back.

'I'm not sure a snack is going to solve much,' said Amelia. She wasn't being hostile, just stating the truth.

'I know, but what else can I do?'

'Your parents came out here to gather evidence, right? Of illegal mining. Seeing as you're the one with the big camera, they should probably have brought you with them in the first place. I'd take as many pictures as you can, if I were you.'

The fact that we still didn't know who had hold of Mum and Dad must have played in my face. Amelia went on, 'They'd want you to document this and put the evidence in the right hands. Theirs, preferably. But if your parents don't make it to the summit, they'd want you to show people the photos there yourself, yes?'

The summit was still a way off, and Mum and Dad would surely make it there in person. I couldn't let myself think anything else, but said, 'I suppose so,' to Amelia all the same.

'Get on with it then – take as many as you can before one of these guards realises Caleb's not as important as he's pretending to be.'

She was right of course. 'I'll take the kids' photographs, you get their names and ages,' I said, and we set to, working our way around the piles of rocks and puddles and holes and sacks and heaps of dirt, everything filthy and alive with apparently pointless physical work of some sort, a termite mound that only made sense when you thought of how all the backbreaking tasks – hacking and digging and shovelling and lifting and pouring and picking and sluicing and sifting – came together in the form of something valuable to sell.

I focused on the kids, tried to take photos that showed the punishing practicalities of what they were doing as well as who they were, and for each kid I photographed, Amelia asked their name. I remember a Fabrice and a Justin, a Gabriel and a Pierre, a Mpenda and even a Sublime, but to be honest I was more bothered about getting well-composed, properly lit, sharp photos than I was about who was who. After we'd photographed about fifteen kids I realised Amelia wasn't writing down the names and made the mistake of suggesting it might be a good idea. She gave me a withering glare and muttered, 'For you, maybe. Just do your bit and let me do mine.'

I'm not sure how long we worked; I got so caught up in what I was doing that I lost track of time. It seemed ages, but probably wasn't long. Still, Caleb managed to ask the gathered guards if they'd heard anything about a visit from a middle-aged white couple linked to his father, and the next thing I knew he was by my side, apologetically giving me the bad news: nobody knew anything at all.

'Also, you should probably wrap it up with the camera. They're getting pretty antsy.'

I glanced over to the gaggle of guards. Two of them were arguing with Francis while a third looked on, and the original man who'd stopped us, still hugging his rifle as if it was a cat, was giving me a proper thousand-yard death stare. Marcel, squatting next to this group, held up one big hand palm down and wobbled it from side to side, the universal 'this is iffy' signal. I turned away and took one last photograph – of the GPS screen, to pinpoint the location of this place for future investigation – before returning the camera to its padded pocket in the bottom of my rucksack. By the time I was done, the guards' argument was audible over the squelching of feet and thump of spades in the hole I'd just photographed.

They wanted us gone, that much was clear. So Caleb and I hurried Amelia up the slope to where Francis and Marcel were now openly pleading with the guards, who'd sort of surrounded them, a bit like a crew of school bullies on the brink of making their move. Caleb either didn't notice or decided not to care. Fair play to him, he barged right into the middle of the men, wagging his finger, and saying, 'No, no, no!' very loudly indeed. Again, it was an impressive act. He looked very entitled. But the guards seemed to have grown; for all his work in the gym, Caleb stood out as puny by comparison.

'What's he objecting to, precisely?' Amelia asked me.

'I'm not sure, but it seems to be working.'

The main guard had taken a couple of steps backwards. Now the others followed suit, the noose of their circle relaxing.

'Take names,' Caleb was telling Francis. 'Tell them my father will be pleased to hear of their vigilance. Explain that we've undertaken this visit on his behalf. They'll be rewarded.'

Francis began relaying all this before Caleb finished saying it, and Marcel somehow got himself between the guards and the three of us while the translation was going on, shepherding us away up the hill with an insistent, 'Suivez-moi!'

We did as we were told and backed away further up the slope. I kept my eyes on the guard with the rifle. Mesmerised by those fidgety fingers, I wasn't exactly focusing on where I was stepping and I lost my footing on the uneven ground and sat down in a pool of sludge. The guards all looked my way when this happened and mercifully found it funny. I slapped my forehead, very clown-like, which made one of them laugh out loud. This gave Francis the opportunity to disentangle himself from the conversation.

'Physical comedy is weird like that,' Amelia said, helping me up. 'I've no idea why, but it defuses tension.'

'Deliberate ploy,' I said.

'Really?' she asked, looking impressed.

I didn't tell her the truth.

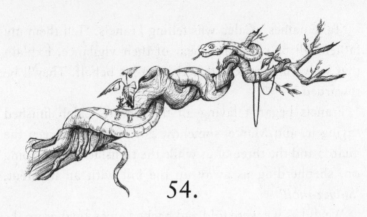

54.

Covered in muck, I led us out of the mine the way we had come, picked up the steep path and quickened our pace despite the gradient, desperate to get out of there. When it became clear that nobody was following, my heart rate dropped by about a third; I hadn't realised it was beating so fast until it slowed. In the wake of panic, a hollow ache spread across my chest. Mum and Dad would be proud of the evidence I'd managed to photograph, but the trip had drawn a blank as far as actually finding them was concerned. Caleb, who'd fallen into step beside me, seemed to know what I was thinking.

'There are other mines, other contacts. This was just the first – what the . . . ?'

I followed his gaze, up the track to where the 4x4 was parked, and did a double take of my own. Where there had been one Land Cruiser, now there were two. Both were painted in the same white-on-green livery of Langdon's mining company. The second had clearly just arrived, its exhaust still pumping out diesel fumes. Both Caleb and I stopped walking. Marcel and Francis and Amelia caught up with us. Francis saw why we'd stopped and gasped.

Both front doors in the newly arrived truck swung open at the same time, as if it was stretching its wings. Langdon's driver stepped out of one, the same guy that had driven us in Kinshasa – I recognised his quick-stepping bandy-legged walk. More slowly, as if moving through water, Langdon himself emerged from the other door. He surveyed the five of us for a moment without saying anything. His shirt was busy, as ever, black swirls on silvery grey today. The corners of his mouth twitched and he gave a little wave.

'Fancy seeing you here,' he said.

I sensed Caleb stiffen, but it was Francis's reaction – he was actually quivering with worry, the scar-lines on his cheeks pinched tight – that made me step up; we'd come here because of me, not them.

'Weird, that he's here too,' said Amelia. 'It's almost as if . . .'

She's so fast at the difficult stuff and yet misses the obvious. I put my hand on her shoulder to stop her saying any more, and stepped forward.

'I'm sorry we came alone. I'm desperate. My parents. I knew you'd be doing everything you could in Kinshasa. The other trail led here. I made everyone come. I –'

'Of course,' smiled Langdon. 'And I'm here as well now, if a bit late, to help.'

'Yes, but it was my decision to come, nobody else's,' I said lamely.

'You seem to think I might have a problem with that?' One of Langdon's eyebrows lifted.

'No, but . . .'

'But?' he said.

I had one motive in that moment, to stop him going down to the mine and talking to his guards. If they let on that I'd been taking photographs, well, nothing good could come of that.

'I think you've shown admirable initiative,' Langdon went on. 'Getting yourself here. Finding your own way.' His gaze passed over Caleb to rest upon Francis. 'Making use of the help.'

Caleb spoke up. 'I gave Francis the order. He just did what I told him to do, Dad.'

The word 'Dad', tagged on to the end of Caleb's assertion, made him sound as young as I felt in that moment. Langdon merely smiled at him, but everything about my uncle's calm, friendly facade felt fake. Beneath it, he was seething, I could tell. The fact he said nothing further to Francis made no difference – the driver would definitely get it in the neck, and soon.

'Either way, I've had no luck turning up leads,' I said, trying to change the focus. 'Nothing at Canonhead, and nothing here either. We talked to the guys in charge, but they hadn't heard anything about a visit from Mum and Dad.'

'I know that,' Langdon purred, pulling out his mobile phone and waggling it from side to side. 'Though this operation has nothing to do with me, I know who runs things here, and we've been in touch.' He waved the phone in a loose north-east-south-west circle and continued, 'The same goes for all the other mining facilities round and about. We've checked. The word is out. Should anybody hear anything, I'll know sooner rather than later.' After a further pause he added, 'I understand why you wanted to look in person, but really there was no need. Your parents would want me to keep you safe, not let you run around the bush. As I told them, it's a dangerous place.'

My hackles rose when Langdon said this. Of course the bush was dangerous. My parents had been kidnapped in it! 'If you don't mind, I'd like to carry on the search in person,' I said, as evenly as I could. 'Francis has done a great job getting us here; he can take us to the next mine too, can't he?'

I shouldn't have made it a question; it gave Langdon the opportunity to say, 'I'm afraid not,' only too easily.

'Why not?' said Amelia.

'I won't be letting you out of my sight again. Your parents wouldn't forgive me if anything happened to you.'

'You said you were here to help,' Amelia said.

'And I am,' Langdon replied.

'How though?' she asked.

'Jump in the truck and I'll explain,' he said, with a smile so fake I wanted to punch it off his face. I didn't though, because climbing into the truck suggested we'd be moving away from here, and that made it less likely Langdon would have a chance to ask the overseers down below what exactly we'd done during our visit. The truck was the lesser of two evils in that moment, so I did as instructed and climbed aboard. Amelia and Caleb followed me. The Land Cruiser's

245

heavy doors clumped shut behind us. My uncle, however, didn't immediately take his seat. Seeing him step in Francis's direction, I nearly jumped out again, but he seemed merely to want to talk to him quietly. I have no idea what he said. Whatever it was, it spurred Francis into action. He immediately fired up the other 4x4. I was relieved to see Marcel climb aboard with Francis before his truck leaped away down the track. Once Langdon and his bandy-legged driver were installed up front, we set off, the second half of the convoy, in hot pursuit.

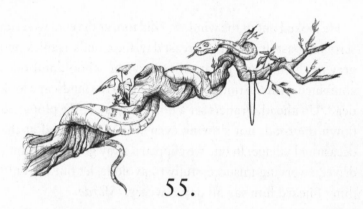

55.

Not long after we moved off, I noticed the locks on the rear doors had dropped into their sockets. That happens on some cars automatically, I know, but in the truck, then, it seemed deliberate. Had Langdon locked us in? I didn't like the idea of that at all.

Though Langdon had promised an explanation he didn't offer one, just sat there in silence up front. At length Amelia asked where we were going, to which Langdon gave the one-word reply: 'Canonhead.'

'We've already been.'

'I know. But I've work to do there before we head back to the capital. As has Caleb.' He looked back at his son with another fake smile. 'You've barely begun!'

Caleb didn't reply to his father. He'd shrunk again, hunched over beside me. He whispered, 'I'm sorry,' and I realised he was beating himself up, thinking this was all his doing. But in fact he'd taken a risk for me, crossing his dad.

'It's not your fault,' I said.

He looked out of the window. I did too, at the endless scrub scrolling past. It was an overcast day, the clouds as thick and grey as the mashed potato they serve at school, and that, combined with the tinted windows, made the landscape look dead. Up ahead, Francis set a blistering pace. We ploughed down the road, not slowing even when we arrived at the occasional village. In one we clipped a stray goat. Langdon's driver, swerving unsuccessfully to avoid it, let out the only thing I heard him say all day, a weary, '*Merde.*'

'That means –'

'I know what it means, Amelia,' I said.

I've no idea if the goat survived. Though he'd swerved, the driver wasn't about to stop. I didn't even care much; in a trip filled with bad days I felt lower than ever – not just frightened for Mum and Dad, but powerless to help – in the back of Langdon's truck that day.

Hours passed, punctuated only once by my phone, which, having caught some random signal, buzzed in my pocket somewhere along the way. Before I checked the screen I willed it to be my parents making contact. But it wasn't. It was Xander. He'd left me a voicemail. I fought back the hope his name conjured: might he have good news?

Surreptitiously – not wanting Langdon to see what I was doing – I pressed the phone to my ear.

'Jack, heads up. Langdon worked out where you are. He's on his way to you, and he's not a happy chap.' Xander's voice, clear as you like, right there in my ear. In most circumstances I'd have laughed at the timing, but not today. 'No news here,' the message went on, 'but I did have one thought:

248

the hotel has CCTV covering the entrance and the lobby. I've asked them to dig it out so we can have a look at the guy who dropped off the ransom note. Probably useless, but I'll let you know either way.'

I knew Xander was clutching at straws with this news, but even so it made me realise how much I wanted to get back to Kinshasa, not just to check out the footage, but to make sure the photos I'd taken of the kids in the mine made it into the right hands. I owed that to Mum and Dad; the fact they were out of the picture for now meant I had to step up. To be speeding anywhere other than the airport, in the hands of a man I didn't trust, was a kind of torture.

We roared back into the Canonhead compound late in the afternoon. I was hungry and tired and simmering with resentment. Caleb trotted over to Francis and Marcel immediately after we arrived, and they all sidled off, keen to avoid his father no doubt. Langdon, focusing on Amelia and me, made a great show of taking us to what he called the canteen, a clutch of plastic tables and chairs set beneath a corrugated roof on stilts. It was empty at this hour. Somebody had wiped down all the tables, but not very well. You could see the patterns where the cloth had cut through the grime. They reminded me of Langdon's shirt. Nobody had bothered to wipe the chairs he pulled out for us though. They were filthy with orange dirt, and the bottles of lemonade and Coke he rustled up from somewhere were also filmed with dust. There was grit in the leftover lunch of chilli con carne and rice as well, I'm sure of it. Caleb joined us as we ate. I was biding my time, watching my uncle. He polished off two bowls of the chilli-slop and tipped half the contents of his hip flask – Jack Daniels, I bet – into his own drink before gulping it down.

'You said you've work to get on with here,' I ventured. 'How long will it take?'

'Not long. A few days. A week tops.'

'Non-specific – unconvincing,' muttered Amelia under her breath.

'You don't want us here that long, getting in the way,' I said quickly.

'Nonsense. You can help Caleb. Think of it as a learning opportunity.'

'Thanks, but surely we'd be better off back in Kinshasa, waiting for news there.'

Langdon tipped his plastic chair onto its back legs, planted his drink on his belly and smiled. 'You decided to take this little trip. You have to live with the consequences,' he said.

'Dad,' said Caleb.

Langdon swivelled towards his son, the fake cheer draining from his face.

'Come on,' said Caleb. 'If you went missing you'd want me to do all I could to find you, wouldn't you?'

From away in the mine a heavy thumping noise struck up.

'What I want you to do, now and always, is exactly what I say,' Langdon stamped the words down in time with the pile-driver, or whatever it was.

Caleb sat very still in his chair for a moment. Then he

looked from his father to me and back again, a decision working itself out in his face. 'I bet you would, I *bet* you would,' he said, also to the beat.

The front feet of Langdon's chair hit the plywood floor hard. 'I'm not sure I like your tone, Caleb.'

'And I'm not sure I care,' Caleb answered. This time his sideways look took in Amelia as well as me. He drew a deep breath and pulled his shoulders back. 'Let Jack and Amelia go,' he said simply.

'Or?' said Langdon.

Caleb rose from his chair. Quietly but forcefully he laid down one word: 'Else.'

My uncle carries the ominous swell of good living beneath his Hawaiian shirts. But although a little out of shape, he has as much weight in his shoulders as his gut, muscled forearms, a rugby-player's thighs. He got up slowly from his chair and stood toe to toe with Caleb. They matched each other in height; if anything Caleb was the taller. But my cousin could not have been more than two-thirds of his father's weight. Breathing heavily, Langdon said, 'Repeat that. I dare you.'

'You don't get it, do you?' said Caleb.

He opened his mouth to go on, but before he could, his father hit him. It wasn't a punch – Langdon's hand was open – but all the same it was a heavy blow out of nowhere, a backhander flung hard. Caleb's head snapped sideways and he staggered backwards. But his feet were quick beneath him, and as soon as they'd stopped him falling they drove him straight back at Langdon. I couldn't believe what I was seeing. With real speed Caleb fired three punches at his father. The first caught him square beneath the solar plexus. Langdon dipped forward in astonishment as the second, an upper cut, glanced off his jaw. The third punch was a straight jab, square in the face. Langdon dropped to his knees, a hand covering his nose. For a second, nothing happened. Then he looked up. His nose and chin were already awash with blood. Caleb took a step forward and stared down at his father. He looked electric with anticipation, simultaneously aghast and ecstatic at what he had done.

I should have got between them but I was fixed to the spot, and before I knew it Langdon had exploded from the floor, throwing all his force head first at Caleb. He roared in fury as he rocketed at him. A memory of Spenser the silverback hurtling at Caleb in the jungle came to mind. Then, Innocent had tried to intervene. Perhaps it was lucky that I was too slow. Langdon barrelled straight into his son, knocked him flat on his back and pinned him down by the throat. His free hand rose, his fist making a club, and struck Caleb once, twice, again and again, about the head. In a frenzy Caleb's knees slammed up into his father's chest, but my uncle wouldn't let go. He was possessed. The weight of those punches, the sound of them – I swear he'd have killed Caleb if we'd let him.

Without realising it, I'd picked up my chair, and now I swung it at Langdon's side with all my might, knocking him off Caleb. The hand gripping my cousin's throat came free. As Langdon tried to right himself, Amelia grabbed his collar and hung on so hard buttons popped off his shirt. This sent him off balance just long enough for Caleb to get a leg free, bunch his knee into his chest and aim the sole of his foot at his father's bloody face. When he unleashed the kick, it flipped Langdon over. He was stunned. Caleb sprang up and lashed out with his other foot, a penalty kick across Langdon's temple delivered with a viciousness that made me gasp. The blow knocked my uncle out cold. He didn't even attempt to break his own fall. His head bounced once on the dirt-encrusted floor, and he lay still.

Caleb dropped to his knees beside his father, wide-eyed with shock at what he'd done. He was clutching his own throat, coughing horribly, fighting for breath. 'Go!' he croaked. 'Find Marcel. He's with the bikes. I told Francis to give him fuel.'

I heaved Langdon onto his side, thoughts clashing. Call a doctor? Try to help? No! Help Mum and Dad. Do as Caleb was insisting. Flee. Stay. What had I just witnessed? Caleb obviously hadn't planned to fight his father, but he'd thought to organise Marcel, and when Langdon struck him his response had been savage. A dam had burst. I felt for my cousin, for Langdon even. I don't mind admitting I had no idea what to do.

'That's right, put him in the recovery position,' Amelia said, helping me with Langdon. She had her fingers pressed flat against his neck. 'His pulse is strong,' she announced, very matter of fact. 'Who knows how long he'll take to come round? We should probably do as Caleb's suggesting . . .'

Caleb's face swam close to mine. His throat was already raw purple and his cheek was swelling up. 'I owed you,' he whispered, his voice sandpaper. 'I'll deal with this.'

'But, Caleb . . .'

'Go.'

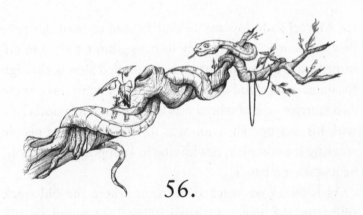

56.

In a kind of daze, I bundled Amelia out of the canteen area and jogged – to have run flat out could have attracted attention – to the perimeter fence. Once we reached it we tracked west, past the horrible container we'd been cooked in, to where I'd last seen the bikes, on their kickstands, amidst piles of pallets and empty oil drums, near the entrance to the mine complex. Marcel was sitting beside them. As soon he clocked us jogging into view he jumped up.

'*Vite, vite, vite!*' urged Amelia, and immediately he was astride one of the bikes. Our packs were there too. The weight of mine, as I swung it onto my back, told me Marcel had thought to refill our water bottles. I unhooked my helmet from the handlebars and just about ripped my ears off jamming it on my head. Marcel's bike coughed to life. So what if Amelia jumped up behind him? We'd make faster progress that way, I had to admit. The rumble of a truck leaving the mine took the edge off the noise of my own bike as I turned the key in the ignition. I motioned for Marcel to follow me so that I could control our pace past the sentry. It was agony to pause, but I waited to fall in behind a departing lorry, and trundled slowly through the gates in its cloud of dust, even managing to wave at the two sentries, one of whom was leaning back in a deckchair with his feet up. Their job was to stop the wrong people entering the complex, not leaving it, I suppose. Either way, he just waved back.

As soon as we reached the spur where the old track split from the bigger dirt road, Marcel cut round me and opened up, firing us into the bush as quickly as the ruts and potholes would allow. He clearly didn't want to be caught by Langdon's men any more than we did. Amelia, her hair bouncing around wildly below her helmet, struggled to hang on to him, and I struggled too; my bike was a live thing I had to wrestle if I was going to keep up. It took such concentration, and was such physically hard work, that I was immediately thrown into a sort of split-screen state. I was super-intent on what I was doing and yet totally distracted by what I'd just witnessed; by fear and by hope, at the same time. What would Caleb do when Langdon woke up? What would I do in his situation? I'd try to restrain him, buy time. Might Caleb have tied his father up? Dragged him into the container he'd rescued us from, even? What would Langdon do to him in return when he got out? What would he eventually do to me? One thing was for sure, I didn't doubt he would want revenge.

We rode without let-up for what seemed days on end. Of course it wasn't – I just lost track of time completely. I suffered a terrible waking dream, or out-of-body experience, in which I saw myself from afar, a speck inching across an enormous and indifferent landscape, a million miles from Mum and Dad, wherever they were; the future as huge as the country we were travelling through, with nothing but a great expanse of loneliness ahead.

I'd never cope without them. And yet did I really think I could find them? It took every ounce of my willpower to keep a tiny flame of hope alive that day. I couldn't afford to give up. Every mile we could put between ourselves and Canonhead counted. Night fell and we battled on. Our headlights swarmed with insects. In the next village we reached, Marcel bartered us a hut for the night. We were up before dawn and would have set off on empty stomachs, but as we were packing up the woman whose hut we'd slept in popped up with three helpings of a sticky, dough-like stuff called fufu, accompanied by a savoury sauce, all served in folded banana leaves. I've no idea what was in the sauce. Not much meat, that's for sure. But it filled a hole in my shrunken stomach, and helped me hang on to that bike, and Marcel's back wheel, all morning.

At some point he must have changed routes because we arrived at a different river crossing, this one served by a crazy motorised raft built out of barrels, bits of tree, planks, even some of those big plastic containers I'd seen people in Kinshasa carrying on their heads to market, which made the traditional dugout seem positively seaworthy. The river lapped sludge-brown between the planks as we wheeled our bikes aboard.

There'd been no signal in the village where we'd spent the night, but I noticed – because it seemed so out of place – that one of the raft guys had a pair of headphones in his ears, and I couldn't believe it when he began talking loudly to nobody, annoying as a commuter, halfway across that river in the middle of nowhere. I turned on my phone. Sure enough, it caught a signal. I waited, but no messages materialised. With just ten per cent battery, I hit Xander's number, willing him to pick up, adrenalin surging when he did.

'Hey,' he said, relaxed as ever.

'Have you seen the CCTV footage yet?'

'Just now, yes,' he said quickly, cottoning on to the urgency in my voice. 'Sorry, though – the guy's wearing a motorbike helmet throughout. He's completely unrecognisable.'

'Did you manage to take a copy for me?'

'Filmed it on my phone.'

'Good. Get out of the hotel,' I said. 'Find us somewhere else to stay. Check you're not followed. Send us the address.'

'Sure thing,' he said.

'Also, get hold of some dollars. I'll pay you back.'

'Right.'

'And call Joseph again. Pay what it takes to have him meet us at Goma airport tomorrow.'

'No problem.'

'Langdon's mining outfit is dodgy,' I explained. 'Full of little kids, and spreading into the national park. He obviously didn't want Mum and Dad to find out.'

'You think he'd kidnap his own family?!'

'No, but it's convenient if they're out of the way until

258

after the summit. And he's been odd about the whole thing from the start.'

'Want me to contact the police again?'

'Not till we get back and I've seen that footage myself.'

'Fair enough,' he said, adding, 'Hang in there, Jack.'

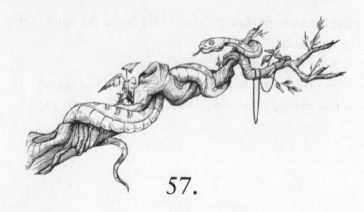

57.

Hanging in – or on – was a Herculean task that day. The track was a snake writhing through the scrub, grass and patchy forest. It went on forever. Occasionally we'd come upon other travellers, all of them baffling in their own way. Here was a man pushing a wheelbarrow full of painted sticks. Hours later, two children alone, neither of them more than three years old. The next person we saw was an old lady arguing with a donkey. It didn't apparently want to take another step. We came to another, smaller river at one point. This one was crossed by a bridge. Quite a broad bridge, in fact, designed to take proper traffic. Marcel paused mid-span for a water break. I shut my eyes and tilted my flask to the sky; the sun broke through the clouds and warmed my face.

'Who would bother to build a big bridge like this when the track either side of it is barely wide enough for a motorbike?' I said.

'The Belgians,' said Amelia. Seeing that I was none the

wiser she went on. 'They were big into infrastructure. Sixty years ago this little track was probably a decent dirt road. Since the Belgians pulled out and the trucks stopped running, the surrounding bush has been trying to reclaim it.'

Mother Nature had done a pretty good job of that. In places the track was no more than a wheel's width, and occasionally it disappeared altogether. But finally it wound back into the village where we'd first picked up the bikes. I was exhausted, dead on my feet, barely had the energy to climb into Marcel's truck. When I shut my eyes all I could see was the bike's front wheel rolling ahead of me, and the constant juddering through the handlebars ran through my whole body long after I'd got off the bike. Marcel seemed unaffected. He put a piece of chewing gum in his mouth and fired up the pickup. I'm ashamed to say I fell straight to sleep. Amelia did too. I felt bad not keeping Marcel company for the last leg of the journey, but I couldn't help it. The next thing I knew, we'd arrived at the airport.

We said our goodbyes to Marcel. I'm not sure I could have found the words to thank him properly in English, let alone French, but I wanted to try, and I made a right mess of it by asking Amelia to say that we were grateful to him for doing way more than we'd paid him to do. She translated his response. 'This was never about the money. He hopes you find your parents. And he believes in what we're trying to do. It's what Innocent would have wanted. Get the evidence out there, he says. Do whatever it takes.'

I offered Marcel my hand. He took it, his palm cool. '*Bonne chance*,' he said.

Walking through the airport made me realise what a state Amelia and I were in; I was already filthy when we left the mine and hadn't changed my clothes since then. Joseph, in his ironed jeans and bright white shirt, did a double-take when he saw us.

'Long story,' I said.

'No excuse!' he replied, leading us to the airport toilet block. 'Nobody flies with me so . . . not clean!'

My spare T-shirt wasn't much better than the one I was wearing, but I stripped to the waist at the sink and got the worst off myself at least. Amelia did better than me in the ladies. She emerged looking fresh-faced, tanned – she'd caught the sun – and her wet ponytail swung cheerfully from side to side as we made our way out to Joseph's plane.

This time our arrival back in Kinshasa really did coincide with a proper storm. The sky filled with black clouds while we were still some way from the airport, a mean weather front closing in. Joseph pushed his aviators up onto his forehead and dropped the plane a thousand metres so fast my stomach jumped. 'We can beat it,' he said with a sideways smile, and began arguing with air traffic control. Raindrops big as marbles whacked against the cockpit glass, loud enough to be audible over the propellers. The storm front was like a lid closing on the runway. Joseph murmured, 'No problem, no problem,' and smiled at us as we descended further, but there were pinpricks of sweat along his hairline. We flew the last kilometre at an altitude of about two hundred metres, crabbing sideways against a horrible crosswind. Being able to see what was going on made the whole thing doubly exciting. I could tell Amelia was worried though; she was gripping the sides of her seat.

'Nearly there,' I reassured her, with the runway a rain-warped streak of grey ahead. Joseph kicked the plane straight at the last second, and the wheels kissed the tarmac amazingly gently.

'As I said, easy,' said Joseph casually, but his relief as we taxied off the apron was obvious.

Once Joseph had fast-tracked us through the airport to the taxi rank, Amelia dug out her phone again. Mine was dead, but she'd thought to keep hers switched off until we needed it. Now she turned it on and showed me the messages that had landed more or less as we did. Once again hope fluttered in my chest: might Mum or Dad have made contact? No, but Caleb had.

His message read: 'Heads up – my dad's on his way. Cx'.

Despite everything, I couldn't help flinching at that 'Cx'. The fact that Caleb hadn't said what had happened when Langdon came round worried me.

'Message him back,' I told Amelia. 'Ask him how it went with his dad when he woke up. Also, ask for Langdon's Kinshasa addresses – both home and work.'

'Yessir,' said Amelia.

'Sorry, but –'

'Don't worry. In the circumstances, you're forgiven.'

As she was writing her reply another message landed, this one from Xander. 'Holed up here,' it read, followed by a link to an Airbnb. Amelia messaged him that we were on our way. I hoped he'd got to the apartment unnoticed.

It seemed to be near to the Gare Centrale, so I asked the taxi driver we hailed at the airport rank to drop us there. I wanted to scope out this new place, or at least look at it from a distance and make sure nobody was watching, before going in.

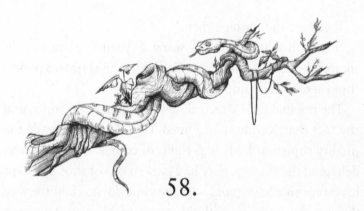

58.

'Gare Centrale' turned out to be pretty close to the Congo riverfront, and the apartment was in a boring-looking five-storey block, with a balcony that looked out over the water. We walked past the building once, eyes peeled, but nothing on the street seemed out of place. A Volkswagen with one wing mirror dangling from its broken bracket drifted by, but a tatty car didn't seem to have anything to do with us. We took the external staircase up to the third floor and knocked on the door, which opened a crack to reveal Xander's face. I could have hugged him, I was that pleased to see him, but made do with a fist bump.

He showed us around, a natural on his crutches now. There was a tiny kitchen diner with a spindly modern table and chairs, a main room not much larger leading out onto the balcony, which I was pleased to see gave a view of the street as well as the river, and a couple of bedrooms with identical Christmas-themed duvets. Whatever. With the main door safely locked, I cut to the chase.

'Let's see the footage then.'

'I was hoping it might show a licence plate on the motorbike or something,' Xander said, pulling out his phone, 'but there's really nothing to see.'

The original CCTV recording was in black and white, and the fact that Xander had filmed it on his phone made the quality ropier still. He was right, of course – the man who delivered the ransom note had parked out of shot and kept his motorbike helmet on, with the visor down, right the way through the argument with the concierge. He wasn't wearing anything unusual, no logo or badge, and I watched the short clip with a sinking heart, right up until the point when the guy was escorted out by security. Something snagged then for me. It was the way the guy walked. He was bow-legged. I'd seen that bandy gait before, recently. It took a second for the penny to drop, but once it did I was certain I knew who it was. Certain and dumbstruck.

'Langdon's driver,' I said under my breath. 'But it can't be.'

'Why not?' asked Amelia.

Xander said, 'You said on the phone that he stood to gain from having your folks out of the way.'

'But kidnapping his own brother? It makes no sense. Not even he—'

'Actually, it makes very good sense,' cut in Amelia. 'Particularly of the ransom. He made a big show of not wanting to pay off the kidnappers, because that's what you're supposed to say, and then he caved, which was weird, unless you're right and that guy is Langdon's driver, because if that's the case, he would literally have been paying off himself.'

I watched that clip many times, the thoughts crowding my head, ironically making it hard to think straight. Dad would surely have recognised Langdon and told him to take a hike. Except of course Langdon would have paid someone else to do the actual kidnapping. He'd never let anyone hurt Mum or Dad though, which was good. Or – seeing how he'd treated Caleb – would he? If I got to the bottom of this, and it turned out to be true, the news would break Dad from Langdon forever. Did that matter? It wasn't as if they were that close anyway. At least I had a lead. And yes, Langdon had a motive: to stop Mum and Dad visiting his crooked mining operation and prevent them giving evidence in the environmental debate. The ransom note was presumably a stunt designed to throw me – and anyone else who cared to look – off the scent. The way Langdon hadn't wanted us to involve the police at first now made a lot more sense.

'When does the summit thing end and the Article 16 decision take place again?' I asked.

'It's Article 16B, and they're voting tomorrow, at 3 p.m.,' said Amelia. 'The vote takes place in the National Assembly. That's the lower house, or legislature. It's situated in the People's Palace, off Boulevard Triomphal.'

Xander blew out his cheeks and looked my way, his eyes asking, *How does she know this stuff?!*

Amelia raised her phone: 'You have heard of the Internet?'

'Yeah, but remembering the detail . . .'

'It's the detail that's interesting.' Amelia shrugged. 'Also, the deadline's kind of important. The summit wraps up in the morning. Janine and Nicholas need to present their

267

evidence there at least three hours ahead of the vote, if it's to influence the debate.'

'Midday tomorrow . . .' I murmured.

'Yeah.'

'We've got to find them before then.'

Even as I stated this simple aim, the impossibility of achieving it overwhelmed me. I was exhausted, wanted nothing more than to slide beneath one of those stupid Christmas duvets, pull it over my head and give up. But there was no time to waste thinking like that. Langdon's driver was the lead, despite his motorcycle helmet. Two could play at that game, I thought.

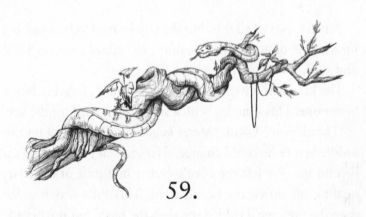

59.

Caleb had messaged Amelia Langdon's address. My recharged phone said it was about five kilometres away. Once she and I had washed, changed and eaten – Xander had thought to liberate a bag of bread rolls and sliced cheese from the hotel's breakfast buffet before he jumped ship – we headed out to flag down a motorcycle taxi. I had some of Xander's dollars safely stowed in the bottom of my backpack. The first bloke we asked wasn't interested, but the second – an old guy with a greasy Lakers cap and remarkably white teeth – I wondered if they were real – took the offer seriously: $200 to borrow his bike.

'*Montrez-moi l'argent*,' he said with a smile.

'Go on then,' Amelia said to me. 'Show him.'

I dug out some of the cash.

Temptation played across his face.

'Plus one hundred deposit,' I said to Amelia. 'Tell him it's just for a day. We'll return the bike to him outside the People's Palace at 3 p.m. tomorrow.'

Amelia relayed all this, but the guy seemed to be weighing up whether or not we were serious, so I added an extra $100 and said, 'Monsieur, please.'

The bike was a wreck: for $400 he could probably buy a better one. This sunk in. With a shrug he handed me the key.

'Thank you,' I said. '*Merci beaucoup*.' I jumped on the saddle before he could change his mind. Amelia climbed up behind me. We left the bike's owner in a puff of exhaust, rattling off down the broad road. This bike was heavier than the ones we'd ridden through the bush, but it worked, and let's face it, I'd had practice. Negotiating the traffic on potholed tarmac was still a lot easier than keeping upright along that snaking dirt path. I'd checked the map on my phone before setting off, and had memorised where the police station, market and our old hotel were in relation to Langdon's place and our hideout flat. I made for the market first, the one where we'd seen the amazing Sapeur guy all dressed up in his three-piece suit, and not because I wanted fake Nikes, sunflower seeds or a set of goat hoofs, though I was pleased to see those stalls still there. No, what I wanted was a couple of helmets, and the woman whose life's work appeared to be selling the most battered of biking lids possible was still at it beneath her pink-and-yellow parasol. She seemed unsurprised to see us, as if white teenagers showed up regularly to buy her recycled helmets. Although her stall was well stocked, not many of her helmets had visors. We found Amelia one that fitted. I had to make do with one that was too big. But that had its advantages. As we threaded our way back through the market on the bike, picking up speed en route to Langdon's place, the breeze worked its way into the helmet and cooled my face.

I found my way there easily enough, though 'there' was pretty unrevealing. Langdon's house was in a side street off a clogged main road. In this little backwater the buildings were set behind gates. My heart sank on our first pass, as I couldn't see anything useful through the metal railings, but coming back down the street slowly on the side nearer the shuttered house I spotted a familiar black SUV tucked in a parking slot behind the railings. Amelia saw it too. She headbutted the back of my helmet, nodding in the direction of the big car. We rolled on past, and I pulled the bike in behind a scabby-barked tree further down the street.

'Pretend we've got a problem with it,' I said to Amelia, kneeling down beside the bike myself.

'But it works fine.'

'That's why I said "pretend".'

I wanted to take stock, see if there was anywhere we could hole up and watch Langdon's house to monitor who came and went. But aside from this tree, there was little cover. We could fake-tinker with the bike for a bit, but do it for too long and we might arouse suspicion. My head was heating up within the helmet, which smelled of someone else's sweat. How could we keep an eye on Langdon's house without running the risk of being caught ourselves?

I'd asked that last question of myself silently, or at least I thought I had, but either I'd muttered it aloud or Amelia was thinking in time with me. 'Easy solution,' she said.

'What?'

'We should split up. There are no turnings off this street. It joins the main road at either end. Drop me off at the southern junction and take the bike to the northern one. We've got phones. If that truck leaves, one of us will see it, and if you move fast, we'll be able to follow it. The bike will be much quicker than a truck through traffic.'

It seemed risky – what if I was too slow and we lost him? – but I couldn't think of a better plan, so we did as Amelia suggested and positioned ourselves at either end of Langdon's curved street. Amelia had an advertising hoarding to hunker down behind at the southern junction. To the north, where I was waiting, there was a mechanic's. I parked the bike to one side of the forecourt behind a truck of threadbare tyres, and waited, and waited, and waited. The storm had long gone and now the sun came out. I sheltered in the shade cast by the truck's cab. The shade moved. I went with it. In time it shrank to nothing on my side of the truck. I waited there sweating as the afternoon wore on towards evening. Just as the light was fading – and my hopes with it – my phone, which I'd had in my hand the whole time, burst into life.

'This end! Now!' Amelia said when I picked up.

I didn't answer, just leaped on the bike and turned the key. The engine spluttered without catching. I yelled, 'No way!' so loudly a woman pushing a shopping trolley full of newspapers past the garage turned around. Not knowing what to do, I stuttered the bike forward three angry paces and turned the key fiercely again, hard enough to bend it. I doubt that in itself made any difference, but this time the tired old engine grumbled awake.

I let out the clutch instantly, gunned the bike round the woman, missing her trolley by an inch, and fired straight through a gap in the rush-hour traffic, heading Amelia's way. She was only a couple of hundred of metres up the road. I wove between two slower motorbikes, dipped around a cyclist and sped past a taxi on my way to pick her up. Catching sight of her running towards me on the verge, I cut towards her and hit the brakes. She swung herself up onto the seat hard before the bike had quite stopped, almost knocking me off. But I held it together and opened up the throttle so fiercely she had to clutch my chest to stop herself flying off the back of the bike as we accelerated away, weaving through the traffic again.

All that happened very quickly indeed, but I was still certain we'd lost the truck. A howl rose within me. It had been a stupid plan. Dad would have laughed at it. In that second, the fact of swerving and the smell of the traffic fumes and the sense of Amelia and I accelerating, on the edge of control, turned into a Mark-shaped warning, and just as I backed off, Amelia shouted, 'There!' pointing frantically ahead of us, at Langdon's SUV, cruising unhurriedly into the sunset.

Two heads were silhouetted in the cab. I couldn't say for sure, but it seemed a fair bet that we were tailing my uncle and his bandy-legged driver. 'Thank you, thank you,' I said to nobody in particular, and dropped back a car or two behind the truck. The job now was not to lose them.

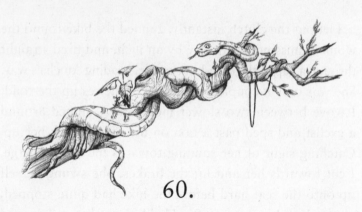

60.

That turned out to be easier than expected, partly because they didn't go far. We were only travelling for about fifteen minutes. Still, it was time enough for the sun to go down. I didn't turn on the bike's headlight. This was helpful, since when the truck pulled to a stop in a half-built neighbourhood, made up of what looked like factories or warehouses, I was able to drift to a standstill behind a van parked on the other side of the road without attracting attention.

'Check that out,' said Amelia.

I was shutting down the bike, rocking it onto its stand. 'What?' I said, peering round the back of the van.

'Them.'

Two men carrying guns had approached the newly parked SUV. When Langdon and his driver stepped down from it, one of the men backed away, an eye on the street, while the other holstered his pistol and stood before my uncle. Langdon's driver handed something over to the guard with the holstered gun. It was a cooler box. Langdon and the guard talked for a moment, Langdon with his hands on his hips, the guard with his arms respectfully at his sides. I couldn't hear anything over the hum of the invisible city, not until Langdon threw his head back and laughed. Something in that gesture caught in my throat.

'Are you thinking what I am?' I whispered.

'I don't know,' Amelia said, baffled. 'What are you thinking?'

'Armed guards. A warehouse in a wasteland. Langdon delivering whatever he's delivering. A cool box. So, food, possibly?'

'Those aren't thoughts – they're observations and guesses.'

'Adding up to?'

'The obvious possibility that your parents are in there.' I turned to her.

'The important word is *possibility*,' she said patiently.

'I disagree. It's *obvious*.'

'Another of your hunches is what it is.'

She was right, but this hunch was all I had.

Langdon raised a forefinger and wagged it at the guard, then spun on his heel. The wedge of light from the security lamp caught the side of his face. There was an odd shadow across his cheek. A bruise, I realised, as he stepped beyond the light and back to his car. I pulled Amelia behind the van, heard the growl of the SUV starting up again, watched its red tail lights bleed out down the street.

'What now?' Amelia asked.

'I don't know,' I said. 'Let's watch for a while. See what those guys with the guns do.'

The answer to that was: not much. Occasionally one of the men would amble across the floodlit forecourt, but then he'd simply stroll back to his position on one side of the building's roller-door entrance, which stayed firmly shut. There was no apparent pattern to these movements. It just looked like two bored guards keeping themselves from falling asleep by making a show of walking around.

'I want to check the building, see if there's a rear entrance, or a window I can reach,' I whispered.

'Yeah, but to do that you've got to cross beneath the light,' Amelia said. 'They'll see you.'

She was right, but there was one solution: put out the light.

'Reckon you can drive the bike?' I whispered.

'I've only been watching you and Marcel do it for about a hundred hours. How could I possibly have learned?'

'OK, OK. When I say, drive it straight to the first junction down there. It's about four hundred metres away if I remember rightly. Anyone follows you, keep going. If not, wait for me there. OK?'

'I should be able to manage that. But what are you going to do?'

'You'll see. Or rather you won't. Shut your eyes.'

'Why?!' she hissed.

'Just do it. And keep them shut. It'll make sense in a minute.'

'All right.'

We were crouched low on the verge behind the van, on scrubby wasteland. I fingered the dirt blindly in search of a decent-sized stone, thinking, *You've got one shot.* The floodlight was on a pole in the middle of the forecourt. Miss it and the stone, thrown from here, would slam into the front of the warehouse. A guard wouldn't have to be a genius to work out where it had come from.

So don't miss.

My hand closed over a solid chunk of something that felt like broken brick. It would do. I couldn't risk stepping out from the cover of the van. Flinging a rock takes an explosive movement, which the guards might spot. Instead I moved carefully backwards until the security light rose above the top of the van. It looked alien, a one-eyed monster rearing up. I was a good ten metres further from the target back here, putting it at the very limit of my range. Was there a less risky solution to this problem? I couldn't think of one, didn't want to think of anything in fact, just took a deep breath and imagined myself in the yard at school, taking aim at the top chimney pot. The trick, at this distance, was to aim well above the target. I had hit that pot before, and I would put this monster's eye out now, or else.

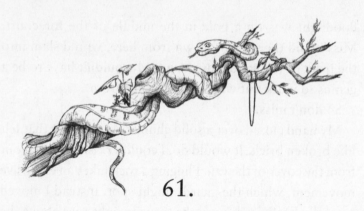

61.

I rocked on my heels, drew back my arm and uncoiled like a whip. Throwing well is all about timing, unleashing from the feet upwards, through the core and back and shoulders, snapping the elbow just so, flicking the wrist. The brick-chunk flew. Too high, I thought at first; I'd never thrown anything with such force. The rock was airborne forever. It sailed above the cone of brightness cast by the security light, black against the night sky. I lost sight of it for an instant. Then there was a crash, as loud as if someone had smashed a wine bottle against a wall, and the light vanished. Night slammed in from all sides, a wave of darkness closing over all of us.

'Nice!' whispered Amelia, opening her eyes.

I froze for a moment, not quite believing I'd done it. But I quickly came to my senses. One of the guards was shouting something. I bundled Amelia onto the bike. Her night vision would be sharp instantly. 'Go, go,' I urged, turning the key for her. I needn't have worried; she shot off confidently down the road. In her wake, on soft feet, I slipped through the darkness and round the side of the building. I must have passed within a few metres of the nearest guard, stumbling out into the road after Amelia. He didn't go far before giving up. In the meantime, I very nearly ran straight into a fence – it clipped my shoulder – but I'd memorised the angle well and I stopped in the darker darkness in the shelter of the warehouse, my eyes already pulling shades of grey from the night now the light was gone.

In fact, I soon discovered I could see *too* well. Edging round the building I realised another floodlight covered the ground to the rear of it. Worse still, there was another guard. Just the one on this side, but he was also wearing a holster and pacing back and forth. I couldn't see the floodlight on this side, not without walking onto the guard's patch, so there was no way I could disable it. And by the time I'd crept back to the front of the warehouse, the men standing sentry there had turned on a second light, this one mounted on the building itself, high above the roller-door, and whereas beforehand they'd looked like they couldn't be bothered, they were now very alert indeed, patrolling the full forecourt in synchronised dog-legs.

I was pinned down, I realised, unable to move either way without being lit up, and at the mercy of any guard who decided to have a good look along this thin strip of darkness squeezed between the side wall and the fence. How had I thought this manoeuvre would pay off in the first place? I wanted to punch myself for taking such a stupid risk. Instead I crouched down low, pressed tight to the corrugated warehouse wall, and wracked my brains for what to do next.

It was then that I heard her. Mum's raised voice, muffled, distant and yet right there.

'But there's no more time!' she was shouting. 'No. More. Time!'

It was definitely her. I pressed my ear to the wall, straining to hear more, but nothing more came, and of course I couldn't yell in reply. Instead, under my breath, I pleaded with her to call out again. The longer she didn't, the more I began to doubt myself. I'd wait, I decided, wait and listen for more, to prove I wasn't mad. Where else could I go after all?

Nowhere. For hours. Right through that awful night I was stuck in a trap I'd set for myself, clinging to the memory of what I thought I'd heard, tormented by the clear and present quiet. It was punctured by occasional traffic noise and the rise and fall of city-hum, but nothing else. I waited there, struggling to stay alert, praying for I don't know what: the guards to go away? Mum and Dad to emerge on their own, unscathed? Help to come?

None of those things happened. It was only when the charcoal wall of the warehouse against which I'd pressed my cheek all night began to turn a lighter grey that I realised I had no choice but to help myself. Careful to angle my phone into my chest I texted Amelia three words: 'ride by slow'.

Instantly I received a one letter reply: 'k'.

And within the minute I heard the drone of an engine, low at first but rising. I'd crept up to the front corner of the building, had one eye on the forecourt, was praying for the guards not to be too close. Either way, I had to go for it, hoping that if they did spot me the sight of a person running away would be more confusing than alarming.

Amelia puttered into view, a slow grey blur.

I waited until the very last minute, then made a sprint for it, dashed straight out of the parking lot and jumped up behind her on the slow-moving bike. Sure I could hear footsteps behind us, a man's voice shouting over the noise of the engine, I squeezed Amelia as hard as I could. She got the message and accelerated. Before we turned the corner I glanced over my shoulder, just in time to see a car shoot off the forecourt and turn our way.

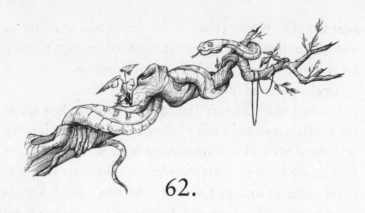

62.

I'll admit it: I wished I'd been driving. I wasn't though – Amelia was. She had her left arm threaded through my helmet strap and the bike slowed down as she wriggled to give it to me. 'Just go!' I wanted to scream, taking the helmet from her and pulling it on. But I knew better than to yell pointless directions at Amelia. She'd be more likely to call me out for being an idiot than speed up.

I needn't have worried. Without the awkwardness of the helmet on her arm she let rip. I'll admit this too: I was amazed how good she was on the bike. It turned out she'd spent the night poring over satellite maps of the area on her phone and immediately she was jinking between buildings, doubling back, bumping us over a railway crossing, and speeding up again onto a dual carriageway. The guards in the car didn't have a hope in hell of catching us. I was still squeezing her tight, I realised, as much in awe as to keep myself from flying off the back.

'Where to?' she hollered.

'Xander! At a speed that won't get us pulled over!'

She hadn't memorised that route, but I worked it out, signalling the way to her as she drove with textbook care through the waking city. We reached the apartment block without incident, parked up outside it and climbed the stairs to the rental. The light was on. Xander, fully dressed, ushered us in. I started to tell him what had happened, but he cut me off: 'Amelia's been giving me updates. I know where you've been.'

'Yes, but neither of you know that I heard . . .'

'Heard what?'

It seemed so improbable beneath the buzzing strip light in that kitchen-diner, but I forced myself to tell them what I'd heard. Xander's mouth fell open as I spoke, prompting me to add, 'I could have been imagining it, I suppose.'

'Unlikely,' said Amelia. 'You're not delusional in other respects.' A smile lit up her face. 'It's brilliant news, potentially at least.'

'Look, we still need to get the evidence to the summit,' I said.

'Already on it,' said Xander.

'How?'

'I copied the photos from your camera to my laptop yesterday while you were in the shower. Amelia's idea. She also texted me a thirty-page report full of coordinates, kids' names, descriptions of them, et cetera, et cetera.'

Amelia shrugged at me. 'I had time on my hands. It was a long night.'

'And while you were sneaking about in the dark, we

283

worked out who your parents would have been trying to influence at the summit: the Mining and Conservation Committee. I emailed the entire portfolio of photographs, plus Amelia's report, to its chairman at four o'clock this morning.'

Like a puppet whose strings had been cut, I collapsed onto one of the spindly kitchen chairs in relief.

'Only trouble is, he's not yet replied.'

I checked my phone. It was only a quarter to seven. 'He's probably not up yet.'

Xander shrugged. 'Maybe.'

I turned to Amelia for reassurance and saw that she'd fallen asleep with her head on her arms, right where she was sitting at the kitchen table. I'd been up all night crouching in the shadow of that warehouse; she'd spent the night working on her phone and waiting to pick me up. Xander too had been at the computer through the small hours. I had that burning sensation in the pit of my stomach I get when I'm properly exhausted; they had something similar, I bet. Everything in me wanted to go back to the warehouse with reinforcements – from where, I didn't know – but I convinced myself that Mum and Dad had been unharmed there until now, and I'd go straight there once I was sure the evidence was in the right hands. What's more, I knew that if we tried to keep going that morning without rest we'd get nowhere sensible, so reluctantly suggested we all turn in, just for a couple of hours. Amelia and Xander took a bedroom each. I flopped down in my clothes on the couch and fell into a black hole so deep I didn't hear my alarm when it went off, partly because my phone had wedged itself down the back of the sofa. When I eventually retrieved it and checked the screen my '*No!*' was loud enough to pull Xander from his bed.

'Eh?' he said, poking his head round the door.

'It's eleven fifteen! Quick, see if you've had a reply from the committee chair?'

'His name's Mukwege,' said Xander, clicking away at his laptop. After a pause he said, 'No, nothing. But look, it's not too late. You can intercept him on the way to the chamber.'

'How? I don't even know what he looks like.'

'You do now,' said Xander, turning the screen my way. He'd pulled up a photo of the politician. Martin Mukwege looked to be an enormous barrel of a man. In this picture he was dressed in a boring suit, but his hair was wild, a great white afro haloing his enormous head. 'He'll be wrapping up the committee meeting at twelve and going to the vote after that. I'll do some digging and see if I can work out any more detail,' Xander said.

Amelia had surfaced with the commotion. She also took in Mukwege's photograph over Xander's shoulder before washing her face at the kitchen sink. I packed my camera into my backpack and downed two pint glasses of water. I was parched. Hungry as well. Xander had got hold of a couple of boxes of cereal from somewhere. Despite having no milk, I ate two bowlfuls of cornflakes on the spot. Amelia chose Coco Pops. She didn't have to say anything for me to know she'd be coming too. I was relieved. Tracking the guy down and convincing him to take me seriously seemed a mountainous task. If – and it was a huge if – we got the chance, I knew Amelia could be more persuasive than me.

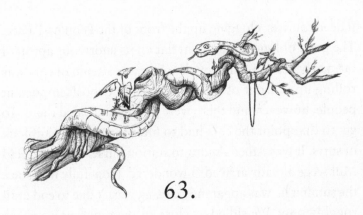

63.

I resisted the temptation to speed us to the People's Palace; Kinshasa's streets, I'd noticed, are full of traffic police just looking for a reason to stop cars, motorbikes, even cyclists, and demand a payment. Better to make like a tortoise than a hare. That gave Xander time to work out that chairman Mukwege would likely be arriving by car also, since the summit was taking place across town. When we spoke, on our arrival, he had a plan all worked out.

'Get rid of the bike and act like a tourist; work your way as close to the entrance as you can and if – no, when – you see him, try shouting, "Cloudburst!"'

'Why?'

'It's what I labelled the file.'

'OK,' I said. 'Wish me luck.'

'Make your own!' he said, trying to buoy me up.

Amelia had been listening in. 'Instead of talking about something that doesn't exist, let's get in position, shall we?'

Mercifully there were no big crowds of protestors, or

287

indeed tourists, clogging up the front of the People's Palace. The great oblong building sat flat on its enormous apron of tarmac beneath a felt-grey sky. A steady stream of cars was rolling up in front of the main steps to deposit important people, however, and there were guards stationed there. To get to that point the cars had to filter through a roadblock of sorts. It was Amelia's idea to station ourselves there. Had Mukwege already arrived? I wondered. Hopefully not, since the summit he was apparently closing wasn't due to end until roughly now. We sidled as close to the pinch point as we dared, and stood inspecting the cars as they came. It seemed a ridiculously long shot, and yet I knew Xander wouldn't have suggested it without having done his best to research the chairman's schedule and movements. Some of the cars had heavily tinted windows. They were agony to let pass. As more and more time ticked away I felt hope draining through the soles of my trainers into the warm tarmac. Twelve o'clock turned to twelve fifteen turned to half past.

'He's late, if he's coming this way at all,' I muttered, turning to Amelia.

Her face was screwed up in concentration. 'If I wasn't here,' she said, 'you'd have given up and missed him.'

I snapped back to look at the next approaching car, and sure enough, behind the driver, was an enormous figure crowned with that distinctive shock of white hair. It had to be him. The car, a huge silver limo, with at least three rows of seats, was rolling along quite slowly. It just kept coming. I approached its side, waving at the driver to stop. In response the car eased forward faster. In desperation, I dashed to the front of the limo and slid across the bonnet: I had to put myself between it and the gate. To avoid running me over, the car had to jerk to a stop. Immediately the front passenger door flung open and a guy with a gun, screaming in French, took a step towards me with the barrel aimed straight at my face.

'*Non, arrêtez, non!*' shouted Amelia.

Her words had no effect; the man just kept coming. He had a crooked nose. Flattened, almost. He wouldn't shoot me there and then, would he? That was a gamble I had to take. I moved towards him – and his open door – yelling, 'Cloudburst, Cloudburst!' at the top of my voice. The bodyguard got hold of me, tried to haul me away. I felt my T-shirt ripping as I struggled, still hollering, 'Cloudburst!' for everything I was worth, which, in that moment, felt like nothing at all. I had hold of the door frame somehow and wasn't about to let go of it – the guy could rip my T-shirt clean off for all I cared.

Lazily, the rear window of the limo lowered, revealing a concerned broad face beneath a white cloud.

'*Qu'est-ce que vous avez dit?*' he said gently, and in accented English, 'What did you say?'

Amelia stepped in. With a showstopping smile and her perfect French she held the big man's attention. I heard my parents' names, the word *enfants* repeated, and a load of other stuff, the gist of which I could follow without understanding all the words. The bodyguard melted away. The chairman climbed out of the limo, towering above us both, six foot eight at least.

'Martin Mukwege,' he said, his voice velvet, offering us his hand. We shook it in turn and did what he said, which was simply, 'Walk with me.'

In English and French, speaking one after the other, fighting to get everything out, we told our story. Our words poured into Mukwege as if into a vault; here was somebody we both instantly had complete trust in. I pulled out my camera and thrust the screen showing the photos I'd taken up at him. He waved it away, saying, 'I received the email, don't worry. Its contents are in circulation as we speak.'

'So you believe us?'

'Of course. The pictures don't lie. The coordinates don't either.'

'And it'll do some good?'

'If I have a say in things,' he said with a smile.

I could have hugged him. With my parents missing, Langdon an enemy, Innocent dead, and distanced from pretty much every other adult I'd encountered on this miserable trip by my poor French, Mukwege seemed a god. There was something absolute about him. He believed us.

'And you say your parents are being held against their will, that you know where they are, that you need help to secure their release?'

I blurted out the street name.

'After the vote,' he said, 'I'll be leaving the way I arrived. Wait for me.'

At that he shot his cuffs and checked the time on his watch. It was plastic and orange and massive, bright against his huge black wrist. He gave us both a friendly nod and strode toward the parliament building.

As Mukwege disappeared inside, taking our story with him, I suddenly felt very alone with Amelia. We stood facing each other before the massive facade of the People's Palace. I felt lightheaded, dizzy with something more than relief and tiredness. Together, along with Xander, we'd achieved something. We may well have done some actual good.

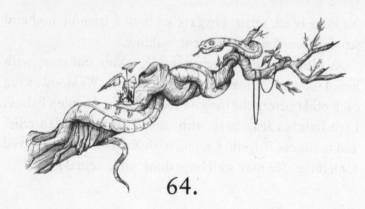

64.

'We need to get the bike back to the taxi guy,' Amelia said.

'Three o'clock, as the vote's happening, is what we told him.'

'You can buy me a Coke or something,' she said. 'While we wait.'

We rode the motorbike to a nearby drinks stand beneath the shade cast by a clutch of dusty trees, and hoovered up a couple of cold drinks each.

We called Xander, filled him in. He was as pleased as we were that his carefully put-together email of evidence had reached its target. After that we just sat and waited until eventually three o'clock wound round and we wheeled the bike to the front of the parliament building again. I wasn't necessarily expecting its owner to show up – he might prefer to keep the deposit I'd given him. But at three on the dot there he was, with his brilliant-white teeth and this time wearing a pristine New York Mets cap. Once he'd looked the bike over and found it satisfactory, he took the hat off, pulled the cash from within and handed it over. I gave him our helmets too; he could always sell them.

'*Merci*,' we said in unison.

Once he'd gone, there was nothing to wait for except Mukwege's return. Now that three o'clock had passed, he would be out soon, surely? And yet he didn't appear. By four I began to have doubts. He'd seemed so genuine, surely he'd come? Four turned to four fifteen, four thirty, four forty-five . . .

'You can't wait, can you?' Amelia sighed.

'No.'

She picked up the phone to Xander and asked him to send Mukwege a message telling him we'd set off for the warehouse ourselves and asking him to follow on.

We hailed a cab, rode it to the spot where Amelia had waited all night and walked from there. My pulse was jumping as we approached the building. It looked so different in the early evening light, more boring, less sinister. I'd planned to stroll past it once and count the guards. They'd not seen either of us the night before so there could be nothing wrong with simply walking by. I doubted they'd do more than glance our way. The van from behind which I'd thrown the rock was still parked across the street. This time we walked in plain view on the other side of it. My feet stopped moving as the full expanse of the warehouse forecourt, smashed floodlight and all, spread out before us. I couldn't see any guards out front at all.

'Weird,' I said.

'Where have they gone?'

'No idea,' I replied. Were they round the back, or inside? That wouldn't make much sense. A nasty thought flashed past: had we spooked them last night, prompting them to up sticks with their prisoners and move on?

Before I knew it I was running across that forecourt, Amelia trailing behind me, making straight for the warehouse's front door. What was the worst those guards could do to me if they were inside? Lock me up with my parents, if my suspicions were right. The big roller-shutter covering the door was down, secured with a padlock through two metal hoops, one in the bottom of the door, the other embedded in the concrete floor. I hammered on that metal shutter, yelling, 'Hello! Hello! Is there anyone inside?'

Bang, bang, bang. Again and again. Until my hand hurt.

'You should probably pause to listen for an answer,' Amelia suggested.

I gave another *bang, bang, bang* and waited.

Nothing. Then, from far away, a distant *thump, thump, thump*.

We looked at one another.

Bang, bang, bang.

Thump, thump, thump.

'Mum? Dad!'

Silence.

Then, from so far away, 'Jack!'

In a frenzy I tore around the building looking for a way in. There were definitely no guards: the place was deserted. There were no windows either, and the only other door, at the rear, was also made of metal and locked shut. While

I was circling the warehouse, searching high and low, Amelia considered the situation her way, and when I next jogged past she pointed at the security light that I'd smashed, at the top of its long metal pole, and said, 'That?'

'What about it?'

'Let's rip it down and use it smash the lock.'

It took us a good half an hour. The pole snapped off its stand easily enough, but the only way through the lock at the foot of the roller door was to chip and stab and gouge the concrete from around the fixing. Eventually we loosened it enough to prise up the bottom of the door, and when the lock gave, the door, counterbalanced from inside, shot up in a clattering rush.

'Mum, Dad!' I yelled again.

And this time Mum's response was louder. It was coming from behind a partition wall, in the middle of which sat another locked door. I was yelling at her in delight, shouting, 'Stand back,' and about to attack that door with the metal pole too, when Amelia pointed to a key hanging on a nail in the adjacent wall. I couldn't get it into that lock fast enough – my fingers were a jittery mess. But eventually I did, and the door swung open to reveal my parents. Mum was right in front of me, crying with excitement. Dad was standing with a hand to his forehead, his face as grey as the breeze-block wall.

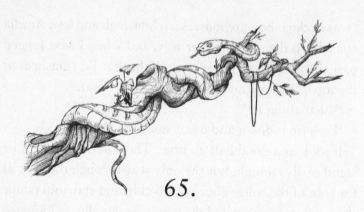

65.

I didn't know where to begin, started talking in a frenzy, gabbling on about Innocent and the mines and Langdon and the safari and Caleb and motorbikes and canoes and child slaves and national parks and photographs and evidence, all in a great rush. Were they all right? Had they been here all this time? Did they know what day it was? Had they any clue who had done this to them and why? They wouldn't believe it! Did they know what I meant about the evidence, and chairman Mukwege, and –

Amelia put one finger on my forearm and said, 'What Jack's trying to tell you is this. Our safari ended in disaster. We returned to find you missing, reported it to the police and eventually paid the kidnappers' ransom. When that didn't work, we went looking for you ourselves at Langdon's mine and beyond, worked out his business is corrupt, that he was responsible for your kidnapping – presumably to stop you finding out the truth and presenting it at the summit – and followed him here. We had no luck getting in last night, but

296

we delivered evidence to the chairman of the Mining and Conservation Committee on your behalf ahead of today's vote and returned just now to find the guards gone. You're free. I think that's the bones of it.' Turning to me, she asked, 'Anything to add?'

I just wanted to know they were OK. Scanning the room, I saw two camp beds, a fridge, a sink, and an open door leading to a little bathroom. They both looked healthy enough, if a bit pale.

'Langdon responsible?' Dad said with a laugh. 'Don't be ridiculous.'

I looked him straight in the eye and said, 'Believe me, he is.'

'You've done fantastically finding us,' Dad said. 'I'm in awe. So grateful. Proud. Come here.'

I went to him and put my head on his shoulder. He hugged me stiffly. Behind him, on the floor next to the fridge, stood the cool box, its lid ajar.

'That's his cool box,' I said.

'Langdon's?' Dad released me.

'Yes. He delivered it to the guards last night. I saw him.'

Dad smiled and shook his head and said, 'This must be some kind of mistake.'

I felt sorry for him. Though they didn't exactly see eye to eye, this was his brother we were accusing. Perhaps we shouldn't have hit him with the truth straight away. Who knew what state he and Mum were actually in, after all this time cooped up? Best not to press the point, not now, I thought.

But Amelia said, 'It's no mistake. The proof is

incontrovertible, I'm afraid. He kidnapped you, his brother. And he also hits his son.'

'Ease up with the allegations,' said Dad evenly.

'Nicholas . . .' said Mum.

'The thing to do,' said Amelia, 'is confront Langdon immediately. You'll see then.'

Dad gave her a hard stare.

'Fresh air,' I said. 'Let's get you outside.'

We all traipsed out through the yawning roller door and stood blinking in what was left of the sun. Mum held my hand. Quite tightly. She looked older in the light, tiny crow's feet crowding her eyes. What had she been through in there? The atmosphere was strange, strained. I noticed neither Mum nor Dad had comforted the other yet, or reassured each other the ordeal was now over. Mark swam up within me for some reason. Why, in a moment that should have been happy, was I full of such aching sadness?

A car pulled onto the forecourt, stately and slow, silver and long. Martin Mukwege's limo. He stepped out of it, unfolding himself to his full size. 'Mr and Mrs Courtney,' he said, presenting a hand, which they both shook automatically.

'Who are you?' asked Dad.

'This is Mr Mukwege,' Amelia answered, as if that should have been obvious. 'He's the chairman of the Mining and Conservation Committee, and he's who we gave Jack's evidence to.'

'I told these . . . children to wait for me,' he said, grinning broadly. 'Possibly I should have guessed that, having demonstrated such resourcefulness, they might find it hard

to wait around for help freeing you. So here I am, too late.'
To me he said, 'You mentioned guards. What have you done
with them?'

'They'd gone.' I shrugged.

'How strange.'

'Not really,' said Amelia. 'If the motive was to keep
Nicholas and Janine away from the environmental summit
until the conservation vote had passed, it makes sense to
abandon the kidnapping about now.'

Mum was looking at Mukwege in open awe, while Dad's
face was closed, apparently in distaste. 'This evidence of
Jack's,' Mum said, 'was it any help?'

Mukwege chose his words carefully, delivering them from
on high: 'It was profoundly influential, yes. I came as much
to offer thanks as I did to help.'

'So,' said Mum tentatively, 'the vote went the right way?'

'It did.'

Mum gasped and took a little step sideways. I put an arm
around her shoulders. She looked up at me.

'By which you mean . . . ?' said Dad.

Mukwege replied, 'There will be a crackdown on mining
in the country's national parks, and a full investigation will
be undertaken into the use of child labour in the industry.'

We stood in silence for a moment. A noiseless plane, high
above us, drew a pencil line across the fading sky.

At length, Amelia, who'd been looking at Mukwege's
limo, said, 'To Langdon's then. Any chance of a lift?'

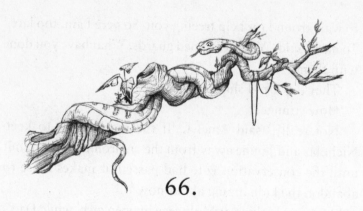

66.

We all climbed into that huge car. Mum and I were pretty
squashed by Mr Mukwege, but so what – we were together
again. The limo didn't drive so much as float on the softest
suspension imaginable; we drifted through the rush-hour
chaos of stuttering buses and meandering motorbikes and
laden-down pedestrians as if in a dream. On the way I
messaged Xander to take a cab there straight away, but
not let himself be seen. The rented apartment was closer
than we were, so he was already there when we arrived
at Langdon's compound, skulking behind a whitewashed
wall to one side of the entrance gate. As the car came to a
gentle stop Mr Mukwege asked if he could be of any more
assistance.

'The lift's fine,' said Dad abruptly, adding, 'Thanks.'

'Well, you have my details,' the big man said.

'Sure,' said Dad, climbing out slowly. He looked as if he
was off to the dentist's. That was understandable, I suppose.
What Amelia and I had told him had obviously sunk in. I

would have felt more sorry for Dad in that moment if he hadn't looked so accusingly at me.

He hung back from pressing the intercom. Amelia had no such qualms. She leaned on it for a good long time, rousing a barked, 'Yes?' from within.

'Langdon, it's me,' said Dad. 'Plus the family.'

Langdon's response was a strange low laugh, before he buzzed us in.

We crossed a bare yard to the front door, Xander's crutches clicking beside me. 'Guess who called this morning?' he murmured to me as we went.

'Who?'

'Caleb.'

A lurching sensation, of guilt and pity, swept through me. 'Is he all right?'

'In his own words: he'll live. Langdon's got him digging in some mine with an actual shovel for the rest of the summer. Can you believe it?'

'Yes. I can.'

'Well, he said to tell you that despite that, he's OK. After what happened with Innocent, he reckons he deserves it.'

'What did you tell him?'

'The truth – that you were worried for him, and grateful for his help.'

Xander was right, obviously. Yet I was more than worried and grateful. For some reason I wanted Caleb's forgiveness. And not just because we were about to expose his father.

Langdon drew the door back and stood framed in the

opening. His face looked worse than it had the day before, but he'd been at a distance then, and it had been dark. His nose was swollen, his left cheek too, the eye above it a mean slit. An ugly brown-purple bruise down the left side of his face underscored everything. The sight of him made me wonder how truthful Caleb had been with Xander. I'd have been willing to bet Langdon had done worse than make his son dig holes. How else would he have punished him?

'Welcome,' Langdon said. With no apparent feeling at all he continued, 'What a relief to see you.'

'What on earth happened to you?' Dad said.

Langdon narrowed his good eye in my direction. 'Ask your son.'

'Can we come in?' Mum said gently.

'Why not?'

Mum looked at him quizzically as he backed away from the door, then followed him into a large white kitchen. We all traipsed behind. The room smelled of disinfectant. Before we'd come to a stop, Amelia, who'd heard what Xander told me as we crossed the yard, said, 'Where's Caleb?'

Langdon snorted. 'Where you last saw him. Making amends.'

He clearly wasn't going to pretend to be surprised by Mum and Dad's newfound freedom. A tumbler of whiskey sat on the countertop between us. He reached for it and took a sip, waiting for the accusation to come, I suppose.

'What's going on, Langdon?' asked Mum, renewed steel in her voice.

'You tell me.'

'We've been locked away –' she began.

'I'll tell you,' I cut in, anger knotting in my chest. 'We know you're responsible for Mum and Dad's disappearance. You had them kidnapped. Admit it.'

Langdon let out a slow breath, looked from me to Dad and said, 'I think not.'

'This is ridiculous,' said Dad, without conviction.

'Is it now?' said Langdon. After a pause, he unleashed: 'What is ridiculous is the havoc these little twits have caused in your absence. I hate to say I told you so.'

'Told you what? Dad?' I asked.

To me Dad replied, 'I don't know what he's talking about.'

'Yes, you do,' Langdon laughed, taking another slug from his glass. 'I said at the beginning, the safest thing to do would have been to lock them up too. It would only have been for a few days. What harm could it do?!'

Mum was rocking on her heels beside me, looking from Langdon to Dad with her mouth open. The shape of the problem, a locomotive bearing down on me through the mist, was coming into focus.

Amelia got there first. 'I don't believe it,' she said to Dad. 'Except I do. You were in on the whole thing.'

'Come again?' said Xander.

'Jack's dad here, together with his brother, had himself and Janine kidnapped on purpose.'

'But why?' I still couldn't fathom it.

'Money, probably.' Amelia was right in Dad's face, sneering up at him. 'I bet you've an interest in Langdon's mines, haven't you?'

'You don't know what you're talking about,' said Dad coldly.

His reserve was supposed to be dismissive, but I could see the lie behind it. So could Mum. With one quick step she arrived in front of Dad and struck him across the face. The slap sounded like the crack of a whipped towel. It stunned Dad. He did nothing in response. Just swayed there for a moment before turning his gaze upon me. He'd never looked at me that way before. No words could have spelled out his hatred as plainly. The air in my lungs turned to ice.

'Yup,' said Langdon. 'We should have kept the lot of them in the jungle. Caleb too. But he had to mess that up with his stupid gorilla baiting. Still, we could simply have rounded them up on their return, as I suggested, even chucked them in the same tank as you.' He was slurring, drunk, happy to repeat himself. 'But no, no, no. Your boy was "too witless" to piece anything together, you insisted. Well, someone pieced it together for him, and he turned Caleb against me while he was at it, and now the whole goddamn operation is blown.'

'From the very beginning,' said Mum. 'The fake storm, the robbery at the airport, the missed meetings. *Kidnapping*. All of it orchestrated, bought, for one purpose: to undermine me.'

'You'll get over it,' Dad hissed.

'My own husband,' whispered Mum.

'My own father,' I said.

Mum looked at me funnily when I echoed her like that. Pity filled her face. She moved closer to me, placed both cool hands on the back of my neck, a huge decision weighing in her face. 'What did you say?' she said.

'My own father. I can't believe he'd do this to you. To us.'

She turned from me to Dad, an utter stillness descending. 'Nicholas,' she said, and paused to draw breath.

Amelia, at my side, took hold of my hand. I could feel Xander's presence in the room too. They were a help. We'd done some good together. I tried to think about that and block out everything else, and I failed. In the near silence, all I could hear was the whine of a mosquito.

'Nicholas,' Mum repeated eventually, 'for as long as I live –'

'*We*,' I interrupted. I knew exactly what she was going to say, but it had to come from me too. I squared up to Dad, stared straight into his eyes, an unexpected sense of relief flooding through me as I spoke for both of us: 'For as long as *we* live,' I told him, 'neither of us wants to see you again.'

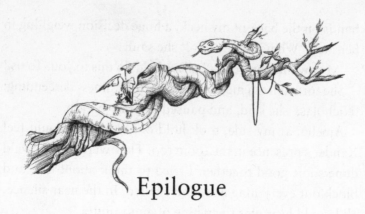

Epilogue

We flew back to London separately. Xander sorted the logistics, changing our flights and organising taxis to the airport while the rest of us packed up in a bit of a daze. He was returning to Nigeria; I'd see him back at school. Amelia, Mum and I made the trip home without Dad. Mum was furious. She spent the journey staring into the middle distance with a determined look on her face.

Over the days and weeks that followed, I tried to help her cope by looking like I was coping myself. Dad decided to take us literally and refused to set foot in the house. He would send someone for his things, he said. This meant Mum and I had to pack up all his belongings, ready for the courier. I took charge. It was surreal to stand before his mahogany desk – I'd not even been allowed near it when I was small – and sweep the contents off its leather-inlaid top into a packing crate.

One of the objects on that desk was a little wooden elephant Mark had carved, copying as best he could one made out of actual ivory which, for as long as either of us could remember, had stood in pride of place under the brass desk lamp. Carving anything out of ivory is wrong; to make an elephant is as wrong as it gets. Mark's wooden version was crudely done, but for a ten-year-old, the age at which he had carved it, that elephant was impressive.

I stood there turning the carving over in my fingers, transfixed. Was it a good thing that Mark died without knowing what our father was actually like, deep down? Was I better off knowing it now? For the first time since the ordeal in the Congo, the feel of that wooden elephant in my hand brought me close to tears. I put it in my pocket. The rest of the desk's contents, the magnifying glass and letter opener, the blotter and glass paperweights – and Dad's prized ivory elephant – I clattered into the crate. Who cared if anything got broken? Desk cleared, I dragged the box into his dressing room and rammed in his handmade suits. A couple of drawers of underclothes went in on top. Seeing the neatly pressed silk boxer shorts and paired woollen socks fall in among the jumble was curiously satisfying. Box full, I went off to find Mum.

She was at the island in the kitchen, focusing on her laptop.

'What's going to happen next?' I asked.

'Hmm?' She sat back on her barstool. 'Well, Langdon's mining operation is under investigation,' she said. There was a glimmer of satisfaction in her eye as she nodded at her screen. 'According to Mr Mukwege, the authorities are likely to confiscate the whole business.'

Though that was of course good news, I hadn't quite

meant the question as she'd taken it. 'I was thinking more of us,' I said.

'Of course. So you'll be back at school in no time. That will be the same as it's always been, more or less.'

She was probably right, but that wasn't a good thing. The idea of sitting in a classroom was pretty boring, and being cooped up like a prison inmate for weeks on end filled me with dread. It must have shown in my face. Mum went on, 'Listen. You'll be fine. And before you know it, you'll be home again for the holidays. I've been thinking about that too. The Congo trip didn't work out that well –'

'You could say that.'

'So we should plan another one, somewhere else, the two of us.'

'It wasn't exactly a bundle of laughs for Amelia or Xander either,' I said.

'You're right. We should invite them too. To do something completely different. Have a think about it.'

She was trying so hard to be positive, I found myself doing the same. What sort of place would best blot things out? From nowhere a picture of Amelia swimming underwater came to me. Turquoise sea, coral reefs, a firework display of tropical fish. Might as well add in some treasure spilling out of a pirate's chest. We should head beneath the waves somewhere. That was about as far from the jungle as it's possible to get.

Mum was watching me closely. 'Any ideas?' she asked.

'As it happens –' I returned her smile – 'yes.'

Wilbur Smith is an international bestselling author, having sold over 130 million copies of his incredible adventure novels. His Courtney Family saga is the longest running series in publishing history, and with the Jack Courtney Adventures he brings that adventure to a new generation.

Chris Wakling is a lifelong Wilbur Smith fan, travel writer and novelist. He is available for events at schools and festivals and for interview.

For all the latest information about Wilbur, visit:
www.wilbursmithbooks.com
facebook.com/WilburSmith
www.wilbur-niso-smithfoundation.org

PRESS

Thank you for choosing a Piccadilly Press book.

If you would like to know more about our authors, our books or if you'd just like to know what we're up to, you can find us online.

www.piccadillypress.co.uk

And you can also find us on:

We hope to see you soon!